STEFAN BACHMANN

A DROP OF NIGHT

GREENWILLOW BOOKS

AN IMPRINT OF HARPERCOLLINS*PUBLISHERS*

A Drop of Night
Copyright © 2016 by Stefan Bachmann

All rights reserved. No part of this book may be used or reproduced in any manner whatsoever without written permission except in the case of brief quotations embodied in critical articles and reviews. Printed in the United States of America. For information address HarperCollins Children's Books, a division of HarperCollins Publishers, 195 Broadway, New York, NY 10007.
www.epicreads.com

The text of this book is set in 12-point Granjon.
Book design by Paul Zakris

Library of Congress Cataloging-in-Publication Data is available.
Bachmann, Stefan, 1993–
A drop of night / by Stefan Bachmann.
pages cm
"Greenwillow Books."
ISBN 978-0-06-228992-6 (trade ed.)—ISBN 978-0-06-244959-7 (international pbk. ed.)
16 17 18 19 20 21 PC/RRDH 10 9 8 7 6 5 4 3 2 1
First Edition

 **GREENWILLOW BOOKS**

To Briony, Beckett, and Milla,
dear friends and champion palace escapists

A DROP OF
NIGHT

I heard it being built. Father's secret
Versailles, a palace beneath a palace. A
world of gilt and crystal hidden deep within
the roots of France. When I was a small
girl, only three or four, I heard the booming
far below, shivering up through the floor.
I watched the tiny furniture rattle inside
my dollhouse and I asked my governess,
Mademoiselle d'Églantine, what it meant.
She told me with great, frightened eyes that
the earth had swallowed something dreadful
and was suffering indigestion. I was not the
cleverest child in France. I believed her.

Aurélie du Bessancourt—October 23, 1789

We are fleeing along the upper gallery when the windows explode. Seventy-two panes of glass burst inward. I am knocked sideways by the force of it, my vast skirts billowing into a banner of flickering silk. For a heartbeat all is silent, echoing and slow-moving, as if I have been submerged suddenly underwater. Rocks hang suspended among the glittering shards, burning clods of peat, flaming torches whirling end over end. . . .

And now everything is noise again, my running feet, my bloody hands, and the growl of the crowds outside.

Mama is shrieking: "Aurélie, do not leave me behind!"

She is coming after me, but she is dressed for a ball, whalebone corsets and thirty pounds of Florentine brocade. She is far too slow. Ahead, Bernadette and Charlotte have reached the stairs. Father's guards are with them, their faces bright with sweat. Delphine huddles against the newel post, fingers digging into the wood, waiting for Mama and me.

"Follow the guards," I snap. The cuts on my palms are small, from glass or from the rocks, I do not know. I press them to my side, wincing, then snatch Delphine and start down the stairs. "All of you, follow them!"

I look back over my shoulder. Mother has almost reached the head of the stairs. She is prancing, snatching things, letting them fall. Her little hands are full of snuffboxes, strings of pearls, and gilt figurines. Frightened to go, frightened to stay.

Outside, I hear voices rising above the others, bellowing orders. I hear *financier* and *porcs* and *le meurtrier*. The slaughterer. I have heard my father called many things, but never that. I wonder what will become of us if we do not make it down. If we are lucky, we will be taken to Paris for trial and be executed before a roiling, toothless crowd. If we are less lucky . . . I see our bodies lying in a heap among the ruins of the château. Moths flit across our dirtied faces and spread their wings over our eyelids. And all in a moment, my life seems very small, a shred of cloth snagged in a hedge, blowing in a hard wind. Soon it will be torn away, and what have I done with my years here? Not very much. Nothing at all.

In the entrance hall, the doors are breaking. Boots hammer the marble, an echoing chorus of hobnails and slapping leather. I know where they are by the sound of them. The music room. The *salle des arts* where the Bessancourts' painted frowns and beakish noses have all been taken down, leaving nothing but phantom squares on the wallpaper.

Mother starts down the stairs. Her shoes are so high she must go down sideways, step by step. Smoke is beginning to drift into the lower passage, bitter as crab apples. I can hear the crackle of flames. The torches must have caught hold of the drapes.

I tap the young guard on the shoulder. "Get her," I whisper. "Drag her if you must, but *get her down*."

He nods; he seems to coil, gathering energy, and now he bolts past me, back up the steps. In the gallery, the flames flare brighter. A door bursts open, frighteningly close. Rough shouts echo toward me, clanking weapons and the thudding march of feet.

"Run, Mama! Kick off the shoes! *Run!*" My sisters are all shrieking at once. Delphine is weeping, tears flowing down her fat baby cheeks.

The old guard swings his musket off his back and trains it up the steps. The young guard has almost reached Mother.

She is so small. He could carry her under one arm. . . . But just as he is about to snatch her, she darts. One step up. One step away.

I freeze, clutching at my skirts. The young guard stares at her, slack-jawed. She shakes her head at him. And now she looks past him, to me.

Her mouth is moving. "Forgive me, Aurélie," she says, and it is only a whisper amid the crashing and the flames. "I wish I were braver. For all of you, I wish I were brave."

"No." I feel a blistering rage surge toward my heart, turning my lungs to ash. "Mama, no, *NO*! Come with us!"

She wipes her face, turns, and climbs back toward the gallery.

They have seen her. The shouts become shrill, grotesque and jubilant, hounds barking before the kill. The flames are roaring. The young guard careens back down the stairs toward us.

A shot rings out.

I scream, but I do not hear it. All I hear is the gunshot, deafening, ringing in my ears. Mother stands transfixed at the top of the stairs, her back toward us.

No, Mama, please no—

She turns slowly, one hand clutching the creamy fabric

above her stomach. When she pulls her hand away, it wears a shining red glove. Her face registers astonishment. The guards are trying to herd us behind a little panel in the wall, a panel with a butterfly in it, wrought in brass, and I am struggling, straining to keep Mother in sight.

"*Mama!*"

The revolutionaries flow around her. Delphine is wailing in my arms. The old guard slaps her. The panel slides shut.

And now there is only darkness, our moving feet and our quick gasping breaths, and we cannot cry, we cannot stop. The guards are pushing us—down, down into the blackness—toward the new palace, to good luck and safety and everlasting peace, where Father waits.

1

I'm scribbling a good-bye note in permanent marker on Mom's stainless-steel fridge. I don't know if permanent marker sticks on stainless steel. I'm thinking maybe I should have been super dramatic and scratched it in with a steak knife, but the marker is going to have to do because in one minute I'm gone. In one minute I'll be in a black Mercedes heading for the airport. In an hour I'll be meeting the others. In three we'll be somewhere over the Atlantic.

Hi family! I mash the tip against the cold surface. The clock above the oven locks on to 5:59 P.M. The sun's setting, oozing gold and pink all over the lawn outside.

I'm going to Azerbaijan, surprise surprise! Why, you ask? Oh wait, no you don't. But you'll hear about it anyway in about three months. In the New York Times. *And* Good Morning America. *Pretty much everywhere.*

Bye, Anouk

It's not funny. It's not supposed to be. It's supposed to hurt. And that last part—Anouk—that really is my name. I don't know who picks up a newborn baby, looks it in the eye, and names it Anouk, but that's me: Anouk Geneviève van Roijer-Peerenboom, pronounced like *"Ahhh-nuke* is falling, everybody run!"

You should.

I pull my woolen granny coat around me and hurry out of the kitchen. A bunch of neon feathers screeches at me from a cage above the bar. Pete the Parrot. Ancient, perpetually depressed, incredibly annoying. Basically my soul in bird form. *Bye, Pete.*

I'm in the front hall. Tires are crunching up the gravel driveway outside. The house feels huge and empty around me, marble pale. I'm a deliberate smudge, an eraser mark on all the sharp lines and sleekness. No one's going to be home for hours. Penny has a ballet recital. They all went. In a perfect world Mom and Dad would come tearing out of their rooms right now, and Penny would show up in a purple unicorn onesie or whatever she wears these days. They'd all lean over the railing like extras from *Les Misérables* and shout and beg me to reconsider, and I'd snap something scathing at them and march myself righteously out the door.

Pete shrieks again from his cage. Good enough.

I hear a car door slam and the driver start up the front steps.

I take a deep breath. This is it. The biggest thing I've ever done. Not vandalizing fridges. And I lied about going to Azerbaijan. *This.* I was picked for it. Picked out of hundreds of other brats and geniuses and entitled, private-school-educated, polo-shirt-wearing bootlickers.

I see the driver's shadow growing against the Venetian glass panes in the front doors.

Go.

I grab my suitcase, click off security, open the doors.

"Good evening, Miss—"

I hand the driver my bag, dart around him, and walk down the front steps. Slide into the backseat of the Mercedes. Pull my toothpick legs in after me. Sunglasses on. Cold face.

The driver closes my door and gets back in, up front. He gives me a quick glance in the rearview mirror, eyebrows knit, trying to sum me up.

You can't, buddy. Don't even try.

He starts the engine. The car eases up the driveway.

The gates are open. We're out on the street, gliding under the bare branches of Long Island winter. I don't look back. *Have a blast at the ballet recital,* I think, and I can actually feel my anger curling like a red-hot animal in the pit of my stomach. *Dance your heart out, Penny. For me.*

2

We're meeting in JFK, in the white-glass-steel world of Terminal 4. We were given very specific instructions:

6:45 P.M.—Arrive at airport. Do not check your bags. Clear security and proceed to the exit at Gate B-24. Your plane will be waiting for you there, together with the other students selected for this expedition. Your chaperone and point of contact: Professor Dr. Thibault Dorf.

I got the fancy blue folder in the mail a matter of hours ago. Reams of thick, creamy paper detailing exactly where we're going, what we'll be doing, what's expected of us. Up until then, I was mostly in the dark, coasting on hints.

I run my fingers over the Sapani coat of arms embossed on the top right corner of each of the pages—a hatchet and flag, entwined with two roses. They're the financiers. They own the château under which the site was found.

According to Google, they're the fifth richest family in the world. Never heard of them. They definitely don't go to my parents' lawn parties. I keep flipping back and forth through the pages like I'm actually reading them. I'm not. I've gone over all this a dozen times, but I don't want the driver to get chatty. If he does, I'll snap his head off, he'll throw me out on the curb or drive us into the ocean, and I'll miss my plane. I'm really trying to be help-ful here.

My eyes dart over the documents. Packing lists. Safety precautions. Something called *Building Good Teams: Clarity, Communication, and Commitment,* which I've skipped every time. They had me take weeklong intensive courses in rock climbing and scuba diving, sign thirty-six pages of contracts, get tested for every major disease and condition known to man, to make sure I didn't have any-thing that might endanger the expedition. On top of that they expect me to be a clear, communicative, and com-mitted person? That's asking a lot.

I hold the papers in front of my face and let my gaze wander out the window. Watch the trees turn to town, now city, red-brick tenements and gas stations, networks of power lines chopping the sky into manageable pieces. I thought the whole thing was a scam at first. That single unmarked envelope six weeks ago, outlining the opportunity, all smarmy and fake. *Dear Miss Peerenboom: The information you are about to read is strictly confidential.* That's as far as I read. I left it sitting on my homework heap for a while. Looked up the name Sapani on a whim. Turns out smarmy and fake is pretty much synonymous with polite professionalism. The Sapani Corporation is huge. It has offices in Paris, Moscow, San Francisco, Tokyo. Based on my SAT scores and past accomplishments, they had plucked me out of the desperate, wallowing masses of New York's private school elite. I wasn't going to let this opportunity pass me by.

So here I am. Following their rules like I'm good at it. They had me do the prep, notified me as I passed each round. I was worried they'd ask for a face-to-face meeting at the end, I'd say something rude, and they'd throw me out the window. They never asked.

We're in Queens now, heading south. I try not to think about home. I was supposed to tell parents or legal guardians about the expedition, have them sign off on it. I didn't. Now that I think about it, it wouldn't have made much difference either way. As far as they would have known, I'd be visiting a fairly regular—though culturally significant—château in the Loire Valley for a restoration camp. After reading the blue folder, I get why the organizers were so stingy about information. This site we're visiting is not just any château. It's on the same level as the Terracotta Army in China. The pyramids. Pompeii. Not as old as those, but huge and bizarre and possibly monumental for the historical community. And so nothing's allowed to leak. No news outlets have been informed yet. Once we're there, we're on a complete social media blackout.

The car is pulling up in front of Terminal 4. I tuck the blue folder under my arm. As soon as the locks click open, I climb out and scurry for the trunk, dragging at my suitcase while the driver is still opening his door. I walk away as fast as I can without looking like I'm fleeing a crime scene, which I basically am. The driver is probably staring after me, scratching his head.

Sorry, man.

I catch a split-second image of myself in the sliding doors as I approach. Tall. Thin. A tiny, vicious-looking, sharp-chinned face. Haircut like a helmet, a severe black bob. Dark rings under my eyes. The granny coat hangs around me like a box, my stick legs punching out the bottom, and from there it's all skinny jeans and witchy lace-up boots with pointed toes that will probably kill my feet in a few hours—

The doors whoosh open, snipping my reflection in half. I step into the terminal. Eau d'Airport washes over me—coffee and dusty carpets, top notes of radiator heating and cheap cleaning products. Passengers, pushing their luggage mountains in front of them like they're doing penance for something, stare at me, bovine and slightly hostile.

I plow into the crowd. *Clear security and proceed to the exit at Gate B-24.*

A young mom dragging two kids bumps into me. For a second I think she's going to apologize, but she takes one look at me and her expression changes— embarrassment-surprise-fear-pride-disgust—all in millisecond flashes. It's almost fun, like watching a slide show. A PowerPoint called *How People React to Other People Who Don't Conform to Their Expectations of Niceness and Civility.* I draw my coat around me and step past her. Slap my passport and boarding pass down in front of the TSA guy. I allow myself to wonder what the other kids will be like. What *they'll* think of me.

The TSA guy starts leafing through my passport. Does a suspicious double take when he sees that nearly every page is full. Aruba, last summer. Dubai, for a paper on migrant workers. Tokyo, volunteering after the earthquake. He eyeballs my boarding pass. Motions for me to step to the side.

Oh great. I move out of the line, eyeballing the boarding pass, and trying to see how it incriminated me.

A TSA woman approaches, red lipstick so bright it's like she just gorged herself on cherries or blood or something. "Follow me, miss," she says in the most bored voice ever, and starts leading me around the endless security queue. I brace myself for deportation, gulag, whatever they do to people these days. The TSA woman positions me right at the front of the line. And leaves. The security people wave me forward.

Oh?

Phone out, coat off, hands up for the body scan. And now I'm in the gate area, squeezing past some punk guy who thinks it's a good idea to travel with studded belts and twelve dozen piercings. He looks at me accusingly, like I'm personally responsible for his poor life choices.

I head into the gauntlet of fast-food restaurants, coffee shops, screaming kids, and snack walls.

Well, that was strangely easy. I think of the last time I was here. I was on my way to a master class on Renaissance literature in Perugia, Italy. Everything was infinitely worse. Dad couldn't take me to the airport—he stays at the loft downtown during the week—and I said I'd order a car, but Mom had to drive Penny to her ballet class so she offered to take me.

I should have guessed this wouldn't end well. Mom doesn't do things for no reason.

They sat up front. Mom was chewing that nasty medicinal herbal gum she likes. She kept leaning across the middle console and tucking Penny's hair behind her tiny, half-gone ear. I wanted to tell her to watch the road.

Later, in Departures, Penny was power texting, her hair brushed forward to hide the scarring on her cheeks. Mom was telling her something about Madame Pripatsky's carpel tunnel syndrome. I was being pathetic, thinking, *Mom? Penny's not even good at ballet. I'm the one going to Italy. Talk to me.*

And I was saying, "Penny, don't forget to feed Pete."

I adore Penny. I shouldn't even be allowed near her,

but she's the only person in the world I'd bother rescuing, if, say, the world were about to be hit by a comet and I had a spaceship. She's the one who gave me the nickname Ooky, back when she was two and the name "Anouk" involved way too much drooling. When she was four, she told me she wanted to be a starfish when she grew up, a blue one, and also a veterinarian. I remember saying she could totally do that because blue starfish skilled in veterinarian work were really rare. She's eleven now. She wants to become principal dancer at the New York City Ballet someday. She can barely walk upright.

I remember Penny nodding to me. Her thumb, tapping away at her screen. Me and Mom, staring past each other. Mom's forty-three. She's got huge hair, like Mufasa. She's charismatic. She can make shareholders, VPs, the hot-dog seller on the curb outside her office building follow her into the void. She wishes I were dead.

We stood like that for maybe ten seconds, and inside I was screaming for her to just turn her eyes a quarter of an inch and look at me.

She didn't. She fixed her gaze on a point over my shoulder and said: "Keep those Italian boys in line." And then she smiled this tiny, grim smile that said: *Serves you right.*

She unwrapped another square of gum. Leaned down and whispered into Penny's ear, like they were friends, or at least a mother and a daughter. I watched them and I wanted to slap Mom, grab her flowing black clothes and shake her until she screamed, until she hated me, because if she hated me at least she'd have to look at me. I stood perfectly still, my skin crackling. "There are three bottles of Moët behind the couch in the basement if you're planning on celebrating when you get home," I said.

I left feeling sick and angry, and hid in the business-class lounge as soon as I got through security. Chewed on blood orange rinds until my mouth hurt. Three of my classmates from St. Winifred's were there, also on their way to Perugia. A trio of perfect brains, perfect nose jobs, and perfect Tiffany jewelry, whispering and throwing glances in my direction. One of them—Bahima Atik, I think—waved. I pretended not to see. I don't feel bad about that. Neither did they. At St. Winifred's you don't have friends. You have allies. You have trade agreements and pacts of nonaggression, and if you're lucky you have one or two people who won't stab you in the back. Unless stabbing you in the back is a prerequisite to becoming president of something, in which case, buy a coffin; you're already dead.

I snap back to the present, and I feel the anger again, nestling behind my ribs like it belongs there. I left the lounge that day like some kind of dark and spiny sea creature, daring anyone to get too close. It's where all this started, I guess. This searching for something colossal, some epic task that would make people move out of the way when I walked down a hall, that would make me fearsome and great and impossible to ignore. I hope this is it.

I could have done a million other things. I could have gone through the Long Island house with a baseball bat and broken all the Kutani porcelain. I could have made party streamers out of Mom's and Dad's sensitive business emails and thrown them around at their next fund-raising gala. I could have picked up drug-addled Ellis Winthrope and flown to LA and sent pictures of our wedding to the whole family. But this is better. It's my coup de grâce. Or maybe just my coup, no grâce.

I look down at my phone. Three minutes until I meet the others.

3

I spot Jules Makra first. He's leaning against a pillar by Gate B-24, scrolling through his phone. We each got a little bullet-pointed spreadsheet in the blue folder, like we're superheroes in a lame cartoon. Age. Skill set. Majors. Extracurriculars. Mug shots so we know how to spot one another.

Jules is tall, gangly. Jittery. Elaborately sculpted black pouf hairdo that looks like he spent ages trying to get it right. It's starting to droop. His earphones are in and his leg is bouncing to a very irregular-looking beat. I tap my fingernails on the handle of my bag. Steel myself and walk toward him, suitcase whizzing behind me.

A second before I reach him, he looks up. Sees me. Grins.

Jules Makra up close: a little bit punk, a little bit hipster. Rolled-up chinos and this weird, bright thrift-shop shirt plastered with Russian dolls and flowers, all crinkled up under a lopsided bomber. His eyes go sharp for a millisecond, little splinters over his grin. He's assessing me.

I assess him back. "Are you with Professor Dorf?"

"Yeah!" he says. He pulls out one earphone and his grin widens. "You're Lilly?"

"No." I glance around for the others.

"Um. You're Anouk?"

No, I'm William Park. I almost say it out loud, but then William Park shows up, so I don't.

I like Will Park's face. He looks like someone studiously observed everything about Jules and inverted it. He's tall, too, but bulky and broad shouldered, and while Jules looks like he's about to pop a shoulder blade out of his skinny back, Will looks self-contained. Calm. Except for his jaw, which is sharp enough to cut stone and slightly tense, like he's clenching it. Nervous, maybe. He's wearing a newsboy cap pulled down low and a ratty old pea coat that was probably shabby chic in the 1920s.

Jules tugs out his other earphone and grins again, only I think he grins wider at Will, probably in the hopes of avoiding the debacle-that-is-Anouk. "Hey!" he says.

"Hey." Will's voice is low. He goes straight for the handshake. He only looks at me for a second before his gaze drops. His eyes are blue.

Jules is frowning, probably wondering what the odds are that everyone on this team is an asocial freak. I sit down on my suitcase. Will leans a shoulder against Jules's pillar and looks out into the crowd. Incredibly awkward silence ensues. One of those silences where everyone knows they're being awkward, but there's nothing they can say to break it, and so they just freeze up and hope for a quick and speedy death.

Hayden Maiburgh shows up next. He's just as tall as the rest of us, but he's another type entirely. The type I like to avoid at all costs. He's wearing a private school blazer and blue-mirrored aviators, and his hair's been lacquered into a brassy swoop. He looks like he's on his way to play polo or bathe in gold bathtubs of champagne, and he grins at us as he approaches, that sort of *Hey, losers* grin some people are born with.

"Hey, losers," he says, and I almost spit out my metaphorical mouthful of water. He's doing one of those fake bro handshakes with Jules, all splayed fingers and fist bumps. Except Jules has no idea how bro handshakes work, and I'm pleased to say the whole thing is failing miserably. Unfortunately, that seems to please Hayden, too, like the handshake is a test and Jules flubbing it up settles the hierarchy. Hayden turns to Will, grinning, ready to do the whole maneuver again. Will is completely oblivious. He grips Hayden's hand, harder than looks comfortable, shakes it once, and goes back to gazing soulfully into the crowds.

I stay on my suitcase. Stretch out my legs and give Hayden a death glare when he glances down at me. Now I look away, like he's too boring even for glaring at. Try to visualize the files in the blue folder, lining everybody up in my head:

Anouk Geneviève van Roijer-Peerenboom. Seventeen years old. Gymnast. Jerk. Speaks five languages fluently, has basic knowledge of eight more, nationally acknowledged teen academic studying art history at NYU. Recent graduate of St. Winifred's Preparatory School in Manhattan. Can now also climb and scuba dive.

Jules Makra. Seventeen. Graphic design student. San Diego, California. Won a prize for drawing a chair or something.

Will Park. Seventeen. Engineering student from

Charleston, South Carolina. Has nice eyes.

Hayden Maiburgh. Seventeen. Philosophy major at Cornell. That's a joke. What does he philosophize about, weight lifting? Juice boxes? The plight of the one percent?

The fifth kid isn't here yet. Lilly Watts. Sixteen. Sun Prairie, Wisconsin.

She arrives three minutes later, and I guess she walks up like a normal person, but it feels like she explodes onto the scene like an anime character, blowing everyone backward in whooshy streaks. She's short and plump. She looks like a hippie-indie American Girl come to life, feathers in hair, colored wristbands, a bedazzled leather jacket with fringes. Except she's also carrying the most enormous hiker backpack I have ever seen. It dwarfs her. Towers over her head. Her nose is shiny, greasy looking.

She takes one look at us propped against pillars and suitcases like a tear sheet straight out of *Vogue* and her eyes pop wide. "Oh my *gosh*." She spreads her fingers, palms downward. "You guys. We're going to France."

She does a little dance. Now she's smiling right at me. "I was literally afraid today wasn't Wednesday. I mean, I couldn't find anyone, and this one time I slept all night and all day and missed an entire twenty-four hours, so I thought maybe I had slept through Wednesday and today was Thursday. I know, *Seriously, Lilly?* But I thought it. Hi!"

She shakes Hayden's hand because he's closest, and she's laughing and jabbering, and Hayden is smiling down at her a touch derisively. I wonder if Lilly notices.

Now she's talking to Jules. He jokes around. They blab. Lilly does one of those shoulder dip things and says "Ohhh, me, too!" and I imagine they're talking about their mutual mastering of the blinding toothpaste-commercial smile.

Lilly gets to Will. For a second she looks like she wants to hug his poor quiet self, but she tucks that thought back into a folder of good-deeds-for-later and instead grabs his hand in both of hers, beams at him, and tells him she loves his historically accurate coat. Right before she gets to me, I stand up.

"Hooray," I say flatly. Do some jazz hands. "We've arrived. Where's Dorf?"

Lilly stops in her tracks. Everyone stares at me.

"We're supposed to meet him here," Hayden says.

"Did anyone else totally fail at the climbing wall part of preliminaries?" Jules says.

"Hi," Lilly says, and waves at me, a tiny, frantic motion.

I pivot, scanning the faces flowing past. We're right where we're supposed to be, Terminal 4, Gate B-24. But the rows of gray waiting seats are empty. There's no flight info up on the screen.

"Maybe we *all* slept through Wednesday," Lilly says. She laughs, but no one else does. I'm actually freaking out a little bit. If I got the wrong day, the wrong time, the wrong airport, if I have to go crawling back home and find out that permanent marker *does* stick on stainless steel—

Something clanks behind me. The metal door to the skywalk, opening. I whirl, see four guys in black suits striding out. They're dressed impeccably, but the rest of them is rough. I glimpse a tattoo snaking above a collar. Silvery scars crisscrossing a row of knuckles. One has an actual chemical-red Mohawk, six spikes rising in angry sunrays down the center of his scalp.

Walking between them is a fifth man. At least fifty. Elegant and scholarly looking, huge as a boulder. He's got a neatly trimmed beard, silvered glasses, a hat. A colorful silk foulard is knotted under his chin. He looks like Indiana Jones if Indiana Jones got old and fancy and bulked up on several hundred pounds of broccoli and protein shakes. He also looks exactly like his picture: Professor Dr. Thibault Dorf.

"Hello, hello!" he calls out. His voice isn't loud. It's deep, a raspy, rich, velvety sort of voice that makes everyone within ten feet turn and stare. Us included. The bodyguards are picking up our bags. Red Spikes is behind us, herding us through the metal door and down the skywalk, and Dorf is saying: "It's wonderful to meet all of you. And all on time! Welcome to Project Papillon."

He has a trace of an accent. Not French. Not British either. I don't know what it is. Lilly immediately latches on to his arm and starts explaining to him how un*believably* excited she is to be here. I look over at the nearest bodyguard type. Vulture eyes. Blond stubble up his face, so pale it's almost gray. He looks like a Norse god. He brings a hand up to his ear, and he's got a headset there, running down his jaw. A light is blinking in it—a thin red strip, throbbing silently, like he's getting a message now. A whisper plugged straight into his skull.

The others are starting to talk, warming up to each other, making friends. I watch the light, and I watch the guy, and I wonder what he's hearing.

Aurélie du Bessancourt—August 27, 1789

Mother was invited down today. No one has seen the Palais du Papillon yet, no one but Father and Havriel and the legions of craftsmen who live in the depths, heedless of night and day, working and painting and sculpting tirelessly by lamplight.

The invitation arrived with much pomp: three footmen in full livery—scarlet coats, gold braid, and silk stockings, the center one bearing a small gilded casket—knocked on the door to Mama's chambers. Mama was in her boudoir, asleep in a patch of sunlight like a cat, and so it was I who leaped up to receive the gift, and it was I who snapped open the lid and peered inside like a great nosy peacock. A single square of paper lay within, cushioned in dried posies and apple blossoms.

My darling, my treasure, my heart, I read. The card was edged with gold, and it smelled so sharply of cloves and rose oil and thick perfumes that I almost gagged.

I request your most excellent presence at the gates to the Palais du Papillon, on this day, the 27th of August, 9 o' clock.

Forever in love, Frédéric du Bessancourt

I replaced the card quickly and dropped into a chair. The reason for the invitation is clear: Father's mysterious palace is nearing completion, and he is eager to show it off.

I hand the invitation to Mama when she wakes and feign surprise when she tells me what it says.

"May I go, too?" I ask, perhaps too bluntly; Mama peers at me, startled.

"No," she says. "No, my sweet, he did not say to bring anyone. He is very particular."

"I am particular, too," I say, frowning in mock seriousness. "Particularly curious." And I laugh, but Mother's smile is weak as watered brandy, and so I do not press the subject. Her quietness does not trouble me. I am as excited as if I were going myself. Last month, Charlotte, Delphine, and I watched the armored coaches approach down the avenue, the horses sweating, gleaming in the sun, the drivers shouting merrily down to the gardeners as they passed. We saw sofas from Paris, spinets from Vienna, bolts of silks and brocade from

London and Flanders, so heavy they bent the servants double, loaded down into the lower passage and disappearing into the shafts and the dark, as if swallowed by some insatiable beast. The palace will no doubt be a wondrous sight. And vast. There were so many coaches. An endless snake of them, all filled to bursting. It seems Father can afford anything he pleases: to grow fat on honeyed quail and petits fours; a wife as beautiful as Mama; four daughters and no sons. A palace that would put the king of France to shame. I wonder if there is anything he cannot have.

Mother passes me on her way out, dressed in splendor like a Venetian Madonna. Her gown is deep, rich crimson, finest silk, like poppies, berries, roses. Her sleeves and bodice are weighted with pearls. Her wig is a mountain of smoke-gray locks, pinned with silver flowers. She is going alone down to the gallery. There, Father and Lord Havriel will meet her. Not even Madame Kretschmer or the maids have been allowed to accompany her. She does not see me as she passes, and I want to call out to her, to say something, wish her luck, but she is gone already, tapping slowly down the stairs. I keenly await her report.

4

We're greeted on the plane by a spindle-thin Asian woman in a pencil skirt and high-collared white blouse. Her eyes are striking—mismatched green and gray vortexes, the pupils wide and black, like someone took a hole punch to a starscape. She's sizing us up. Her gaze is borderline scary, like she's weighing meat.

"Miss Sei," Dorf says. "Chief science officer from the Sapani Corporation. She'll be assisting with the expedition."

Her tongue clicks against her teeth and she strides away down the body of the jet, waving for us to follow.

We do, and I watch her shoulders moving in a square under her blouse. Next to me, Jules lets out a low whistle. "We are *definitely* traveling first class."

I'm assuming he's referring to the iPads in the armrests, the flat-screens showing screen savers of beaches and waterfalls, the random potted mango plant next to the jump seat.

Miss Sei ushers us into a lounge, all white leather and shiny black wood. Sofas curl along the walls like huge Persian cats. A bar stands in one corner, three Art Deco stools and a bunch of brightly labeled bottles poking up like glass chimneys. Red Spikes, Norse God, and the others file past us, through a glass door and into the jet's next compartment. Miss Sei gestures us toward the sofas and follows them, wordless. Dorf pauses. He smiles at us.

"All yours!" he says, and sweeps his big hands out on either side. "I'll see you in Paris, bright and early tomorrow morning."

He ducks after Miss Sei. A door slides shut. We're alone.

Wait, that's it? No introductory speech? No "Welcome, young chickadees"?

We sit in a semi-catatonic daze for about a millisecond. And now Jules says: "This. Is. Awesome," and sprawls himself all over a sofa, and it's like no one even thinks this is bizarre. Lilly bounces from barstool to mango plant to waterfall screen saver, cooing appreciatively at everything. Hayden goes to the bar and starts clinking through the bottles. I sit down on a couch, hook one leg over the other, and watch the carnage.

Will eases himself onto the sofa next to me.

Neither of us speaks. The pilot tells us to prepare for takeoff. I glance over at Will. His hands are on his knees. His eyes are serious, like everything he's seeing is an epic tragedy. *I agree, Will.*

Jules and Lilly are on their phones, laughing about something, and I get sour grape-y for a second, wondering if they remember the contract stipulations about no social media and no sending pictures, or if they're just doing whatever and hoping they won't get caught.

Will clears his throat. I glance over at him. He clears his throat again and says: "There aren't any seat belts."

His voice is gorgeous, deep and quiet, and it has a slight drawl, the *a*'s and *r*'s softened to buttery nothings.

"Nope," I say.

Silence. That must have been his entire repertoire of small talk, so I decide to help him out. I wave toward the others. "Gonna be a blast, huh. Nine hours with these people? And then two weeks. And then another nine hours. What we really need are cages. And tranquilizers."

He peers at me. His eyes go a shade bluer and a shade curious.

"Cages and tranquilizers!" I say again, louder. The engines are revving up. The lights on the runway spread away in twin orange lines, like well-trained fireflies.

One of Will's eyebrows cricks a little. "No. But seat belts would be a good idea."

Um . . . right. I don't know how to communicate with people who don't understand sarcasm. Supposedly you can tell the intelligence of someone by how well they recognize humor. I don't know if it's true, but I live by that. It's a comfort to assume that when people don't think you're funny, it's because they're just stupid people.

"Okay." I scoot an inch away from him and slide my headphones on. "Good talk."

End of that relationship. I hit the screen on my iPod. Music flows.

I watch the cabin slant as the plane takes off. Will doesn't move from the sofa, which strikes me as awfully gallant of him, considering I just scratched his name from my mental Book of All Things. I close my eyes and wonder if maybe I could get along with these people. It's not impossible. People make friends sometimes, just by accident.

"Hi!" Lilly squeaks, and practically pile-drives herself between Will and me. "We didn't really meet before. I'm Lilly. Hi."

My eyes snap open. I was listening to Ingrid Michaelson, and I was at that part of the song where you can actually hear the smile in her voice. *Let's get rich and buy our parents homes in the south of France.* I love that part. I listen to the whole song for it.

"Hi," I say. I don't take off my headphones.

"What's your name?" Lilly asks. She smiles at me encouragingly.

"Anouk," I say. "Didn't you read your folder?"

Lilly's smile splinters a tiny bit, but somehow she keeps it in place through sheer force of will. I look at her curiously. She doesn't *seem* brilliant. She doesn't seem like she can climb a wall or scuba dive, either.

"That's a cool name," she says. "Is it Russian?"

"What?" It comes out annoyed. I slip my headphones down my neck. "No. Dutch, I think. Or Flemish."

"Ooh, my aunt lives in Flemings!" Lilly says. "Yeah. In Wisconsin." She touches my knee and gives me another smile, like living in Flemings, Wisconsin, is an accomplishment.

It is. I don't know how anyone does it.

"Congrats to your aunt," I say, moving my leg. "No, really, Flemings, Wisconsin. Wow."

Lilly's eyes go sharp. For a second I think she's angry, but nope: it's the same look she gave Will before deciding to not-hug him. Only this time she's decided that whatever my problem is, it's not going in the good-deeds-for-later folder. It's going to be dealt with *now*. She pulls her scuffed-up chucks onto the sofa, wraps her bedazzled arms around her knees, and starts talking. It's like watching waves come in on a beach, or someone vomiting after a party: endless, and you wonder where it all comes from.

Will looks over at us, slightly alarmed. Now he gets up and moves to a different sofa. *Take me with you!* I want to scream, but he's not so good with mental telepathy. And Lilly's nowhere close to done.

She talks about baking quinoa vegan brownies. Her alternative-hippie homeschooling parents, whom she clearly adores. A 3-D-looking tattoo of a fly on her arm, which she now realizes was a bad idea because it makes her look like she has the plague or is demonically possessed. She was grounded for getting that tattoo, and when she was done being grounded she got a second tattoo on the sole of her foot. She sang The Beatles' "Yellow Submarine" in her high school's talent show and didn't win. She doesn't actually show me the tattoos. And why is she still in *high school*?

I throw my head back and stare up at the little lights in the ceiling. Lilly's barely even breathing between paragraphs. She's definitely too enraptured by her own stories to care that I'm being socially abominable. Her voice becomes a buzz in the background. Everything becomes a buzz. Air systems, jet engines, the clinking of glass—all of it fades into a single flat line of sound.

I sit up. Glance around. It's so weird. Like an eerily slow-moving dream. Hayden is lying on a sofa, sipping Orangina through a straw. Will and Jules are next to each other, and Jules seems to be trying to make conversation, and Will seems to be trying not to die of awkwardness. I look to the sliding panel that separates us from Dorf and the rest of the jet. The glass is frosted, shot through with clear strips. I see a sliver of Miss Sei—a leg, some skirt. One eye wide, watching me.

There's a beeping, sudden and shrill, and sound envelops me again. The captain's voice breaks through the speakers: "Miss Sei, Professor Dorf, we're coming up on some turbulence. Would you like to—"

A commotion on the other side of the glass. The speaker goes off in our compartment, but I can still hear it, muffled, in the one ahead of us.

I shiver. Lilly looks over at me, questioning. I slide my earphones back on and turn the music up loud.

Aurélie du Bessancourt—August 29, 1789

Mama returned to her chambers well past midnight. I heard her on the stairs, the noisy clatter of her shoes as she hurried up, her door creaking shut. An airy, velvet hush descended. But still the château seemed to groan and shift, as if some small object at its heart were pacing, unable to come to peace.

The next morning Mama joined us for breakfast. Her face was drawn and pale, her eyes oddly watery. I should have realized something was not right. Were I not such a fool, I would have silenced my sisters with a severe look and we would have eaten quickly, communicating solely through glances and the tapping of silver, and then fled to dusty, unused guest rooms where we could discuss the matter in private. But I wanted dreadfully to hear tales of the new palace. When my sisters crowded around her I joined them, asked Mama if the palace was very large, and how many candles it must take to light the hallways, and was it warm in the depths, or bitter cold, and was there a *salle d'Apollon* like the one in Versailles?

She would not speak a word. She sat gingerly at the table, peeling an orange with a paring knife, cutting it into neat, jewel-bright wedges, and when the servants brought her a bit of fried liver in a painted china dish, she blanched and pushed it away. We continued to chatter mercilessly. We would not cease. And after a while Mama began to weep, putting her hands to her ears, and the orange lay on the table, a knobbly spiral of peel, and the rich flesh within hacked to bits.

5

Exhibit A—I had a boyfriend once. I was fifteen. He was fifteen.
He had green eyes and floppy hair and liked Vampire
Weekend, and if that doesn't guarantee a life of shared
bliss, I don't know what does. We were going to get married. Move to the West Village and have zero children
and drink tea and live a life of bohemian ennui. It didn't
happen. Green-eyed Boyfriend was expelled for pouring
lighter fluid all over the bike stands and setting them on
fire. Not even to protest anything. Just because. It was
okay, though, because he didn't know we were getting
married. I never actually talked to him. The height of
our romance consisted of me ignoring him all the way
through chemistry, and the instant I heard about the bike
stand incident I was over him anyway. People who are
dumb enough to light bike stands on fire are not people I
want to share a lifetime of bohemian ennui with.

Exhibit B—Two years earlier, when I was thirteen, I went to the library and checked out all the books I could find on sociopaths and bizarre human psychology. The librarian probably thought I was deranged, but I wanted to be sure. I figured if I had a medical reason to be mean and angry, things would be simpler. It turns out having medical reasons to be mean and angry doesn't actually help you become less mean and angry. It doesn't fix you.

I lean my head against the window of the black Mercedes and watch the landscape rush past. It's an endless conveyor belt—frosty green fields, gray sky. We're whooshing along a six-lane highway. Behind us are two more Mercedes—long, low cars with tinted windows. Ahead is another. We're like a shiny, furiously speeding funeral procession.

Jules is lying on the seat across from me, staring up at the ceiling. Professor Dorf and a driver are up front behind darkened glass. Will, Lilly, and Hayden are one car behind us. I'm starting to regret this arrangement. Jules is much too effusive for me. He has this way of laughing loudly and then looking at me cautiously, like the only reason he laughed is because he wants me to laugh, too. I don't like that kind of pressure. Still, it's better than being in the other car. Lilly's trying to drag Will out of his shell, and I don't know *what* Hayden's doing. He didn't stick with Orangina for long on the plane ride, and his reaction to all the alcohol was to become very slow and buzzy, and speak in short, dramatic sentences about the sky and the tarmac. But maybe he's knocked out cold by now. I wish Jules were knocked out cold.

He's just being friendly, Anouk. He's just a nice person. It's possible. But this is where Exhibit B comes into play. I don't believe in the whole "deep down people are basically good" notion. I think deep down is where people are the worst.

"And so for our social sculpting class this one guy got a bunch of horse manure and mixed it with Plasticine until it was this really glossy brown, almost like chocolate, and he put it in a bear-shaped mold and called it 'Poo Bear,' get it? It was, like, a commentary on how culture is packaged to look appealing but is basically crap. It was brilliant." He raises his eyebrows in admiration and looks out the window.

"Except Winnie-the-Pooh isn't crap," I say. "Winnie-the-Pooh is amazing."

"What? It's not about Winnie-the-Pooh, it's— You're missing the point."

"No, I'm not. 'People say nothing is impossible, but I do nothing every day'? *That's* brilliant. If Mr. Social Sculptor wanted to be all clever and subversive, he should have made a shampoo bottle out of crap, called it 'Sham-Poo,' and it could have been a commentary on all the toxic chemicals in commercial shampoo, and then he could pretend he's a crusader against multinational cosmetic corporations instead of just skewering children's books he's probably never read." I click my tongue. "Missed opportunity there."

"Don't you study art history?"

"Is that a legitimate question, or are you trying to shut me up?"

Jules laughs. I know he's doing that inquisitive little sideways look right now.

I keep my gaze fixed on the landscape outside. We landed at Charles de Gaulle Airport about 10 A.M. Paris time and were whisked straight from the tarmac to our waiting motorcade. We didn't even have to go through Immigration.

I get a quick blur of kebab restaurants, bright signs, and concrete-block houses as we pass through a town. Jules starts talking about bands I've never heard of. I wonder if he's just trying out subjects until I latch on to something. Sorry, my life consists of reading Tolstoy in original Cyrillic and watching foreign-dubbed Hollywood movies on repeat until I understand the dialogue through context. Also dreaming up Machiavellian revenge. Also being irritating and pretentious. At least we have that in common.

I slip the blue folder out of my bag and page through it. Jules starts talking about a book, still staring at the ceiling. ("It's called *The Beauty of Chartreuse on the River Styx,* and it's about quirky teens who fall in love and die.")

I see Lilly's one-sheet:

Lilly Watts—skill set: audio and visual sensitivities.

What does *that* mean? That she can see and hear?

I flip further. I really want to be sleeping right now. I didn't even doze on the flight over. I changed out of my pointy witch shoes at the Paris airport in favor of some sensible-looking crepe-soled brogues, but my toes still hurt, and all I want to do is lie down on the black leather seat and conk out. I force myself to read:

Very few records of the Marquis du Bessancourt and his family have survived. Many of their papers were likely destroyed to avoid capture and the widespread repercussions against aristocrats during the Reign of Terror. Surviving documents show that Frédéric du Bessancourt was born in 1734 as the only legitimate child of a local nobleman, later rising to prominence as a banker and businessman under Louis XV of France. At this time, he also gained a reputation as a scientist, natural philosopher, and a frequent lender to the king and his successor, Louis XVI, financing much of the monarchs' lavish lifestyle. In 1774, the marquis married Célestine Gauthier. They had several children.

All records of the Bessancourt family cease after 1789. They are never mentioned again, either in revolutionary propaganda or in prison registries in and around the city of Paris. It is at this time that we assume he and his family fled underground, escaping France shortly afterward and reestablishing themselves under other names in England or Germany. Construction on a subterranean palace may have begun as early as 1760 in the vast caverns under the ancestral château. The palace, known at the time for unknown reasons as the Palais du Papillon (Palace of the Butterfly), has sat untouched for two hundred years. It lies below the water table, in bedrock, inviting *the possibility that some areas are partially or entirely submerged. We have no definite idea how large the palace is, how structurally sound, how safe. Regardless of its current state, it will be a treasure trove of revolutionary era detail and perhaps the most significant discovery from eighteenth-century Europe in history.*

We are pleased to have you with us on this momentous expedition and hope that this project will be a rewarding and enlightening experience for every one of you.

It's signed with an illegible scribble. Underneath is written, helpfully:

The Sapani Family

"Hey?" Jules is looking at me. I wonder how long I've been ignoring him. "You okay?"

I drop my head against the window again and make some indeterminable noise against the glass. For some reason he takes that as a no.

"You know," he says, as if pondering some major philosophical revelation. "You're a weird one. Normal people would be like, 'Yayyy, going to France with an awesome person named Jules and also exploring a two-hundred-year-old site, yayyy!'" He waves his hands with each *yay*. "I can't figure you out."

"I can't figure me out, either." I watch a twisted old tree by the side of the road grow closer, larger, gone. "Also, normal people didn't go on this trip. Just so you know."

He's probably making a face, being weirded out. I don't care. I do care, but at some point you have to stop caring, or you become Chernobyl-dead-zone levels of crazy. I *am* excited to be here. I can't wait to get into the palace, start discovering things, forget about New York, forget about college and the next sixty-plus years of my life that I have yet to muddle through. I just don't know how to communicate that to people.

"So, what are you here for?" Jules asks. "What are your stakes?"

I jam my feet up onto my seat and stare at the tips of my sensible brogues. I can't actually tell him. What am I going to say, that I'm being all Huck Finn and running away? Rebelling against the status quo, searching for redemption, trying to find an identity outside of being a punching bag for my dysfunctional family's psychoses? Because that's what I'm here for, and I don't need him to tell me that what I really need is therapy/some people have actual problems/those shoes are Prada, how could you possibly be unhappy?

"I'm here for the experience," I say. Lie. "And to practice my signature forging." I sling a wrist across my forehead. "Those selection rounds, *whew*! Got any dotted lines requiring signatures from parents and guardians? I'll sign them for you."

"You forged your parents' signatures? Do they even know you're here?"

"They think I'm in Azerbaijan. I left a note."

"Can I ask you a question?"

"No."

"What's wrong with your parents?"

"Look, Jules? You're nice and everything, but you need to mind your own business."

The Mercedes rumbles through some road construction. Bright cones flicker past like little lighthouses, gone in an instant. My chest feels tight. I don't look, but Jules's expression is probably bordering on disgust by now.

"Well, you certainly look like you've had a rough life," he says. "Malnourishment. Constant threat of war. No clothes but what you could scrounge out of the charity bin. How did you ever make it this far . . ."

"What?"

"Nothing. D'you think it's strange they're letting teenagers into a find like this? I mean, they could have gotten some veterans. Famous art historians or something. Doesn't it strike you as odd?"

I squint at him. "There *are* going to be famous art historians and veterans. Dorf's here. And anyway, we worked for this. We have qualifications. I'm sorry you have such a low opinion of your skills, but I feel like I've earned this."

I don't. I don't feel like I've earned anything.

"You're saying you're right up there with the greats and they couldn't have gotten anyone better if they tried?"

"I'm *saying*, no one's been down there yet," I snap. "I'm saying there haven't been many tests or age verifications, and no one knows anything until we get down there and start combing the place. So until then, yeah, teenagers are a great option. Good night."

I curl myself into the corner, and I feel empty, straight-up miserable. *Four chances of friendship down, zero to go. Good job, Ooky. Diligent as ever.*

There's this special talent humans have that they can be unhappy no matter where they are. No matter who they're with and what they have. Or maybe that's just my talent.

I pretend to fall asleep. Jules isn't talking to me anymore anyway.

Aurélie du Bessancourt—October 6, 1789

The market women marched on Versailles yesterday. They killed two guards, relieved them of their heads, and mounted their grisly trophies on pikes. "Like apples on a spit," Guillaume told the servants gathered around him in the front hall, and a gasp went up, a frantic chorus of rustling aprons and whispered oaths.

We were not supposed to hear, my sisters and I, but we stood at the crack in the music room's doors and listened.

Guillaume had been at Versailles, waiting to deliver a message from Father, when news came of the market women's approach. He claimed to have seen the queen herself running for the hall of mirrors with the young dauphin. He said that the royal family had fled to Paris, that Louis XVI was as good as headless already.

My sleeves stick uncomfortably to my wrists. My mouth is dry. I hurry my sisters out the other side of the music room, and I try to distract them with fumbled card tricks, but I cannot focus and I drop the deck. Father has already left the château, gone down to the Palais du Papillon. Again a casket was sent to Mama, an invitation asking her to join him in the depths. Again I intercepted it:

My *darling*, it said, the writing splattered and uneven, ink beads on an ink thread, as if Father paused many times during the forming of each letter to consider the next.

It is no longer safe to remain in the château. I have heard whispers, received letters. A storm brews in Paris that will rain blood and ruin on France as it has not seen in a hundred years. Soon there will be looting and death and chaos. The king will be beheaded and his wife as well. A wave of human filth will flow across the land. But you have nothing to fear, ma chérie. For such a catastrophe as this I built the Palais du Papillon: so that no matter what terrors befall the world, our way of life shall go on, the beauty and tranquillity of our grand culture preserved forever. I promise you, you shall have every comfort in the palace. You will be safe, my treasure. You will be cared for.

Your husband,

Frédéric du Bessancourt

But Mama would not go. I had heard her pleading with

the guards he had sent for her, heard her anguished sobs, so desperate and grating, I could hardly imagine them coming from one so small.

"Why?" I asked her again this morning when I caught her alone in the upstairs gallery. "Mama, why will we not go to the palace? We will only be there a short while, surely. What has frightened you?"

She answered me this time, taking my hands and squeezing them until I thought my fingers might snap. "The servants," she said. "They have such dreadful faces."

She might as well have held her tongue for all that helped me.

6

Our convoy pulls into Péronne a little after 11:30 A.M. I peer up at the buildings as we drive down the main street, at the ivy climbing the brick facades, the *boulangeries* and *pâtisseries* and *fleurists*. Freezing rain drips off every mansard roof and verdigris-touched gutter. A woman in a vivid red head scarf turns to watch our convoy's approach, then looks away quickly. It's so quiet.

I expect us to park at the tiny hotel, but we don't. The cars continue down the street, gliding silently. We leave Péronne behind. After about twenty minutes, we turn through a pair of tall iron gates and down a country road. Security cameras swivel as we pass. I look back and see the gates closing behind us.

I tap the glass that separates us from the driver and Dorf. No answer. I look at Jules. He's fallen asleep, knees pulled up to his chin.

I watch the trees slide by, bare and wintry. The road is long and utterly straight. Our convoy slices down it, sleek black cars reflecting the branches and the sky.

We're approaching something: a wide white house squatting at the end of the avenue. It's a château, stark against the muddy greens and grays of the countryside.

I nudge Jules with my foot. "I think we're here," I mumble.

He doesn't wake up.

The cars pull up in front of the pale château, curling like a fiddlehead around the wide circular driveway. The locks on our doors click open.

I step out into the cold. Car doors are opening all around, disgorging Red Spikes, the other bodyguards, Will. Miss Sei is clicking toward me.

"Where are we?" I ask her, looking up at the house. It's symmetrical, two floors, square windows. Probably mid-nineteenth century. Solid and big and old, like a country stronghold.

"Château du Bessancourt. It's part of the Sapani portfolio," Miss Sei says. It's the first time I've heard her talk. She has a perfect cut-glass English accent. She opens Dorf's door. Murmurs something into the dim interior.

Turns back to me. "They bought it several years ago and began a restoration. That's why you're here. Professor Dorf will explain inside."

"Wait, we're staying *here?*" Jules is climbing out behind me, groggy, his hair sticking up in wet-cat spikes.

Dorf chuckles and unfolds out of the passenger seat. "Of course!" He stamps twice on the cobbled drive. His leather wingtip shoes are polished to mirrors. "This is our site. One hundred feet below us lies the entrance to the mythical Palais du Papillon. Best be close by, I thought."

I stare at the cobbles. Peer up at the house again. Somewhere in the blue folder it was mentioned that the original château burned to the ground during the revolution. This one must be the replacement. It's weird to think about French people in wigs and stockings running around here a couple centuries ago. That there was another world here before us, people going about their lives with no idea what was coming for them. I look back down the avenue, stretching away, nothing on either side but trees and fields.

Hayden and Lilly walk up, Lilly jabbering, Hayden glowering straight ahead like he wants to punch something.

"Everybody?" Dorf says. His voice hangs in the frozen air, dull and muffled. "Listen, please. This will be our base of operations during the expeditions. While the Sapanis are not here at the moment, we will be guests in their home. Be careful and conscious of that while you are staying in the château. Now. There will be attendants to bring in your luggage. Follow me."

Lilly slips back into one of the Mercedes and shoulders her huge backpack.

"He said leave it," Jules mutters to her, and I see her look at him like, *Over my dead body.* We follow Dorf up the steps to the dark, polished doors. They're carved with hatchets and roses, just like the coat of arms on our documents. We step into the high, echoing hall. Miss Sei and the four bodyguards enter behind us. I'm still not sure why the bodyguards are here. I get that the Sapanis are rich and powerful, but it's not like there are going to be paparazzi leaping out of the hedges and sticking microphones in our faces.

The floor is tiled in black-and-white marble. The walls are paneled in dark wood. The air is cold. Damp. The kind of air that comes when no one's breathing it, when it just sits and stagnates like still water.

I'm walking right beside Dorf. He leans over. "Anouk," he says quietly, pleasantly. "It's really wonderful you could be here. We were worried we wouldn't fill the last spot, but then, there you were! And with such a fortunate family! We're so pleased for you." He spins, and his voice goes up about ten decibels. "Everyone! Miss Sei will take you to your rooms now."

I stare at him, confused. He smiles at me, all conspiratorial like we're total buddies, and ducks through a low, ornately carved doorway. The door clicks shut.

What was that *about?* My heart is beating painfully inside my chest, a tiny mallet against bone.

"Anouk," Miss Sei says. I turn. She's waiting at the foot of the staircase, watching me. "Please rejoin the group."

She starts up the stairs, six-inch heels going off like a pair of nail guns. I hurry to catch up with the others.

"Dinner will be served at five forty-five tonight." Miss Sei looks straight ahead as she talks, eyes fixed on a point in the middle distance. "Not all the staff has arrived yet. I'm sure you'll forgive any lapses in hospitality. Please feel free to freshen up and rest in your rooms. Be ready to meet Professor Dorf in the entrance hall at five-thirty. That is all."

Jules casts a halfhearted look back down the stairs toward the cars and the luggage. Lilly pats the strap of her backpack and smiles sweetly at him.

We arrive at the second-story hallway. Miss Sei opens a huge door. "Mr. Maiburgh, Mr. Park, Mr. Makra. This will be your room. Miss Peerenboom and Miss Watts, please follow me."

She heads down the hallway again, and I catch a glimpse of her face, like a mask, tense and frozen. If I weren't so heartless, I'd probably feel bad for her. Babysitting teenagers is a big step down from chief science officer of the Sapani Corporation. I would be seething, too.

She doesn't say anything as she opens our door—just stands next to it, watching us with those glimmering eyes. I slide past her into the room. Catch a whiff of something coming off her, bitter lemons and rosemary, like really strong soap. Under it is another smell, duller. Chemical.

As soon as the door closes and Miss Sei's footsteps have retreated down the hallway, Lilly shrugs off her backpack. Lets out all her breath. Collapses on the bed like she just ran a marathon. "This is *so* weird. Did you see this place? It's like Hogwarts. But bad."

I stand stiffly, looking around me. The ceiling is high, fifteen feet at least. Dark green silk covers the walls. Tassels and silver brocade pillows drip off everything. And it's cold. I can hear the whisper of an air system, but all the heat must be rising to the ceiling, curling under the sumptuous plasterwork. I definitely can't feel it down here.

Lilly laughs suddenly and rolls off the bed. "So what do you think of the boyyyys?" She crawls on hands and knees over to her backpack and starts digging around in it. "Hayden's stuck up, but I think he's just insecure. Like, he needs *friendship*."

I don't bother answering. As usual, Lilly doesn't care. She pulls out a very large, clear plastic toiletry bag and resumes her crawl.

"I like Jules," she says. "He's hilarious."

"Of course he's hilarious, have you seen his face? It's called overcompensating."

Lilly stops crawling. Looks over her shoulder like I just ate a puppy. "That's not cool, Anouk. It's not." She stands and walks the rest of the way to the bathroom, her expression closed up like a box.

"What?" I say, spreading my arms in a *Hey-don't-*

shoot-the-messenger stance. "People who are considered less attractive by society have to find other ways to make themselves desirable. It's science."

"It's mean." She tugs open the bathroom door and disappears inside. I hear the rush of a faucet. When she speaks again her voice is flat, echoing through the door. "D'you know what was up with the bodyguards?"

Apparently she's done discussing boys with me. At least she can take a hint.

"I was wondering the same thing," I say. "They don't want anyone to know what they found here—"

"But then why invite students?" Lilly appears at the door, rubbing something furiously into the ends of her hair.

I turn to the window. The light outside is lead gray and flat, like it's already evening. The trees make a tight square around the property. Jules asked that exact same thing. I brushed him off, but it's a valid question. What *are* we doing here? Why Lilly? Why me? Why the others, all of us so completely different from each other? Blue folders in the mail, embossed letterheads, and thick stationery go a long way toward making things seem sensible and official. And I really wanted this to happen, so I *told* myself it was sensible. Like people who believe in daily horoscopes or pass on chain letters. Like people who do non-sensible things.

Lilly goes back into the bathroom. Shouts: "This place is *bare*. I don't like it. And there's only one towel. Did you check for Wi-Fi?"

I study the massive four-poster. It's as big as a whole room by itself, but there's only one. I'll be sleeping on the couch, I guess.

"If there is, I doubt they'll let you use it," I call back, and wander to the window, digging my phone from my pocket. At least ten Wi-Fi options line up on the screen. All locked.

I toss my phone onto the nightstand. Lilly comes out of the bathroom holding a cup of amber liquid. She's clutching it in both hands like it might escape.

"They have brandy," she says, awestruck. "In the *bathroom*."

"I thought you said it was bare."

"Yeah, but *brandy*."

She takes a sip, makes a face, and sets the cup down on a dresser. It's going to leave a ring, but I don't say anything. My head feels heavy. Lilly gets busy pulling chargers and cable tangles from her backpack. I crawl onto the bed. I don't really plan on sleeping. I just lie there, staring up at the canopy. Drift in and out of consciousness. At some point I pull the covers up over my shoes and jeans. . . .

I dream I'm floating in a black expanse of water. Only my face and hands break the surface. And slowly something else rises to the top—a girl in a sumptuous dress, only she's facedown, her back like a velvet island, her cold fingers brushing mine, and I start to thrash, the black water boiling around me—

7

I wake up feeling like a slug. This is what happens when you sleep in your clothes—you get that nasty, greasy mixture of chilliness and warmth, and you remember all the times you slept in airports, car seats, on Ellis Winthrope's cracked-leather couch, braving the smell of rank tennis socks and stale chips because you didn't want to be home, *you really, really didn't want to be home—*

I blink a few times. Roll onto my back. The room is dark.

"Lilly?"

I rub the heels of my palms into my eyes. Kick off my shoes and pad to the bathroom. "Lilly, what time is it?" The bathroom is solid marble. One side of the sink has been taken over by a jumble of bottles and candy-colored makeup tubes. There's the decanter of brandy Lilly was talking about. It's mostly full and Lilly is definitely not here.

I take a quick, scalding shower and poke my head into the bedroom. Lilly's backpack looks like it ate an entire wardrobe of jean jackets and tie-dye and feathers and then threw up, which is a pretty understandable reaction. My luggage still isn't here. I thought Dorf said someone was going to bring it up.

I look out the window. The light is completely gone now. I scramble out of the bathroom, wrapping up in the lone towel as I run for my phone. Hit the screen. *Crap.* It's 5:25.

I tear back into the bathroom, drag on the same clothes I flew here in. Skinny jeans, chunky-knit gray sweater with a kangaroo pocket, the brogues. Hope dinner isn't a formal affair. Open the hall door. And almost knee Lilly in the face.

She's sitting right outside, cross-legged on the floor. Jules and Hayden are with her. They were talking, but they all stop as soon as I step out and stare up at me with too-round eyes.

"Hey," Hayden says after a second. Grins his stupid 1940s movie-star grin.

I step around them and head for the stairs. "Hey,

Blue Eyes," I say, in a way that I hope also communicates *I hate you.*

I don't know why I'm angry. Big surprise that they didn't wake me up for their discussion round. What was I expecting after the last twenty-four hours?

I pass Will as he's leaving the boys' room. I start down the stairs. I wonder what they were talking about. Probably me. Something along the lines of *Anouk is going to be such a pain, and maybe we should just burn her at the stake right now.*

The hall is empty, the columns forming shadow triangles across the checkerboard floor. I drop into a chair in front of the massive, cold fireplace and lean over the armrest. Rifle through a basket of magazines and newspapers. Will isn't exactly bursting with friendliness, either, but I bet no one was talking about that.

Lilly comes down a minute later and sits next to me. Glances over surreptitiously like she's trying to think of something to say.

I pick up three newspapers and spread them over my lap. They're all from today, unwrinkled and unread. The headlines are about car accidents, bombings, a head of state looking constipated about something. I start drafting better headlines in my mind, proper daydream-y screamers:

THE FRENCH PHARAOH: EIGHTEENTH-CENTURY BILLIONAIRE BUILDS A TOMB OF EGYPTIAN PROPORTIONS

MAD MARQUIS: A SECRET HISTORY

UNEARTHED! A DRAMATIC TALE OF UNDERGROUND PALACE FULL OF MYSTERY AND EXCLAMATION POINTS!

"I was going to wake you up," Lilly says quietly. "I was, I just forgot. I know you think we were talking about you, but I swear—"

"I actually don't care," I say.

I slap down the newspapers and dig for my phone. My pocket's empty. I left the phone upstairs. I look around for a clock. There's one across the hall, twelve feet high, dark and thin, like a loner Goth kid at a jock party, standing in the corner, spiny hands creeping over a pale face.

I can feel Lilly peering at me, hurt. I don't know what to do. The ticking is weirdly loud and harsh. My brain must have been filtering it out, because I didn't notice it a second ago.

Will comes down the stairs, looks at Lilly and me

and the empty chair next to us. Deems the waters too dangerous. Leans against the wall.

Hayden and Jules come down.

At precisely 5:30, a door opens and Professor Dorf and Miss Sei come snapping toward us over the marble.

Aurélie du Bessancourt—October 18, 1789

We remain in the château like ghosts. It is so quiet here,
the gardens and the park slowly succumbing to neglect and
silence. All five of us—Mama, me, Bernadette, Charlotte,
and Delphine—are draped across the sofas or curled on the
rugs in a tense sort of stupor. The servants have all been sent
down. I watched them crowding the staircase, a procession
of cooks and maids in dirty aprons and snowy caps, butlers
in gleaming livery, musicians, wigmakers, and tailors, their
faces stiff as funeral masks.

Mama is pretending that all is well. She dresses for din-
ners that are not served, thanks maids and footmen who
are no longer here—pantomiming desperately to us that we
are not alone in the path of thousands of starving, angry
peasants.

Yesterday I went into the lower passage and stared at
the little panel, the secret way into the Palais du Papillon.

I saw Father's motto, picked out in tiny brass letters along the cornice, almost invisible: *To Good Luck and Safety and Everlasting Peace.*

"We should not stay, Mama," I say, sitting up, and every head but hers turns to stare at me. The windows are open onto the park. A breeze is whispering in, warm at first touch and then chilly. "We should take the carriage to Croisilles or go down to Father, but we must not stay here alone. What if someone were to come?"

No one answers. Bernadette and Charlotte do not seem to understand the danger. They have never gone a hot day without parasols or a cold day without fox fur. I fear they think themselves invincible because of it. Delphine knows something is wrong, but she is six. I could not bear to tell her my worries. It is Mama who should worry with me, who *does* know but will not tell me. She should be helping me organize our escape, hurrying to bolt up the château, and yet she continues on her frivolous course like a horse in blinders. I feel I could scream.

"We will die if we stay here."

The words leave me like a battering ram. At my feet, Delphine gasps. Charlotte and Bernadette look up from their poetry, startled. Mama glances at me, her eyes wide and limpid. Her voice trembles when she speaks, but her words ring pure and clear: "Everyone dies," she says. She turns to the window, her beautiful face in profile, the sunlight playing across her long, pale neck. "They are cutting off heads, you say? It is a quick way to go. A mercy."

8

The double doors open, and Dorf leads us into the dining room.
Miss Sei turned down a hallway seconds before we
reached it. Guess she's not mingling with the riffraff this
evening.

The dining room is huge. The size of a tennis court.
A massive table runs down it, polished walnut with an
explosion of peonies and greenhouse hyacinth at its center.
Candelabras stand on either side of the flower arrangement. They're not lit. The lights are in the walls, in the
ceiling, thin strips of LED tucked behind panels, illuminating everything with a soft amber glow. It's like we
just stepped into one of Tolstoy's endless dinner scenes,
except it's high-tech and attended solely by underdressed
teenagers.

We pull out our chairs. Lilly decides she wants to sit
next to Will three seconds after she's situated herself next

to Hayden. Shuffling and scraping chair legs ensue, followed by some annoyed looks from Hayden. Now we're all in place, and silence settles like dust.

Dorf clears his throat. "Your parents have all been informed of your safe arrival. We will be keeping them updated and will have a complete folder prepared and sent to them before your return. Once the media embargo is over, they'll know as much as everyone! I think they'll be quite pleased with what you are capable of."

I hate how he talks. Like we're not even real people. Like we're a row of dumbbells with painted faces, supposed to nod and smile at his performance.

"The palace," Will says. He's fiddling with the silverware, straightening it on the starched linen napkin. "It must have taken decades to build. Versailles took fifty years. How could they have kept something so huge a secret?"

Dorf smiles. "They couldn't. At least, not entirely. There were reports of a great undertaking in Péronne, and certainly local rumors, but many historians thought it was simply another tall tale fabricated by Paris revolutionaries. Slander was rampant against the aristocracy. An underground palace as large as the Sun King's court but buried a hundred feet down was probably too ridiculous and excessive a luxury to even consider."

"When was it found?" Hayden asks. "And how did you hear about it?"

"The entrance was discovered about two months ago," Dorf says. "Quite by accident. They thought it was a sinkhole at first. A Mr. Gourbillon was in charge of this house's restoration. He and some of the workmen came down one morning and found a ten-foot crater in the wine cellar. They started digging and found a chair. Then a room, wallpapered. They had stumbled right into one of the palace's higher antechambers. Mr. Gourbillon called the Sapanis' people. The Sapanis' people called me."

Lucky that the Sapanis' people didn't call the police. The police would have issued a statement and this place would be crawling with AFP and treasure hunters and bearded adrenaline-junkie hipsters with huge cameras.

"And why did the Sapanis call *us?*" I ask. Jules shoots me a look like *Really? Now you're going to bring this up?* I ignore him.

"The Sapanis are very keen on nurturing deserving youth of today," Dorf says. "They have multiple foundations and scholarships set up in a variety of fields. They wanted to give you all an opportunity. And they have."

"That's nice of them. Why aren't they here at the château if they care so much?"

Dorf looks at me curiously. "Anouk, the Sapanis are busy people. I'm sure you read your dossier. Their corporate empire spans Asia, Europe, the United States. One of their technology firms may have designed the processor chip in your phone, the engines in the plane that brought you here, the air-filtration system in this very room. Surely you'll forgive them that they didn't come running the moment you arrived."

Jules snorts, starts coughing violently to hide his laughter.

I stare at Dorf, stone-faced. "I don't expect them to come running for me, no, but for the unsealing of a massive underground palace? Yeah, I'd stop designing air-filtration systems for that."

Dorf twinkles at me. I want to punch him. "Would you? Well, I'll let them know. In the meantime, they've entrusted me with your care and the direction of this expedition, and that will have to be enough for you."

He didn't answer my question. At all. Lilly looks over at me, frowning slightly, and I'm not sure if she's frowning about what I said or what Dorf said. The silence stretches—

—and breaks: three waiters walk into the room. Cream satin waistcoats, gold buttons, little bowties. Each carries two silver bell-covered dishes. They place them in front of us, swoop the bells away, and file out as quickly as they came.

One whiff, and I don't even care about Dorf anymore. In front of me are three dainty bowls, one soup, one prawns, one green steamed vegetables dusted with red threads of saffron. I smell roasted garlic and sweet chili and spring onions.

The table lights up with sounds of clinking silverware and sliding china.

"Has anyone been down there yet?" Hayden asks between mouthfuls. "The file said the palace was sealed up. Have you been inside?"

"No." Dorf isn't eating. He's flicking around on the glimmering surface of the table next to his plate, and I realize he's got a tablet there, razor thin. His fingers skid over the screen. "We found the Bessancourt coat of arms in the antechamber. A butterfly with eyes in its wings. That particular coat of arms ceased to exist after 1792, so it didn't take long for speculation to begin that this was the actual Palais du Papillon. We did some GPR scans and charted out a rough outline of the palace. The antechambers lead to the shafts, which lead to what we assume is the main entrance, but that's as far as we've gone." Dorf glances up. "And yes, Hayden, it is sealed. We have no idea what's on the other side."

He holds up the tablet. On it is a photo, so harshly lit it looks black and white. It shows a huge, ornately gilded set of double doors. The handles are knotted together with massive rope. A dark, fist-sized lump is fixed to the center. I think it's a wax seal.

A hush falls over the table. I stare at the screen. Tomorrow we'll be standing in front of those doors. Breaking the seal. Going in.

"Um . . ." I swallow a prawn without chewing. It hurts. "Obviously the Bessancourts had those doors sealed *after* they left, right? They escaped to England and lived happily ever after. We're not going to find a bunch of corpses down there."

"We do think the Bessancourts escaped to England, yes. In 1802 a man named Friedrich Besserschein died in northern Yorkshire. The village records list four surviving daughters, and they also state that Mr. Besserschein was a foreigner born in 1734, the same year as Frédéric Bessancourt. We *think* that was Frédéric Bessancourt. And no, unless the entire palace is airtight and there was an expert embalmer present when it was sealed, there will be no corpses on this expedition."

Dorf sets down the tablet and smiles. "Now. What we *will* find should be far more interesting. The marquis will have brought down with him everything he wanted preserved. That should include an extensive collection of art and manuscripts, servants, his wife and children." Dorf chuckles, like equating wives and servants to paintings and manuscripts is actually hilarious. "And they will have brought jewels, wardrobes, favorite musical instruments, toys, diaries, medicine. If it is even slightly intact, the Palais du Papillon will be much more than only an architectural wonder. It will be a feast of historical detail, an entire banquet of eighteenth-century French life preserved just as it was, waiting for us to study it."

The waiters are back. I've barely started my soup, but they're whisking it away and a new bell-covered dish is set in front of me. Tender green asparagus this time, so tiny and bright they're like plastic children's toys. A silver teaspoon heaped with caviar. A seashell full of hollandaise sauce.

"We'll be distributing your equipment in the morning," Dorf says. "You'll find the schedule in your rooms when you go upstairs. We will be rappelling into the palace from the wine cellar at nine o'clock sharp, so make sure you get a good night's sleep. Set your alarms, eat a healthy breakfast. . . ." He trails off, looking amused. "And from there, who knows? Whatever happens, whatever we find down there, this is going to be the experience of a lifetime."

Jules and Hayden look at each other like *Aw, yisssss.* Will peers gravely at his plate. Lilly eats a single nub of asparagus and swoops her hair over her shoulder. I don't know what to do. Something is off here. I don't know what it is, but something feels wrong.

Aurélie du Bessancourt—October 23, 1789

We locked ourselves in the library when we heard them: heavy boots in the lower chambers, voices calling to each other. I have been dreading this for days—strangers following the avenue up from the muddy road; hungry, bird-eyed people shattering a window latch, creeping in—but now that they are here, my heart twists in terror.

"Perhaps they are monarchists," I say hopefully.

No one answers. Mama sits like an unfinished fountain nymph, her face stony and expressionless, Delphine clutched in her lap. Bernadette and Charlotte hunch together on the sofa. All of us are staring at the locked doors.

The footsteps approach the second floor—the iron snap of hobnails on the staircase, echoing up into the gallery. When they reach the library, Delphine cannot stop herself; a noise escapes her throat, high and piercing, like a kitten's mew. It is impossible not to hear. The handle to the library rattles. Fists begin to pound viciously at the doors. I watch the wood splinter around the hinges. When no one goes to unlock them, the doors are kicked down.

Two men rush in, clad in Father's colors, red and gold. Guards. One of them is ancient, weathered like the figurehead of a ship. The other is hardly older than I am, his face chiseled, a strand of dark hair fallen from under his hat, stuck in a curl to his forehead. Both are dripping sweat, breathless.

"Madame Célestine," the younger one says. "Mesdemoiselles." He nods quickly to my sisters and me. "They are coming."

Mama sits up in her chair, wide-eyed and frozen, like a rabbit before the butchering. Delphine clings to her, burying her face in Mama's side and watching the guards keenly out of the corner of one eye. Bernadette and Charlotte look on from the sofa, their arms wrapped around each other, the lace of their sleeves trembling, though their bodies seem motionless.

I stand. "Are you sure?" My voice is weak; I clear my throat. "Father said they would not come here. He said he had made an agreement, a pact with the *Assemblée nationale* that we would be left alone."

The old guard speaks, his voice gruff and sticky. I am

afraid he is going to spit on our floor: "If you wish, my lady, step outside and inform them of this agreement. Six hundred fishwives from Paris are coming through the park as we speak. I am sure they would be thrilled to meet you."

The old guard's face is scarred and pitted with age and disease. He is making no turns toward civility. In that case, neither will I.

"What of the delivery road at the back of the kitchens?" I say. "Did you come on horseback? Can you drive a carriage?"

The guards exchange glances. "Mademoiselle, you misunderstand," the young one says. "We are not from the estates. The marquis sent us; we are from . . ."

From below. From the palace. That means it is too late for carriages, too late to flee. Father will not be spared from the revolution. His bribes did not work.

I turn to Mama, but she is already standing, her petal mouth pinched. "I will not go," she says before I can even speak. "Aurélie, I will *not!*" She leans down over Delphine, strokes her cheeks and her dress, almost frantically. "Do not ask me to, Aurélie, do not ask me—"

A rumble is growing outside. The sun is almost gone, the last shades of bronze fading behind the poplars. I hear them approaching now, shouts and singing, rough voices drifting in the quiet of the park.

I cross the distance between us, snatch her hand, and drag her toward the door.

"I am not asking you, Mother. We will not die here. I will not, and I will not allow you to, either. Hurry."

9

Our dishes are removed again. Tiny finger bowls of lavender water arrive, followed by perfect, rose-colored orbs of pomegranate sorbet in martini glasses.

I'm just finishing mine, slipping my spoon along the edge of the glass, when one of the waiters returns. He's carrying a tray of crystal water glasses on small pewter coasters. The coasters have pills on them, dark red and glimmering, like droplets of blood. The waiter sets one coaster down in front of each of us. Whispers out. I catch a glimpse of a tattoo on his neck, a black swirl disappearing under his collar.

"What's this?" I pick up one of the pills. Watch the air bubble in its center shift.

Dorf reaches for his coaster, puts his palm to his mouth, and throws back his head. Swallows. "The palace is one hundred feet below the earth's crust," Dorf says, dabbing his mouth with his napkin. "Uncirculated air can be very dangerous. These are to counteract possible microbes and toxins that can develop within a sealed environment."

Except his coaster was empty. I know it was. The waiter brought six glasses. Six coasters. One of them had no pills on it. Dorf's.

My skin goes cold. "That's ridiculous," I say. Try to keep the tremor out of my voice. "You can't immunize yourself against poisonous air with a couple of pills. Our bodies will start digesting these right away. The effects will wear off in our sleep."

Dorf's gaze falls on me, and for the first time I see annoyance in those calm gray eyes. He doesn't say anything. Lilly's gaze darts between us. *Did she see what I saw?*

But Hayden's already picking up his pills. "Bottoms up," he says, and downs them. I stare at him, watch the straight-razor angle of his jaw work as he swallows. I kind of expect him to sprout claws, horns, maybe fall off his chair and start writhing on the floor. He doesn't. He pounds his chest twice and grins at me, as if he's somehow proving me stupid.

Is he?

Lilly and Jules both pick up their pills. Glance at each other. Jules swallows his and Lilly, not wanting to be left behind, follows suit. Dorf smiles at me again, that sickening *you're-a-joke* smirk. "See?" he says. "Nobody died."

At the edge of my vision I see Will looking philosophically at his pills. Does *he* at least sense anything off?

Nope. He downs his pills, too.

I stare at the one resting in my palm. *Red-dark-red-dark*. And suddenly it looks like a puncture, blood blooming out of my skin.

I'm not overreacting. Something's wrong. I grab the other pill and shove my chair back. The legs screech against the floor.

Hayden is starting to move weirdly, like he's underwater. His head lolls against his chest. He flops upright a second later with a weak laugh, but this isn't funny. Everyone stares at him. Everyone but Dorf.

His eyes are fixed on me.

"Anouk?" he says, and his voice is rock hard. "Sit down. Take the pills."

Aurélie du Bessancourt—October 23, 1789

We whirl down the stairs, deeper and deeper into the earth, and all I can see is Mama turning away from us, the blood soaking her gown.

They shot her. The bullet ripped through flesh and sinew, lodging amid the pearly snakes of her intestines like a speck of coal, a black seed sprouting death. In five minutes she will no longer be able to breathe. In ten she will be gone forever. . . .

"Aurélie," she screamed. *"Do not leave me behind."*

But I did.

Above, I can hear the roar of flames as they consume the château, becoming steadily quieter, as if we are leaving chaos and gunpowder behind us, descending into another world entirely.

Our only light is from the open lantern in the old guard's hand. The hot stench of it catches me in the face as I descend—animal fat and dirty rags and kerosene. Bernadette hurries behind him, dragging at her skirts, her tongue clucking like a goose as she cries. Charlotte is close at her back, doing the same, always her sister's little shadow, even in distress. Delphine and I are next. The young guard brings up the rear, pushing us onward in a dogged panic.

10

I don't sit down. I tuck the pills behind my teeth. Taste the gel casing, smooth, cold on my tongue. And run for the hall.

This was not part of the contract. Undisclosed drugs were *not part of the contract*. I'm going to get my phone and I'm going to call someone. I don't know who, but someone needs to know where we are.

"Is there a problem, Anouk?" Dorf's voice floats into the hall. "If there's a problem, just let me know—"

I see a glass door at the far end of the hall, facing the border of trees and the fields. I could make a run for it. I taste something bitter on my tongue. The pills are dissolving, trickling into my mouth.

Crap-crap-crap, get rid of them, get out of here—

I turn, see Miss Sei striding across the hall toward me. She's got Norse God and Red Spikes with her and they look freakish, dangerous, streaks of moonlight and shadow from the windows slashing across their faces.

I cough and spit a thick red glob onto the stairs. Wipe my mouth and stagger up them.

I'm so slow. What is *happening*? I can still taste the pill, can feel threads of numbness spreading into my cheeks. I reach the upper hallway, stumble down it, my hand on the wall.

"Anouk, what's the matter?" Dorf's voice reaches me, slowed down and warbling, from downstairs. "Why don't you get some rest, it's been a long day—"

I swear he sounds like he's grinning. I fumble with the door handle, burst into my room. I need my phone, I need to call Penny—

I crash into the side table, almost knocking over the lamp. Swipe my hand over the marble top. The door is wide open. I hear them in the hallway. *Where's my PHONE?* I whirl, glance around the room, swaying.

I see the drapes. Chairs. Pillows. No wrinkled sheets. Lilly's monstrous hiking backpack is gone. The bed is made. There's a water ring on the mahogany.

I heave myself toward the bathroom door. Collapse against the frame. A dull, pulsing pain explodes inside my skull. The sink is polished, empty. No bottles of mascara, no tissues, no toiletry bag. Everything's been cleaned. Wiped down.

The pulsing becomes a beat, drowning out my thoughts. I'm on the floor. I see shoes approaching, black and shimmering, like beetles, swarming toward me. My pupils must be dilating, my vision going blurry clear-blurry.

Please, no, Mom-Dad-Penny, someone please help me—

And I'm gone.

Stairs to the Palais du Papillon—
47 feet below—October 23, 1789

I see Mama in my mind's eye, crawling down the gallery. Her beautiful gown is stained with blood and soot. She is coughing, weeping, and ash is whirling like a winter storm, filling the gallery. It coats her face and lashes, turns her to a statue of white and gray. In the distance the flames flare, red-hot and hellish.

We cannot leave her. We cannot leave her behind.

I stop. The young guard collides with my back. Delphine squeaks in surprise.

"We must go back," I whisper. "We must go back for Mother."

"Mademoiselle, we cannot—" The young guard tries to guide me onward, but I dig my fingers into the stone on either side and refuse to move. It is foolishness, I know it is, but she is my mother. In Versailles they murdered two guards, and they were not even noble. I hope to God they have not yet taken her head.

"Mademoiselle, if we return we will all be killed." The young guard's face is strangely exquisite in the torchlight, his expression not unkind. His words slide off me like water.

"I will go alone if you will not help me, but I will not leave her to be burned."

"Please, mademoiselle. Baptiste!" The young guard calls after his companion. *"La demoiselle, elle—"*

I hear the old guard pounding back up the steps, shoving past my sisters, the rushing sound of his lantern as it flares. I do not move my gaze from the young soldier.

"Please help me," I say to him, and my voice is a pitiful-thin thread. "We cannot leave her. If Father were to hear that we had abandoned her to the *révolutionnaires*, he would—"

The old guard grips my wrist, dragging me savagely about. "Your father will do *nothing*," he spits. "The Marchioness Célestine was driven to hysteria by the sight of her burning home. She could not be reasoned with, ran back to fetch her jewels, and was killed. That is all your father will hear, do you understand?"

His teeth are like china, gleaming in his leather face. I recoil from him, try to twist away, but his fingers only tighten further, digging into my skin.

"I asked you, mademoiselle, if that was clear. I trust that even in my brutish, peasant French you understood the question."

"I do not believe you are in a position to command me, monsieur. Do not come if you do not choose to, but—"

The old guard turns my wrist so that my elbow points into the air and I shriek with the pain. My eyes fly to my sisters, panicked, as if I can do something to stop them from seeing, from hearing. They stare back, Charlotte's mouth hanging open.

Somewhere high above, an echoing crash. The old guard lets me go and I stumble, gripping Delphine. "Move," he says. "*Rapidement.*"

And we are hurrying down the stairs once more. Tears spring against my eyelids, hot and shameful. Confusion and fear twist into a knot in the pit of my stomach. I focus on the jacket stretched across the old guard's back, the lantern fumes flowing in stinking swaths up the stairs, the soot dotting on my sisters' necks like fleas. *Mama, please, please be safe.*

We pass under an archway. It is becoming difficult to breathe. The air is not warm, but my skin feels sticky beneath the layers of satin and lace. The stairs are becoming wider, the treads not so steep and narrow. Everything around us is rough, ugly stone.

We arrive at the bottom and move down a tunnel, round

and ribbed like the belly of a whale. Ahead I see a room: a small cube, mirrored on all four sides. Someone is standing in it. A man. My hand tightens around Delphine.

The guards hurry us forward.

The man's shoulders are so wide they seem to push at the seams of his black frock coat. His arms are like tree trunks. His back is toward us, but I recognize him now: Lord Havriel. The quiet giant at my father's side, the steward of his great wealth and the keeper of his secrets.

Lord Havriel turns toward us. He is strangely elegant despite his size, like a dancer. His face is square and serious, framed by a dark beard neatly trimmed. He is almost Father's age, but not half so decomposed.

"Mesdemoiselles," he says, and he moves forward, his hand going to his waist in preparation for a bow.

He stops. His eyes skip over our bedraggled party: the old guard, Charlotte, Bernadette, Delphine. His eyes stop on me.

"Where is the Lady Célestine?" His voice is soft.

"She ran back to her rooms, monsieur," the old guard says quickly. "There was nothing we could do, she—"

Havriel stiffens. "She is still in the château?"

The old guard shifts from boot to boot, but he does not answer. The younger one nods, once.

Havriel's eyes twitch, only the slightest bit, a blink and a focusing. And now he is growling, and I feel Delphine flinch against me. *"Non, espèce d'imbéciles. Qu'est-ce que vous avez fait?"*

He begins to pace. There is hardly any space in the little mirror room, but he does, tight circles, his black-trousered legs cutting like scissors. "You must get her. Get her down here at *once.*"

"My lord, she would not come!" the old guard says desperately. "She was hysterical, she refused!"

Havriel stops and spins on the young guard. His eyes are dark, flashing like storm clouds. I have never seen him anything but calm—at dinner parties or during ceremonies of state, with King Louis and his Austrian wife, with everyone preened and brushed out, proud as peacocks, Havriel was the silent one, the austere figure in black, a vast quiet presence, sipping wine, whispering into Father's gnarled red ear. . . .

"You will return at once to the surface," he says, and suddenly his voice is dangerous and low. "I have orders to seal the Palais du Papillon. If you come back alone, you will be locked out, and believe me, your role in the rescuing of our dear *noblesse* will not be appreciated by your kinsmen in Paris."

The young guard clutches his musket. He swallows, staring at Havriel. The older guard stares, too, but there is something dreadful in his eyes, a mixture of fear and utter hatred.

"You are sending us to our death for a madwoman—" he begins, and Havriel whirls on him and bellows: "Go! And pray she is yet alive!"

They leave us, ducking back through the doorway, and now they are sprinting away, silhouetted in the tunnel.

As soon as the sound of their feet has faded, Havriel's shoulders slump. He turns to us, and the many deep grooves in his face soften. But there is worry in his eyes, and a question, too, as if he does not know exactly what to do with three weeping girls and one staring, sullen one. I do not know what to do with him, either. I take Delphine by the shoulders and turn her away. "All will be well," I murmur, leaning down next to her ear. "They are going back for Mama. They will bring her safely down."

I face Havriel, gathering the courage to speak. Havriel has pulled a bell from one of his pockets. He bows his head to me, as if in apology for what is to come. He rings the bell and a peal breaks forth, splitting the air in two, like a trembling silver thread. I hear footsteps almost at once, fast approaching. Not from the stairs. From somewhere beyond the mirrors. From the Palais du Papillon.

"Children," Havriel says. "Stand and face each other. Quickly."

My insides twist. "What?"

"Do as I tell you," he says, and he is moving swiftly, lighting a lamp, adjusting the flame.

I pull Bernadette next to me and position doe-eyed Charlotte across from her. On any other occasion Bernadette would hiss at me, tell me she is only two years younger and that I have no right to boss her, but even she knows better than to do that now. I place Delphine in front of me and try to smile at her, try to look as though I am not frightened out of my wits.

People are entering the room. I hear breathing, the crinkle of starched linens, the whisper of soft feet on stone. I want to scream with the closeness of them, the stifling weight of their bodies in this tiny space.

I see the mirrored wall behind Delphine. I see Mama, blurry in the glass. *The servants have such dreadful faces,* she whispers.

It is not Mama. It is Havriel, and someone else, and he is murmuring, "Quickly. Quickly!" and now I feel breath against the back of my neck and the scratch of cloth. Fabric slips down across my hair.

"What is this?" My voice is shaking. "I will not be blind-folded! I will not—"

It is not a blindfold. It is a sack. The black cloth slides down over my eyelids, blowing out the room like a candle. Hands spin me in circles. Delphine is no longer in my grasp.

"Delphine?"

I am forced to walk, bundled along.

"Delphine, where are you?" I reach out blindly, but I cannot find her.

What did you fear, Mama? What is down here?

Bernadette makes a small noise at my side. I try to reach out to her, but someone has me by the shoulder and is guiding me swiftly forward. We are passing through a door. I feel its shape around me, the change in the space.

"Keep your arms in," Havriel says suddenly, from somewhere to my left.

I draw my arms in tightly against my body, and a whirring, trickling sound surrounds me, as though I have just stepped into a dripping grotto. We walk for many minutes. The space no longer feels close and claustrophobic, but vast and cold. I hear the click of doors opening. And now we are in a room, and I feel the deep warmth of a burning fire. I smell lamp oil and spiced wine and wood. I smell—

"Frédéric?" Havriel says, and my heart quails.

Father.

I can smell his perfume. I can count on the fingers of one hand the number of times I have spoken to him, but the smell of him, the threads of it hanging in the château after he has passed through its halls, the hint of it on Mother when she is sad and ghostlike: I would recognize it anywhere. It is the smell of roses, lilacs, the sweet, thick burr of lilies on the very edge of rotting. A heady, oily scent, dried and dried again until it is an atmosphere, oozing from his every pore.

"Frédéric," Havriel says again, moving away from us. His voice is gentle, as if consoling a small child. "Frédéric, your children are here. Aurélie and Bernadette and the others. Your daughters."

And now I hear him: "Children?" he whispers, his voice wet and weak, echoing behind his tin mask. "But where is Célestine? Where is my wife?"

11

I wake with a gasp, the air ripping into me. It's freezing cold. I'm lying on something hard. My eyes are open, but all I see is blackness. My mouth tastes raw. Bloody.

I don't move. I don't know if I *can* move. And now I'm scared, every nerve ending flaring, setting my skin on fire. Images flash across my vision: a glinting red pill. Wrinkled sheets, straightening from one second to the next. Dorf smiling, his lips forming words: *the experience of a lifetime,* he says, and toasts us.

Maybe I got away. Maybe I got out into the fields and hid and that's why I'm cold.

But I didn't. I ran upstairs and—

They caught me.

Oh no. No-no-no. This was stupid, freaking idiotic; I swallowed some of the pill juice. I was knocked out.

I'm so dead.

The air is perfectly still. The surface under me is smooth, glassy. I listen, the blood hammering in my ears.

I'm not alone. Somewhere close by, someone is breathing. Multiple people.

Who? Are they watching me? My heartbeat speeds up. I'm sweating despite the cold. My mind instantly jumps to kidnappings, human trafficking, eighties horror movies with meat hooks and dusty lightbulbs and gallons of blood. But you don't fly in murder victims and slaves to France on a private jet and let them eat at your table. You don't send them reams of embossed stationery.

I uncurl one hand and move it slowly across the floor. *Don't panic, Ooky. You can figure this out. You can get out of this—*

Something slithers against my fingers. I jerk back. Cloth. I touched cloth, felt the faint warmth of skin. Someone's lying next to me. A foot away.

It's Jules.

I can smell his hair, that sharp, floral pomade he was wearing. I sit up, relief burning through me. Ease myself onto my knees. *Please don't notice I'm up. Whoever's here, please don't kill me.* I crawl forward. My fingers find Jules's face, and I clamp my hand over his mouth.

"Jules," I whisper. He tries to shrug me off, but he doesn't wake up. "Jules!" My free hand jogs his shoulder. Now his eyes must have snapped open because he's struggling, grunting.

"Jules, shut up. It's me."

I move my hand and pray he won't start screaming. I keep the other hand on his shoulder so he stays down.

"Anouk?" His voice is a cracked whisper, scared.

"Wait. Be quiet." I crawl a little farther, come to another body.

This one's Lilly. I can just make out her blond hair, lying against the dark floor. I shake her. She comes up quiet, with a soft gasp. Hayden's next. He doesn't wake up at all. I shake him, press a finger to his pulse and feel the rapid pump. He's alive. *So why isn't he moving?*

I keep crawling, a hard knot of pain springing up in my head. Will is curled up like a huge puppy. I barely touch him, and he rolls onto his back and stares at me.

I can see a bit more now: the outline of Will's face, and the shapes of the others sitting up, looking around blearily.

"Guys?" I clear my throat as softly as I can. Dig my

fingernails into my palms. "They drugged us. They took us somewhere; we need to get out."

Lilly sobs, high and strangled. "Where? Get out of where?"

"I don't know. Just keep quiet. Move slowly." I feel the tension prickling around me like an electrical storm, rising toward full-blown ignition. I keep my voice low, all on exhale, no sudden spikes in case someone's listening: "Don't panic. Don't panic."

Jules stands and knocks against a wall. The sound is hollow, beer bottles rolling against each other on the floor of a car. We're using more air now that we're awake. I can already feel the space heating up.

"I don't have my phone," Jules says. "They took my phone!"

I go back to Hayden and kick him hard. I don't care if it hurts; we need to move *now*. I see a pinprick of light spark to my left. Lilly has a key-chain light in her hand. She's crying over it, shining it directly into her eye.

"Oh, *thank you*." I grab it from her. Point it over the walls. I see a person facing me, and for a second everything inside me shrivels in stone-cold terror. But it's just my own reflection. The walls are mirrored. We're in a room—a small cube—and everything from the floor to the ceiling is mirrored.

"Help me find a way out," I gasp. Start stumbling around, feeling along the glass for seams. I don't know how much time we have, but the people who brought us here do. They'll know exactly how long the red pills last, and what they plan on doing to us afterward, and if ours have already worn off they'll be coming soon. It occurs to me that the mirrors might be two-way. Someone might be right on the other side, watching us.

I find a seam in the corner of the chamber. Dig in my fingernails and pull. Nothing moves. I start to sweat. We're piling over one another now, a bunch of squirming guinea pigs in a cage.

"Anouk?"

I swing the light around. Right into Will's face. *Crap.* He raises a hand to shield his eyes. "There are chairs," he says, and gestures.

I spin the key-chain light.

Yep. Two chairs, facing each other. Spindly gilt Louis XIV things, starkly out of place against the glass. *Were they even there ten seconds ago?*

No, they just randomly appeared, Anouk. Of course they

were there. I go to one. Try to pick it up. Maybe we can use it to go ballistic on the glass. It's bolted to the floor. I drop down. There are thin grooves surrounding the legs, marking a square.

I shine the light up. The ceiling is glass, but it's not completely mirrored like the walls. I can see myself in it, my face a pale oval, eyes wide. And I can also see *through* it: the faintest ghost of a mural, floating just above.

A butterfly. The wings are wide and ragged. In each one is a human eye, peering down.

"Look up," I say. "Look!"

The eyes are positioned exactly above the chairs.

"Somebody go sit in that chair. Anybody, go!"

Jules and Lilly are hyperventilating. Will frowns at me. Frowns at the chair. Goes to it. I sit opposite him.

Nothing happens. I don't know what I was expecting. I guess because the chairs are the only anomaly in the room, it stands to reason that they're somehow related to—

A sharp *clack* splits the air. The chair drops under me, one inch. Lilly lets out a soft screech. My hands clench the seat, so hard my knuckles pop. I stare at Will. His chair dropped, too.

"Um . . ." I swallow. "Okay, that was—"

Clack. Again, louder this time, a pistol shot of sound. *Clack. Clack.* Something's moving under the floor, behind the walls, all around us. Will's eyes lock on mine.

I open my mouth to say something, but the noise is getting louder, deafening. The whole room shudders.

The walls are moving backward and apart. Behind them are more mirrors, and they're moving, too, sliding one after another. An alarm goes off. A harsh, screaming siren.

I launch out of the chair. So does Will. Nothing stops. I whip around. Lights are flickering on, dull and fluorescent. The room definitely isn't a cube anymore. I can see down a hallway now, double-glass walls, ribbed with cables and tubes of light. The three other walls have opened onto a maze of mirrors. A labyrinth, as far as the eye can see. Abruptly, the siren cuts out.

Nobody moves. Nobody breathes.

I hear footsteps. Coming toward us. Several people, boots pounding, and behind them the unmistakable *click-click* of stilettos.

I spin to the others. "They're coming," I whisper. "They're coming!"

Hayden is still on the floor, spread-eagled, fast asleep.

I go down on one knee, slap his jaw.

He doesn't move.

They're almost here.

12

We drag Hayden five feet, drop him, and run. Into the maze of mirrored panels in a rustling, whispering group. The key-chain light's weak beam is almost hidden inside the knot of legs and bodies. My heart is mashing painfully against my ribs.

Where do we go? Where-where-where?

Three panels in, we stop. Huddle. I look back over my shoulder. The mirrors are two-way. I can see what used to be the cube room, the chairs standing in the open now. Hayden, sprawled on the floor.

I click off the light just as Miss Sei emerges from between the mirrors.

She's accompanied by four figures. Identical, tall, wearing black bodysuits and dark helmets, like motorcyclists or riot cops. The visors are dead black. Red lights thrum steadily along their jawlines, *bright-dull-bright-dull*, like gills opening and closing. They're all carrying large cases.

We need to get out of here. In two seconds they'll realize Hayden is the only one on the floor.

Two seconds are up.

Run!

But I'm rooted. So are the others. I watch Miss Sei scan the area. Her gaze rests on Hayden. And now the riot cop/motorcyclists are surrounding him and one of them is opening a case, drawing out some sort of black tubing, a wire-thin stretcher, what look like medical instruments in vacuum packaging. Miss Sei kneels next to Hayden. Lifts his head and strokes a thumb over his brow, almost tenderly.

With her other hand she reaches into the open case. For a second I think she's going to help Hayden. Get him onto the stretcher, take him someplace safe—

She's holding a nozzle. Long. Barbed. A silver needle extends from its tip like a stinger. Her mouth twitches into a smile. And now she drives the nozzle into the base of Hayden's skull.

His eyes snap open. He starts choking, gurgling. His back arches. He raises his arms like he wants to shove Miss Sei away, but Miss Sei pulls a trigger on the nozzle and Hayden drops, flat on the floor like a ton of concrete. The helmeted figures descend. Medical tape snaps around Hayden's wrists. Another injection, this time from a syringe. The nozzle, attached to the tube, stays in place. They're lifting him, black gloves digging into his neck, his arms.

No. No, this is not happening. . . .

I clamp my hand to my mouth. Slowly, I turn to Lilly, Will, and Jules. I want them to tell me this is a joke, that Miss Sei didn't just stab Hayden with a gas nozzle, *that she didn't just murder him.* They stare back at me.

I look through the mirrors again. Hayden's on the stretcher. His chest isn't moving. His eyes are wide, glazed. Miss Sei is standing, wiping her hands on a white cloth.

They killed him. They killed Hayden and if we were still on the floor, if we'd taken a few more minutes to wake up, they would have killed us. They're still going to kill us.

Miss Sei hands the cloth to one of the riot cops. "Find the others," she says, and her voice is chillingly loud. "They'll be slow on their feet."

I haven't cried in years, but I feel like I might now.

There's a pressure building behind my eyes, burning. *We need to go,* I mouth silently, but I'm still staring through the double mirror. *We need to go!*

The helmeted figures turn to scan the mirrors. One faces us. It can't see us through the mirrors, can it? But it's right there, blank visor pointed directly at me, and what if we're visible in a reflection, what if that thing turns a quarter of an inch and sees us huddled here—

I move back from the glass. The others do, too. It takes a step closer. Tilts its head. "Go," I say, and it hears, and we're running, our feet like gunshots against the floor. The mirrors seem to fan out on all sides, multiplying us a million times. A black shape cuts across our reflections.

"Run!" I shout. "Into the corridor!" I don't know where it goes, but we can't get lost in this maze. I slip around one of the glass panels and sprint forward. The corridor shears away in front of me, disappearing into a point. I glance over my shoulder, get a brief impression of the group, Miss Sei in front, marching toward us. They're not running. It's like they already know they have us, like we don't have a chance. There seem to be hundreds of them, mirrored over and over again, an army of doppelgangers.

Miss Sei raises a hand, shouts something, a vicious spike of a syllable.

I face forward again—

A helmet figure is right in front of me. I swing under its arm as it tries to grab me. Will hits it a second later, body slamming it against the wall. I hear glass splinter.

"Where do we go?" Lilly screams.

I have no idea. They're moving faster now, passing Miss Sei. I hear their boots pounding the floor.

We're nearing the end of the corridor. Up ahead is a massive door, like a bank vault. A huge circle of dull blue metal. It's slightly ajar.

"Come on!" I yell. "Get through the door and close it!"

Another glance over the shoulder: Will has disentangled himself from the helmet thing, is stumbling into a run. Farther back, the other helmet things are searing down the corridor, their arms chopping the air. Their speed is incredible, inhuman. Miss Sei is holding a gun now. It's pointing directly at me.

I reach the door and slip through the gap.

"Get in!" I scream. *"Come on!"*

I hear a shot, the ping of a bullet glancing off metal.

Jules and Lilly dart through, start heaving against the door. Will reaches me and we grab the edge, our fingers straining. The hinges are oiled, slick as silk, but the door weighs a ton. We throw ourselves against it.

"Don't!" Miss Sei shouts, and now her voice is different. Scared.

Out in the corridor, one of the helmet figures pulls ahead of the rest. It's freakishly close, speeding toward us. I see its visor through the narrowing crack, a curved pane of night, the slice of red light throbbing along its jaw. Black fingers curl toward me, ready to grip my face, crush my skull.

Miss Sei screams, *"Don't!"* one last time, shrill and desperate.

The door slams into place, and I jam the bar home.

13

We're in a hall. Huge and cavernous, a cathedral of shadows. Lilly and Jules are racing into it. And now I'm spinning back to the door, scrabbling with the other bolts. They're solid steel, radiating out of the center of the door, locking it into the wall. *Three, four, five* . . . Will and I slam them into place. I hear more locks, smaller ones clicking into place, the hiss of air as we're sealed in. I collapse against the metal, gasping.

There's no other sound. Nothing from the other side of the door. Nothing in this vast new space. The silence presses around me like an actual weight, solid and icy.

I raise my head. Jules and Lilly have stopped about twenty paces in. I can't see a light source, but somehow it's not pitch-black. The walls are marble, black and green. They remind me of some sort of digestive organ, darkly translucent, veins pulsing just below the surface. The ceiling is a vault of gilt and crystal. I still have Lilly's keychain light and I raise it, flicking it across the expanse. It catches on golden leaves, marble hands. Portraits and mirrors glimmer, chairs and Chinese-style vases twice as tall as a person. It's like it was built for giants.

I let my breath out slowly. "Jules?" I call out weakly. "Lilly, wait."

I start toward them, tripping all over myself. Jules has his hands tangled in his hair. He's bobbing around like he can't decide between throwing up and staring around in awe. Lilly is sobbing "Wow" over and over again.

I glance down. The floor is a huge mosaic, fitted together out of thousands of marble tiles. Enormous wings. Human eyes.

You've got to be kidding me.

I reach Jules and Lilly. "They're going to kill us," Lilly whispers. She looks at me beseechingly, her face streaked with tears. "They're insane, they—"

I'm not listening. My brain is spinning, twisting into a single thread of thought. *This is the Palais du Papillon. It's not lost. It's right here and it has a very twenty-first-century vault door and fluorescent-lit glass corridors. They were lying, lying from the moment they contacted us—*

Out of the corner of my eye I see Will moving toward us. He's favoring one side of his body, limping slightly.

"What about the expedition?" Lilly sobs. "We were supposed to pick up our gear by 9 A.M.—"

"Lilly, there *is no expedition*," I snap. "Don't you get it? They drugged us. They tricked us into coming here. We just barely escaped being murdered, okay?"

The voice in my head is changing, getting shrill: *You can't stay here. You've been kidnapped by psychos. RUN!*

But I don't move. My body feels a thousand miles away. Lilly and Jules are both on the floor now, dazed. I'm just standing, stiff and scared, my hands clenched at my sides.

"We should hide," Will says. "We don't know who might be down here."

"*Down* here?" I mimic. My voice sounds spiky, mean. It's not supposed to. But that's the only way I know how to talk. "How do you know we're *down* anywhere, Will? How do you know where *down* is?"

"The butterfly—" he starts, gesturing at the floor, and I laugh at him.

"The Bessancourts' coat of arms? But you're assuming the Bessancourts ever existed in order to own a coat of arms. You're assuming we weren't lied to every single *second* by the Sapanis."

Will moves a little closer to me. He's wearing a watch, one of those bulky mountaineering ones. He sidles up, cautiously, and hits a button on it. Shows me the green-glowing screen.

Elevation: 88 feet above sea level

"So?" I say. I don't know what that means. I'm an art history major, not a freaking Girl Scout.

Will hits another button. Coordinates appear on the tiny screen. "I checked them when we got out of the cars," he says. "The coordinates are the same. We're right where we were yesterday. Except Péronne is two hundred feet *above* sea level." He looks up at me. "We're a hundred and twelve feet underground."

Lilly's standing up, craning her neck to get a view of the watch, still bawling.

Will shows her. A second later he switches off the screen. "The battery's solar-powered," he says quietly. "It's going to die soon."

I have the urge to scream *Just like ussss!* while spinning maniacally over the marble.

Instead I mumble: "I don't get it. They didn't have to

do all this. They could have just dragged us off a street somewhere, or hacked us up in a parking garage—"

Will doesn't answer. Something else does. Somewhere in that huge, unbroken silence, something is creeping over the floor toward us, skittering like an animal. Lilly breaks out in a fresh, high-pitched sob.

Images rush into my mind: huge, muscled zombies dragging rusted chains. Carnivorous plants. Shape-shifting insects. Every cliché I've ever seen on one of my late-night movie-watching binges. *Please don't let there be carnivorous plants down here. Please don't do that to us.*

Click.

The skittering breaks off. A red pinpoint of light pops up about thirty feet down the hall, glimmering.

I stare at it, holding my breath.

The light's in the wall. A panel snapped back, and now a square of embedded machinery is exposed, coils of gray metal tubes and that red lens, staring out like an eye.

"Sealed for two hundred years?" Jules breathes. "Really?"

To the right, I hear a second click.

I jerk around, staring through the dark. Another red light has popped up on the opposite wall. A steady, round glow. And now the red light buzzes out of it, slicing across the hallway in a pure, thin cut, as if someone slit open the darkness. A hologram springs up in the center of the hall. We gape at it, huddling together on the floor.

"Children."

It's Dorf. The hologram isn't detailed, no eyes or nose discernible, but I recognize the sloping shoulders, the hugeness. "Reopen the blast door." His voice is low and quick and utterly clinical. "This is for your own safety. Reopen the blast door and let in the security team—"

The hologram casts a grainy, fuzzy red light over our faces.

"Can you hear me?" Dorf says. "We have a visual on you. Open the door and let in our security team. I cannot guarantee your well-being otherwise."

"Our *well-being*?" I almost choke on my own sarcasm. "If you were concerned for our well-being, maybe you shouldn't have *murdered Hayden*, how's that for an idea?"

"Anouk," he says. He *can* hear us. He pauses. Turns, maybe to someone else in the room he's in. "Listen to me," he says, in that same cold, urgent voice. "This should not have occurred. It is *vital* that you follow my instructions exactly. Turn around. Return to the blast door. Unbar it as quickly as you can. If you do not open that door, you *will* die. There is nothing we will be able to do to help you. You're being clever now, thinking, 'Well, I'll die either way,' but believe me, there are ways to die so terrible you cannot possibly comprehend them."

"Yeah?" I say, and I feel a hysterical thrill rising in me, making me brave and giddy. "Well, we're not opening that door."

The hologram seems to stiffen, darken. "Anouk, this is not a game. You have not locked us out; you have locked yourselves *in*. You have approximately three minutes to live—"

"And if we let you in, we have one," I say.

"What happens in three minutes?" Jules whispers. "What are they going to do to us?"

"He's bluffing," I say, like I have a clue.

"Children, open *the door*." Dorf's voice is tense now, his control slipping.

I start walking toward the red eye in the wall. Wrap my fingers around the key-chain light, locking it behind my knuckles. I reach the panel. Above the red light is a camera lens.

"Come and get me," I say under my breath. Grit

my teeth and smash my fist into the tech panel. Glass crunches. It hurts, but I don't bleed. The hologram flickers out.

Everyone's on their feet now. I hurry back to them. We have about five seconds of silence, and now two more panels slide open, farther down the hall. Two new lights blink on. The red lines collide. Dorf springs up a second time.

"You don't know what you're doing," Dorf says, and the cool sheen in his voice is completely shot. "A team of trackers is being dispatched from the other end of the palace. They are three miles away at present. Wait for them to arrive and do not, I repeat, *do not*, go farther into the hall. The palace is not a safe environment. There are rogue assets loose within, and we cannot risk a meeting, we—"

"Trackers?" Lilly asks, her eyes wide, the whites huge in the darkness. "What are trackers? *What do you want from us?*" She shrieks the words, jagged and raw throated. There's something in her hand—a pointless, useless bracelet. She hurls it at the hologram. It passes through with barely a blip and skitters away over the marble.

Jules is starting to fidget, and now he runs straight for the hologram, all skinny legs and rage, like he's going to tackle it. He tumbles through, twists, falls on his back.

"Stop moving!" Dorf shouts. *"Do not move!* Someone open that damned door!"

I race toward the next red eye, my fist raised. Will is going for the one on the other side of the hall. We smash into them at almost the same time. The hologram blinks out a second time. But Dorf's voice keeps coming, echoing through the hall—*open-the-open-the-door-don't-DON'T-MOVE—*

And I snap the trip wire. I barely feel it. A slight tug against my ankle, and the speakers cut out. The hall goes silent. Almost.

Under the thumping of the blood in my ears, I hear something—a hurried ticking, like a pocket watch. *Tick-tick-tick-tick-tick,* somewhere in the walls.

14

I stand perfectly still, trying to place the origin of the sound. It seems to be coming from everywhere at once, rippling through the huge space.

"Uh—" I look down at the severed wire, coiled on the marble. "Guys?"

A sharp *clank*. The sound intensifies, thumping now, rolling along the paneling. I imagine the hall as a huge aquarium; there's a squid just beyond the walls, its tentacles batting along the glass. Lilly sees the wire at my feet. She looks up at me from where she's crouched on the floor, wide-eyed.

"What did you do?" she whispers.

The rumbling stops. It's replaced by a gentle, shimmering hum.

My head snaps around. The sound is coming from the far end of the hall.

Sssss. A hiss, like Penny dragging her mangy toy crocodile over the floor by its tail. Like fingernails sliding through a groove, sand pouring through an hourglass.

Will and Jules turn slowly. Lilly stands, twisting toward the sound. I stare, paralyzed.

At first it looks like a thin strip of mirror, two hundred feet away, stretching from one side of the hall to the other. Except the mirror is rising. And now it's coming closer.

"Anouk, what did you do—?" Jules starts.

It's not a mirror. It's a wire. A single glinting wire, skimming approximately five feet above the floor. Not fast. Not slow. I stare at it, transfixed. And now it reaches a tall oriental vase and slices through it like butter.

My skin turns to ice.

"Duck!" I scream. "Duck, duck, get DOWN!"

I slam to the floor. Flip onto my back. The wire sings over me. The others are sprawled in a circle around me, shoes squeaking against the tile eyes of the butterfly. "We need to get out of here," I say, panicking. "We need to—"

I push myself onto my palms. At the far end of the hall is a door. Huge, gilded, set in an ornate marble frame. It seems to be glowing dimly in the shadows. I hop to my feet. Will is right behind me.

"Move!" I shout. "Get to the door!"

I glance over my shoulder. The wire has reached the end of the hall. It pauses. Another *clank*, reverberating down through the expanse. And it's coming back. Two feet lower. Twice as fast.

Lilly's on her feet now. Jules isn't.

"Run!" I scream. *"Get up, run!"*

Will heads for Jules, jerks him upright, and we're off, sprinting down the center of the hall. In front of us, three new wires emerge from above the golden door and drop down, shooting along the tracks on either wall. All different heights.

Lilly shrieks, looks like she wants to turn around. But the other wire is still approaching from behind.

"Watch the ones ahead and I'll watch our backs!" I yell at her, and we run together, me stumbling over my feet trying to look back over my shoulder. The original wire is moving faster than the others. I see it shimmering ten feet away, speeding toward us. I fall and pull Lilly with me. Wriggle onto my back, knocking my elbow hard on the floor. The wire passes a hair's breadth above my nose. I'm up again, leaping the second wire, ducking under the third. Lilly's not with me anymore. She's wailing, on and on, like a siren, but where? *Is she hurt?* I can't see anything. I can't look back.

A fourth wire is coming toward me, three feet above the floor. It slices through chairs, another vase. It's vibrating, shivering back and forth, blindingly fast. Will is ahead of me. He's running straight for it. And there's another wire. A fifth wire I didn't see, sliding low over the floor. He's going to duck the high wire and the low one is going to take off the soles of his feet.

"Will, look down—" I whisper.

He's four feet away.

"Will, *jump*!"

A second before the wire catches him, he sees it. Leaps. The one following it dips down. And somehow he's turning, spinning onto his back, still in the air, slipping over both wires. He hits the floor, rolls, and he's running again, full speed for the golden doors.

The hall is a grid of wires now. Nine. Ten. Dropping out of the wall above the doors and speeding toward us. They're not following a pattern. Some are going forward, some back. Some shift in their tracks, clacking a foot higher. I don't know where anyone is, can barely see in the blackness.

"Jam the tracks!" someone's shrieking. "We need to jam them!"

It's Lilly, behind me.

I drag myself across the floor toward the wall. Look up.

"What is this place . . . ?" I breathe.

What I thought were decorative inlays in the panels is a network of grooves, a complex track system going up about six feet. The wires are attached to wooden nubs. I watch one of them buzzing along its track toward me. There's a clicking sound. It's like it knows I'm here. The wire shifts into a new lane a foot lower.

This place was *designed* to kill.

"Anouk!"

I duck the wire. Spin. Lilly's heaving something onto her shoulder—a chair. She throws it at the nearest wire, and for an instant I want to scream at her. The chair touches the wire. It's intersected neatly. Butchered chair legs come sliding across the floor toward me.

Oh. Jam the tracks. I get it. I grab a leg and mash it into the track just as a wire swoops overhead.

It doesn't stop. The chair leg, pinched between the nub and the wall, goes squealing away down the tracks.

Somewhere to my right I see Jules, a ragged outline in the gloom, ducking a wire. Will up ahead. Lilly behind me.

I hear a sharp *ping*. The jammed nub has stopped. But only on one side. The nub on the opposite wall is still moving. I watch the wire stretch, creaking. . . .

"DOWN!" I scream, and everyone drops and rolls into a ball just as the wire snaps and goes whipping back through the wall. Something snatches at my ankle. Blinding pain explodes up my leg.

I push myself onto my hands, clenching my jaw. I see what's coming.

We're dead now.

An entire wall of wires, eight feet high, two inches between each wire, is speeding toward us down the hall. There's a space where the broken wire should be, but it's five feet off the ground. The gap's only six inches wide. There's no way we can get through that.

Will is running back to us. I glance over at Lilly and Jules. I can't see their faces, but they're just standing there in the dark, calm suddenly, staring as the glinting wall approaches. I wonder if this is how death happens. Minimal drama. A simple cause and effect, and the universe ends for you. I see our bodies after the wires have passed through them, blood spattering our faces.

I close my eyes.

Another earsplitting *clack*.

And I'm seeing light. Not light-at-the-end-of-the-tunnel crap, but actual golden light, blazing through my lids.

My eyes snap open. Two inches in front of us, the wires have stopped.

Sconces are flaring to life along the walls, spreading down the hall. The chandeliers are blooming into balls of light high above. Sweat drips off my face. The wires hover, shimmering. All we can do is stand here, four in a row, staring into the blazing, beautiful glare.

Palais du Papillon, Salle d'Acajou—
126 feet below—October 23, 1789

Thick fingers find the sack's hem and drag it off my head. I
am standing in a dark room, a jewelry box of red plush and
smoldering gilt. My sisters are with me. The ceiling is tented,
a canopy of ribbed silk. Dim lamps hiss softly along the walls.
Father sits at the center of the room like a troll king in his
lair, huge and hulking upon a delicate chair, one leg hooked
over the other.

He is as enormous as Havriel, but that is where all similarities between them end: where Havriel is a mountain
of calm and shadowy grace, Father is like a boar after the
hounds have caught it, heaving and fighting and grasping for
life, though the chance for that has long since fled. He wears
a splendid coat of cherry red. On his head is a chalk-white
wig. His mouth is in perpetual motion in his powdered face,
shivering and twitching, forming silent words that he does
not utter, and he holds a small tin mask full of herbs and

perfume to his nose even as he speaks. He has always done this, for as long as I can remember. The doctors say it will stop the plague, influenza, any sort of sickness from befalling him, but he looks a fool for it.

His hands have begun to tremble, the rings on his fat fingers clinking against the arms of his chair.

"My wife," he says again. "Where is she?" He attempts to rise, collapses. Small black eyes skip across our faces and linger on the empty air at my side, as if he expects to see someone there.

Havriel's knuckles tighten around the blindfold in his hands. "Frédéric?" he says gently. "Frédéric, you must listen to me—" He goes to Father's side.

"Where *is she*, Havriel?" Father hisses, and beside me Delphine jolts upright. She must have been dozing as she stood.

Havriel lays a hand on Father's shoulder. Father shrugs it off. Again he tries to stand and again he fails. "Where is Célestine? It promised we would be safe, the wicked thing, it promised—"

"The guards are with her as we speak," Havriel says quickly. "She did not want to leave the château, but they will no doubt bring her safely down—"

"They shot her," I say. My voice is just a thread, but it jerks Father's head up like a puppet. Havriel does not turn. He has gone deathly still.

"She did not want to come," I go on, louder now, and my voice turns taunting, bitter. "She was afraid. She was so afraid she was willing to die rather than come into your paradisical underground realm. Why might that be, Father, pray do tell?"

But Father is no longer listening. He is shrieking. He curls in the chair, his spine contorting, his hand scrabbling up the cushion as if he seeks to climb over the back of it, and Havriel is gripping him, and Delphine is whimpering.

"Frédéric, calm yourself! They are bringing her to safety as we speak! We do not know the extent of the damage—"

"They shot her!" I shout. "They shot her, and if they had not, she might have done it herself!"

I'm crying, and as I move toward Father, Havriel spins.

"Stay back, Aurélie," he spits. "Stay back."

Havriel's bell rings. A door opens. Someone is here. The sack falls again over my eyes. I'm being bundled away, and I don't know where my sisters are, but suddenly my body is wax and twigs and straw hair; I am a drained, brittle husk, too tired to fight. I walk on and on, through echoing halls, my feet aching inside my shoes. It feels as if I walk for days, soft hands guiding me through the dark, and yet I can still hear Father screaming.

15

We stagger away from the wires, examining our bodies for wounds. My foot feels like it's been sawed off. I pull up my pant leg, bracing myself for partial amputation, exposed muscle, the works. I've got a cut just above the knob of bone in my ankle. It's tiny, the size of a fingernail clipping. The definition of anticlimactic.

I collapse against the wall next to Jules. He's testing his hand, watching it swell red and shiny where it caught his fall. Lilly's on her knees in front of the wall of wires. Her head's slumped to her chest, hair hanging lank over her face. I can't see if she's hurt. She's breathing, at least.

I lean back against the wall and close my eyes.

"What do they want from us?"

It comes out in a rasping, grating croak.

No one answers. I roll my head to the side, try to catch Jules's eye. "I'm serious, what? Why didn't they just kill us in the mirror room? Or at dinner? Or on the freaking airplane? And why are there traps? Dorf said they could see us, they know we're here, so why did they stop the wires? Why didn't they just finish us off?"

Will eases himself down next to us. He has a cut on his arm. One of the long sleeves of his T-shirt is sticking to his skin, soaked dark and glistening. He rips the other sleeve along the seam at the shoulder and starts tying a tourniquet above his bicep, the knot held between his teeth.

"They don't want us dead," he says.

I see the barbed nozzle, sliding into Hayden's skull.

"Really?" I say. "Because they sure wanted Hayden dead."

Will pulls the tourniquet tight, wincing. Jules has his head between his knees. All I can see of him is his black hair, hanging toward the floor. I feel like throwing up, and I also feel like I want to smack someone, or argue and figure things out, but everyone is just *sitting here*!

I stand abruptly, ignoring the pain in my foot. "We need to get out of here."

Jules starts gasping. He's sobbing, his head still pinched between his knees. Will glances up at me. His eyes are clear and still. He's not crying like Jules, but I think he might if no one were around.

I look to the golden doors at the end of the hall. They seem to be flaming in the light from the chandeliers, gathering it. "So *get up!*" My voice bounces through the hall, cold and hollow.

Nobody moves.

I start toward Lilly. I saw Hayden die, too, and I'm all for the four stages of grief and periods of mourning and all that, but I also don't want to be murdered. I grab Lilly's wrist and practically drag her to her feet.

"What is your problem?" Lilly sobs. "We almost—"

"Yeah," I say fiercely. "We almost died, and we're going to completely die if we don't get moving!"

As if in response, a series of metallic pops echo behind the walls. Lilly and I freeze. The wall of wires starts sliding back along their tracks. They're not whirring anymore, not vibrating. It's like watching a wounded animal drag itself back into its hole. They reach the end of the hall and rise up, coming to rest in their slots above the golden door. Taut. Invisible.

"Will, get Jules," I snap over my shoulder. "Dorf said they were dispatching trackers from the other end of the palace. That means there *is* another end."

Somewhere behind me, Jules speaks, his voice bitter: "You want us to just walk through those doors? Is that your plan? And what about Dorf? He said there's something down here. What if whatever he warned us about is right on the other side—"

"It's that or Miss Sei and her gas nozzle, so puzzle it out."

I've got Lilly by the arm and we're moving quickly across the floor. The golden doors loom, spiny and vaguely surreal, Rodin's Gates of Hell. They're like a gold-drenched nightmare—gilt faces, contorted bodies, wings and hooves and claws, all struggling up through the golden mass. Jules and Will catch up, Will supporting Jules even though Jules's swollen hand is in no way impeding his ability to walk. We stand in a row, breathing hard, staring up at the doors.

"Maybe it's a trap," Lilly whispers. "Maybe it's rigged."

I put my hand against it.

"Maybe," I say, and push.

16

It's not rigged. Or if it is, whoever's controlling this place decides not to kill us. We slip around the golden doors. Will closes them behind us as quietly as he can.

This new room has nine more doors—three in each wall, not including the one we just came through. Everything is bone white. The ceiling, the walls with their curling plaster moldings, the circular table in the center . . . everything. The only color comes from a massive bowl of fruit on the table, a Dutch still life of grapes and oranges and ruby-colored apples, rich and vivid against the whiteness. Nothing else. It's utterly silent.

I glance around. I'm guessing it's some sort of antechamber, but it's not like any I've ever seen or read about. It looks drained somehow, desaturated, like an unfinished bit of computer animation. The ceiling is a butterfly again, a white one. This time the eyes are almost closed. Not sleepy. Sly. Catlike.

"They can't do this," Lilly breathes, and the words feel like a disturbance, a ripple in the dead air. "They can't get away with this. Our parents know we're in France. They don't know where exactly, but my mom will find out, and she is going to dig this place up with a spoon if she has to—"

"See if they care. Our boarding passes were enough to completely skip U.S. security. That's a whole different level of rich."

"They still must care about being caught, though," Will says. "Otherwise why the big lie? Why bring us here in the first place?"

"And then let us get away," Jules says.

"They didn't let us get away," I answer. This room is creeping me out. I have to force the next words out. "I don't think we were supposed to wake up. I spat out most of my pills, which is probably why I regained consciousness sooner. And then I was able to wake you up, too, and Hayden—"

Hayden wasn't so lucky.

"We were supposed to die in that cube room. But we escaped."

"So now what?" Jules asks.

"Now we hide," I say. "Dorf said they were three miles away. Those things, trackers, whatever—if they're anything like the guys with Miss Sei, they're fast."

I walk to the table and grab an orange. I expected it to be fake, dangerous, maybe explode into poisoned barbs and skewer my hand. It doesn't. I can smell the sharp tang of the oil from its peel, rubbing off on my fingertips. I stuff it in my sweater pocket, grab an apple, a bunch of grapes. Will takes a pear cautiously, eyeing it like a puzzling mystery.

"Dorf said they could see us," Jules says. "They might be watching us right now."

"Most likely." I pivot. I have a weird sensation as the room turns around me. The air is so still, but now that I listen—really listen—it's not a dead silence. It's charged, thick with a sharp, buzzing energy. The hairs on my neck stand on end.

I squeeze my eyes shut. Open them. "Which door? Pick one, any one."

Will points his pear toward a door in the left wall. I head for it.

My brain starts up a panicky chant: *There is no right*

door. *They don't want us dead yet, they don't want us dead—*
I drag on the door's handle, peer into the next room. It's a salon, the place where fancy French families receive their guests. Crusts of gilt. Red brocade wallpaper. Stained-glass wall panels and crystal chandeliers. Chairs waiting like empty mouths.

I walk in. The others follow at a safe distance.

"Thanks a lot," I say, without turning. "Wouldn't want to be killed along with Anouk if the room is rigged, right? You guys are *dolls*."

This room has three doors, the one we came through and two in the far wall. What we're doing is stupid. Running around randomly until we feel like we're a long way from our starting point is not hiding, and it's not going to keep us safe. Just because we don't know where we are doesn't mean they don't.

We're going to have to prepare for the worst.

I run over to the marble fireplace and try to lift myself onto the mantel. It's taller than I am. I can't get a footing on the smooth sides. I try again, slip off like a dork.

Jules hurries over. "Uh, what are you doing?" He's staring at me like I should be put down for rabies.

I ignore him, drag a chair over, climb onto the seat. It

creaks under me. I make it onto the narrow ledge of the mantel and start toeing my way toward the center. The others are probably contemplating leaving me behind as a peace offering to the psychos at this point. I don't care. Above the fireplace, fixed inside a decorative coat of arms, are two swords—curved sabers with spun-gold hand guards, making an X.

I grab one and try to slide it out. It doesn't budge. I pry at the coat of arms. Unlatch it from the wall. *Whoa.* It's heavy. I tip back. Realize I'm going to fall off the mantle if I don't let go of the shield. Whirl and let the whole thing drop.

It clangs against the floor, deafeningly loud. I leap down after it.

"Are you crazy?" Jules hisses, and Lilly is turning circles, twisting frantically at one of the feathers braided into her hair.

"Weapons," I say. "You should find some, too."

I have no idea how to fight with swords. I can do a flawless dive roll and speak at length about the Florentine masters during the early stages of the Italian Renaissance, but I'm pretty sure whatever those trackers are, they will not find that impressive. Still, swords are better than no swords, if you ask me. I brace a foot against the edge of the shield and pull with all my might.

Lilly catches on. She starts ripping drawers out of a side table, rummaging through them. Will goes to an armoire in the far wall. I get the first sword loose and rip it free.

I rub my thumb along its blade. Not very sharp, but the tip is. It will do some damage if I jam it in hard enough. I wiggle out the second sword. Lilly comes over with a long, ivory-handled letter opener. Will has a gorgeously curled fire poker. Jules has nothing, so he picks up a porcelain statue of a lady holding a parasol, because it's closest, and waves it menacingly.

I grab it from him and smack it back down. Hand him Will's fire poker, and since Will's hand remains opened, like he's still trying to catch up mentally with the sudden lack of fire pokers in his life, I replace the fire poker with one of the swords. Lilly grabs the other sword. I think subconsciously I wanted it, but whatever. I slide the letter opener into my jeans pocket. Hope I don't impale myself while walking. Face everyone.

It's kind of sad. We're like a group of overzealous mercenaries in a low-budget sci-fi movie, accessorizing with household items.

"Great," I say. "Let's go."

I head for the door on the left. Slip through it. It's like stepping into a picture frame, a 3-D masterpiece. The room isn't large, but every inch of ceiling and walls is painted with massive landscapes in oil: shadowy, visceral scenes of myths and betrayals, twisting figures and roiling bits of cloaks and darkness.

I know what this reminds me of: a miniature Sistine Chapel. I went to the real one at the tail end of the Italy trip last year. Rented a rooftop apartment in Rome and drank Montepulciano and ate pancetta with olives and pretended I was a grown-up. I had dramatic conversations with my parents in my head, screamed at the late-night revelers down in the street, the whole shebang. And when I visited the chapel, worming my way between the tourists, I remember tipping my head up and feeling like all those bodies on the ceiling were watching me. Here it's worse. They're closer.

I want to keep going—the others are already moving past me, drifting through the room—but something about the pictures makes me pause. The brushstroke faces look angry. The figures are fighting, locked in battle, their eyes so deep set in their skulls they're almost black. The skies are bruised, the trees warped.

I imagine the trackers, streaking toward us through rooms just like this one.

This room has four doors. One in each wall.

The air still has that odd, prickling feeling.

And a man is standing in the corner. Bleeding. Watching us.

17

For a second I think I'm imagining him. Bone thin. Red-rimmed eyes. Standing like a twisted angel against the baroque gilt and oil paintings behind him.

There are rogue assets loose in the palace—

And now Lilly sees him, too, and it's like her brain is telling her one thing and her eyes are telling her another thing, because she's walking straight toward him, saying, "That's not—that's not a person—"

And now she shrieks so loud it hurts my ears, *"Who-are-you-who-are-you?"*

And everything snaps. The others see him. We're all running, trampling over each other trying to get to the nearest door, desperate not to turn our backs on him. He's plaster pale. He's wearing knee breeches and a ruffled, loose-hanging shirt, and the blood is drenching it, slicking it to his skin.

He doesn't move. He watches us, and his mouth drops open. Words start tumbling out of him, frenzied and desperate: *"Reine,"* he says, shivering. *"Mere de misericorde, notre vie, notre joie, notre esperance, salut. Enfants d'Eve—"*

We're crashing into a long, high gallery.

I hear: *"Nous crions vers vous de fond de notre exil—"*

It's a French prayer, but it sounds mangled, dark, and in my head Dorf is laughing, screaming, *You didn't lock us out; you locked yourselves in!*

I whip my head around, almost fall into Jules's back. The pale man is still standing, grinning. And now he follows. His eyes fix on mine. He's charging toward us, feet pounding the floor. I face forward, running with all my strength.

"What's he saying?" Lilly screeches.

I look back again, my vision bucking drunkenly. *Four to one, four to one, if he catches up we can—*

He's hurt, but those milk-white arms are corded with muscle, and his gangling legs are carrying him toward us like some bony, fast-moving spider. He's still muttering, staring straight at me.

We reach the end of the gallery. There's no exit. What we thought was a door is a three-dimensional illusion painting depicting the gateway to the Elysian Fields. This room is a dead end.

You have got *to be kidding me.*

I look back. The pale man is fifteen feet away. Lilly drags her sword out and starts swinging it in front of her in wide, frantic arcs. "Stop!" she shouts. "Don't come any closer. Anouk, *speak French to him, what are you waiting for?*"

I spin. *"Arrêtez!"* I shout. *"Arrêtez, n'approchez pas! Ne vous—"* Don't come any closer, don't—

He skids to a stop about five feet away. And everything goes silent. The others turn slowly. The man stares at us. A drop of blood, dark as wine, rolls from his fingertips and splashes to the floor.

"Who are you?" I ask in French, and it comes out in an awkward yell. "Are you with the Sapanis?"

He tilts his head. His eyes are bruised and bloodshot, and something about them—the way they're pinned freakishly on my face—makes me want to crawl under the floor.

"What do you *want*?" I ask again.

The man blinks at me. And now he seems to cringe in slow motion, bowing elaborately, one leg forward, one arm swept back and up, his gory hand extended toward me like a pantomime. He takes a step closer, another one, his head still lowered.

"Don't touch him," Lilly whispers. Her sword is extended toward him, the blade shivering.

"Trust me, I don't plan to . . . *Écoutez*," I snap at the pale man. "What happened to you?"

His eyes roll up to meet mine. For a second they're sharp. Now they're brimming, dripping tears and he's inching toward me, fingers trembling, blood splattering the floor.

"*Aurélie*," he croaks. "*Aurélie*."

"Who's Aurélie?"

He doesn't answer. Drops onto one knee and wraps his long arms around himself, head hanging. He's so thin. His spine stands out like a little mountain range down his neck, strangely reptilian. "*Aidez moi*," he whispers. "*S'il vous plaît, ayez pitié. J'ai tellement peur.*"

"Help me," Will translates softly. "Please, have pity. I am so afraid."

"*He's* afraid?" Jules practically shrieks. "What about us? Dorf said there was something down here. That thing could very well be it. What if he's infected or something?"

The pale man tips sideways and clatters to the floor. His breathing is getting shallower, quick, weak gasps. His skin is turning a disgusting gray-purple color.

"He's going to bleed to death," I say. It comes out cold, flat. I don't know what the proper reaction is to meeting a terrifying person on the verge of death in the palace of your kidnappers. My brain is telling me to run back to the Sistine Room, pick a different door, and forget we ever saw him, but—

"What if he can help us?" I step toward him cautiously. His breaths are so quiet now. A line of blood is creeping away from him across the floor, like a finger, reaching for us. "What if he can tell us what we need to know to get out of here?"

"Are you crazy?" Jules whimpers. "No, no, no, we are on the *run*, okay? We are going to be killed."

"Jules, look at him. He's hurt. He's in the same boat as we are, and he's probably been down here longer—"

"It might be a trick," Will says. "If he's faking it—"

"Then I die gruesomely and you guys know better for next time. Win-win." I'm not waiting for a decision by committee. I pull my letter opener out of my pocket and walk up to the pale man. He raises his head, looking at me from under his lids. His skin is almost translucent now from loss of blood. Patches of red are blooming around his eyes and on his neck. His fingernails are thick and yellow.

"*Aidez-moi,*" he wheezes again, barely audible. "*Aurélie, aidez-moi. . . .*"

I crouch and hold his gaze. "Can you get us out of here?" I say in French.

He begins nodding, but his eyes are glazing over. "*Oui, mademoiselle, oui!*"

"Okay. *Un accord.* You help us and we'll help you, got that?"

He's sobbing, grasping for my hand, tears dripping, mixing with the blood on the floor.

I jerk away and force down the bile rising in my throat. "If he tries anything . . ." I turn to the others, "we knock his brains out and run. Until then we're going to help him."

18

He smells disgusting. A mixture of sweaty and grimy, New York City streets in summertime and something bloody and metallic that I can't quite place. I'm trying not to breathe—trying not to touch his skin accidentally and throw up everywhere—as I wrap swath after swath of pine-green velvet from some drapes around his arm. It's like I'm in *Gone with the Wind,* being all nurselike and mid-nineteenth century. Give me some hoopskirts and I'll kick Melanie right out of town.

"More," I say, and throw my head back, staring up at the ceiling. "I need more cloth."

We're one door over from the Sistine Room now. A little hexagonal sitting room with a concert harp standing in the center. The drapes were hanging in front of some fake mirror windows that I assume are supposed to trick you into feeling less enclosed, except they do the exact opposite. You see drapes and a window-shaped object, and you expect to be able to look through it and gaze out into the sky or wide-open fields, but you don't. You see yourself. It's disturbing.

Will tears another strip off the drapes and passes it to me. I gulp air and dive back down, tying bandages as fast as I can.

The blood is coming from a deep gash running from the base of his elbow to his wrist. It's on the top of his arm, just a flesh wound, but it's bizarre. It's not a cut. Not a bite. It's wide and smooth at the edges, a trough, almost like something burned him. Slowly.

"He said he can get us out of here?" Jules mutters over to me. He's hunched next to Will, trying to find the seams in the curtains. "And yet we can't believe anything he says. So explain to me, why are we helping him again? We can't trust him!"

"We're not going to trust him." I tie another strip of velvet around his arm. Hear a wet squelch as I tighten, and feel my stomach roil. "We're going to make sure he doesn't die in the next five minutes and then we're going to have him save our lives whether he wants to or not."

I glance at the pale man's face. His skin hangs in folds,

but I don't think it's from age. He's like one of those Vietnam POWs in archive footage, or an extreme mountaineer after a hard climb. Exhausted and depleted and sick. I see why his eyes seemed bloodshot before. The dark irises are weirdly broken, as if they've begun to spread into the white. I think of the zombies in arthouse-y British apocalypse movies, how the characters look right before the infection grabs hold. I want to put this guy in a glass containment cell and talk to him through an intercom. He has other wounds on his body, too. Older ones. Tiny, hairline cuts on his neck and forehead and on the palms of his hands that have healed into delicate satiny scars. White as fish bones.

"We need to go!" Lilly whines. She's standing next to us, shifting from foot to foot and brandishing her sword like an angry garden gnome.

I knot the last strip of velvet around the makeshift bandage and stand quickly.

"We're going. Can you walk?" I say to the pale man. *"Pouvez-vous marcher?"*

He nods, but he doesn't stand. Will helps him up. Lets him go. His leg cricks grotesquely, and he almost drops again. Will catches him.

"By *yourself*?" Jules asks testily.

Will holds him up, and we start to walk across the room. Slowly. Okay, maybe this was stupid.

"Take us to the exit," I say in French. "The way out. *La police pour nous, l'hôpital pour vous.*"

He shakes his head wildly.

"What d'you mean 'no'? Yes! Like, right now!"

"Not yet," he says, lowering his head, squeezing his eyes closed, doing that bobbing bow again. "Not safe. We must hide! They are coming!"

"He says we need to hide?"

"Where? Where do we hide?"

"Follow," he says, and now he rips out of Will's grasp and begins to hobble unsteadily into the Sistine Room, through the doors, back toward the white antechamber. We hurry after him, Will going right up to his side in case he wants to make a run for it. We're slamming through doors, through an endless string of sumptuous rooms. Drapes, gilt, paintings, and furniture pass in a blur. We're in a narrow corridor, the walls paneled in dark wood, the ceiling ribbed with gilt, patterned as if it's made up of massive dragonfly wings. The pale guy stops in front of a double door. He starts nodding, gesturing toward it.

"Safe?" I ask, tapping a hand on the wood. "We'll be safe in here?"

He stares at me, eyes twitching. Jules turns, staring down the corridor.

"Safe!" I repeat, urgently. *"Est-il sécuritaire?"*

Something's coming. I hear it now that we've stopped—far, far away, but getting closer, the unmistakable sound of pounding feet. Doors opening. And that humming's back, sudden and sharp. The same humming I heard in the bone-white antechamber, but louder now—a thin, fuzzy line of sound, rising painfully. Whoever's approaching, they can't be more than five rooms away. In a few seconds they'll be bursting into the corridor.

The pale man is freaking out, and so is Jules. The hum is a bone saw now, cutting into my brain.

Unless there's a contingent of Sapanis on the other side of these doors, draped over chaises longues and sipping the blood of infants from martini glasses, this is where we're hiding.

I rip open the doors. Will grabs the pale guy, Lilly grabs Jules, and we're all piling into someplace big, someplace dark—

Palais du Papillon—Chambres Jacinthe—
112 feet below, 1789

They have separated me from my sisters. I cannot remember the moment it happened. Perhaps I went mad for a short while after meeting with Father, or perhaps I was simply too tired and battered with grief to notice, but they are gone now. I remember the dry click of our shoes on wooden floors, Delphine's soft crying, and the swish of Charlotte's and Bernadette's skirts as they held hands and comforted each other. A door, creaking open and shut. Crawling into the cold sheets of a bed. When I woke, I was alone. I have been alone ever since.

Nine days since I have seen the sun.

Nine days since Mama died.

Nine nights in these close and muffled chambers.

Nine scratches on the wood behind the bed canopy.

I feel as though I have been buried alive.

My tomb is lovely. It consists of two rooms. The hyacinth

rooms, so says a scroll above the door, the *chambres jacinthe*. There is a bedroom, lavish in colors of pale green and rose. There is a boudoir draped in blue silks, with a great curling fireplace of snowy marble. I tried to climb up the chimney on the second day, but there was a grate only four feet from the ground and no way to loosen it. I still wonder sometimes where it comes out, whether there are chimneys poking out of the earth in the middle of Péronne's woods far above.

Or perhaps it is a fakery, like the mirror windows and the drapes. Perhaps it goes nowhere. I have never seen the fire lit.

My rooms are connected to each other by a tall gilt doorway. There is a small toilet through a panel by the bed, and the door from the boudoir leads to a hallway. That is all I know. The door to the hallway is always locked, and no one has entered or left by it since I arrived.

The servants do not use the doors. They have their own clever system and I never see them, even during the day when they bring me luncheon or tidy one of the rooms. Every night, I go to sleep determined to doze lightly and to wake at the smallest sound, but in the end I sleep like a rock, and in the morning my clothes are cleaned and the lamps have all been trimmed and there is breakfast waiting for me. I have discovered how they do it: when I move from the bedroom to the boudoir or vice-versa, the door will click shut behind me, locking. I can rattle and hammer as much as I please, but it will not open until it wants to; and when it wants to, the room beyond is always empty of anybody. I will find dishes of pastries and bowls of fruit, cups of thick cream, freshly starched petticoats, little pots of tea, and sometimes a new volume of poetry or tales. But the one who brings me these gifts is always gone.

Of course I looked for the secret panel that lets them in, and of course I found it. Two rooms can hold only so many secrets, and for only so long. But alas, the panel is locked from the other side. I pried at it until my fingers bled, and the next day there were bandages and a greasy brown salve on my nightstand.

I had half a mind to throw them across the room, another half to break my toes against the wall and scream until I was hoarse. I would have, had I thought it might help. But there is no use being childish. I have searched every nook and every cranny for a way to escape. I have left desperate notes, and shouted to be released, and I have cried all my tears away. No one is listening. I have nothing to do now but go mad. I feel I am accomplishing that, at least. I am becoming like the batty old dowagers at court, wandering from room to room or sitting half lost in the heaps of their finery with nothing to do but mutter and glance disapprovingly at the young, happy people they had once been, and wished they could be again.

Sometimes I write on the paper provided. Often I stare at my own reflection. It is poor company. During the first several days I would peer at the false windows and pretend I was speaking to Mama, would imagine the dry click of my sobs was her soft tutting and the swing of the clock hands were her fingers, running through my hair.

"Do you think we will get out?" I would say to the glass, and then I would answer in a lovely, foolish voice: "You will get out, Aurélie. You are clever and you are brave."

I have stopped doing this. Not even the dowagers were quite so mad.

Last night I thought I heard Delphine crying. "Aurélie?" she wailed, somewhere faraway, and I sat straight up, listening until my ears rang, but I heard nothing more. I got out of bed and pressed my ear to the door. I woke on the floor nine hours later, and now I think that perhaps I dreamed it.

Today, I rise at my usual hour and dress behind the silk screen. It is nearly impossible to dress without a servant; I miss half the buttons, but it doesn't matter. I don't know why I bother anymore. Perhaps I will never see anyone again, and I might walk about in a sheet like a Roman princess. Perhaps I will die down here, an old spinster far underground, by then utterly delusional.

I am already having the strangest dreams. Flashes of teeth and butterfly wings, folding open and closed. Delphine with her hair grown wild and vast, tangled with silver forks and toy rocking horses. Mama, pulling a bullet from her breast.

Breakfast is waiting for me in the boudoir when I am finished dressing. Hot rolls and butter, honey in a crystal dish, and a bundle of glossy black grapes. The grapes taste of ashes. All the fruit here does. I wonder if Father grows them in little jars in a laboratory. Havriel said they sealed the palace, closed it up against the blood and ruin of the revolution, so I doubt they are coming from Lyon, as they used to. I pluck a few grapes and eat them. I sit down and butter a roll. The silverware makes soft clinking noises in the silence.

It is different down here, the sound of silence. On the surface, silence is a vast, full thing. It is alive, pulsing with the movement of the sky and the world and the stars. Here the silence is closed and tight. Everything is louder, every breath and every step. It makes it difficult to breathe and difficult to step, and perhaps that is the point. I throw down the roll after two bites and go to the writing table.

I am trying to escape, still. I have come to the conclusion that I have two options. One is to discover how the servants come in and out, which I have done, catch them in the act, beat them senseless, and escape through the secret panel. The second is to wait for someone—Havriel or Father—to come in the regular way, beat him senseless, and leave through the door.

I know the servants are only in one of the two rooms at a time, and that the doors lock whenever they are there, preventing me from ever stumbling upon them face-to-face. I know there is a panel in the boudoir and another in the bedroom through which they enter. They will not speak to me through the door. They will not answer my notes, no matter how kindly I write them and how many francs I promise them.

But I have a new idea. A servant will come again today to clear away the breakfast dishes, and this time I will be lying in wait.

I sit at my desk, dip my pen, and write a few words on a square of paper:

Roses

Viper

Whipped cream

I pause. Pretend I have forgotten something in the bedroom. Slip out of my chair and move toward the door. I take
special care not to look at the mirror as I pass it. I doubt they
are watching me through it, but I will not have them suspect.
I go about the bedroom, singing to myself. I move away from
the door, casually. Almost at once it begins to creak shut
behind me, as if guided by invisible hands.

I wonder if it has something to do with the floor. Perhaps
weight on the boards, or simply a watchful eye and a lever.
It makes no difference. As soon as the door begins to close,
I spin. A heavy wad of stationery is crumpled in my hand. I
drop to the floor and jam it between the door and the frame.

The lock snaps out. It does not catch. *Perfect.*

I feel a thrill of fear as I press my back against the wall.
There may be several servants; perhaps someone is standing
guard, and I will be hopelessly outnumbered. But if I do not
try, I will never know.

I hear the panel in the boudoir opening and footsteps pad-
ding across the floor. Slowly, I move forward to look through
the crack between the door and the frame.

I see the boudoir, tranquil and empty, like a doll's room. . . .

I wait, hardly daring to breathe. I do not see anyone, but I hear movement, the slide and tinkle of plates, the whisper of table linens. I reach for the heavy bronze vase in the corner next to the door. It is with this I plan to do the beating. It is too far away. I slide over the floor toward it.

When I return to the door, I see the servant. A leg. A hand. He is standing, facing the bedroom door.

I want to curse. *Was I too quiet? Does he suspect, does he see that the door is unlatched?*

The floor in the boudoir creaks. I glimpse a heel again, a leg. The servant is turning away, moving to another part of the chamber. I ease the door open, barely a fraction of an inch.

I see his back now. It is a man in fine livery, a waistcoat and white stockings. He is clearing away the breakfast dishes, replacing them with marbled wafers and candied fruits that have been cut into bright squares, like soft jewels. He is young. The slope of his shoulders is vaguely familiar to me, as are the brown curls on his head. *Have I seen him before?*

An unpleasant needling sensation besets my shin. I try to shift my position as delicately as possible. The floor gives the tiniest of creaks. When I look again, the servant is gone.

My eyes dart throughout the room. I did not hear the panel close. *Has he gone?* He must not escape. Not before I catch him. I wait, frozen in place, gathering the courage to burst into the room. I take a slow breath—

His face appears between the door and the frame, exactly level with my own. Our eyes lock. I rip the door wide and hit him hard across the side of his head with the vase.

He goes spinning to the side, loses his balance, and crashes to the floor. I lunge at him again. He raises an arm in defense. "Stop!" he shouts, and now he seems to remember himself, and says more quietly, urgently: "Stop, mademoiselle, please."

I stare at him, wide-eyed. He is the guard. The young guard who tried to save Mama. He is not a day older than I am. I whirl and head for his secret panel. It is closed, but surely not locked.

I tug on it. It does not move.

I go back to the boy who is just starting to stand, wobbly on his legs. I raise the vase again.

"I don't care who you are," I say. "I don't care what they told you. I am held prisoner here. My sisters are lost. You will help me find them."

19

It's a library. Long, dim—a shadowy gallery of books. It's got that same faint ultraviolet glow that the hall full of razor wires had—just enough to see by, but still somehow pitch-black. The ceiling arches into a map of the heavenly bodies, gold-leaf planets and star creatures against a blue plane. Mahogany bookshelves reach all the way to Cassiopeia's toes, twenty feet above us. At the end of the library is a massive marble fireplace. The floor is thick with pelts and furs.

Gross. It's like a freaking Narnian battlefield in here. I swear one of them is a polar bear.

"The doors," Will says, and we huddle around them, trying to get them locked up. A floor peg is jammed into its rut. That's all we've got. All that's standing between us and the outside.

"They're coming!" Jules whispers, high-pitched and

panicked, and Will and Lilly start dragging a massive table toward the doors. The noise is excruciating. I run over to help. We lift it the rest of the way and shove it crosswise against the wood. Jules hooks his fire poker through the handles.

We back up, our hands tight around our weapons. My head feels like it's about to blow off like a firecracker.

I can't hear anything from the other side of the doors. No footsteps. Nothing but that scratchy, almost subliminal whine. It's like they stopped right outside the doors, or kept running. The pale man has turned into a weird statue again, his shoulders tense, fingers curled and posed like he's trying to imitate one of the painted figures in the Sistine Room.

We wait, frozen. Minutes pass. My joints start to feel like chewed-up rubber.

"Are they gone?" Lilly whispers.

Or are they waiting right outside? I imagine them out there, inky figures standing like black pillars, silent and tense.

"I think they kept going," Will says under his breath. "We should keep barricading the door. In case they come back."

We break into frantic motion. The wood floor squeaks. Will stacks a few heavy chairs on top of the table. I climb up them and heave an eight-legged bureau with peacock mother-of-pearl reliefs on top. Then a leather-padded stepladder. A footstool. We climb higher, higher, until the entire twelve-foot-high doors are covered with a grid of furniture.

As I'm scrambling down I hear something from outside. An awful rough, grating sound, like claws on wood.

I freeze, clinging precariously to a chair, one foot dangling in the air. My eyes flick frantically toward Lilly on the other side of the stack.

The sound seems to go on forever, *scrrrrtch-scrrrrtch,* echoing in the hallway, so close to the other side of the door. Finally it breaks off. It doesn't pass, doesn't fade into the distance. It's just gone.

I hop the rest of the way down, land quietly on the pelt of a wolf. Jules catches my arm and pulls me upright. Mutters in my ear, his breath hot: "You need to talk to him." He cuts his eyes toward the pale man. "What was that outside? You need to ask him why they brought us down here."

I nod. Will gestures toward the back of the library and we move farther in, our group splitting around side tables and sofas like water. My feet sink into fur and bristles, skin-crawlingly crunchy. The pale man stays close to me, still limping along, his wounded arm cradled against his chest.

We reach the huge marble fireplace and press ourselves into the shadows of one of its carved pillars. The library is silent. The pale man stands slightly apart from us, staring at the doors. I inch over to him.

"Hey," I say. *"Ecoutez-moi.* We've been kidnapped. We're American citizens, and we need to get out of here. We need to know what's going on."

My heart is pounding, ridiculously loud. The pale man doesn't answer. Doesn't look at me.

New tactic: *"Je m'âppelle Anouk,"* I say. *"Et vous?"* Psychology 101. Treat your subject like he's a human being. Pleasantries before business. Better yet, business disguised as pleasantries.

"Moi?" the pale man rasps. Still watching the door. And again, softly: *"Moi. Qui suis-je . . . ?"*

Who am I . . . ?

His eyes widen. He looks lucid, frightened, like

someone waking up from a nightmare. *"Je suis perdu,"* he says. *"Perdu dans l'ombre."*

I turn to the others.

"He said he's lost," I say. "Lost in the shadows."

"That's a terrible name," Jules says, and almost simultaneously Lilly twists her hands together and whispers, "Uh, fantastic, so are we."

I turn back to the pale man. "Fine. You're Perdu. Pleased to meet you. Were you kidnapped too? How do we get out of here?"

Perdu starts to giggle, his head tipping back. An ugly sound crawls out, like his throat is full of broken glass.

"You cannot leave," he says. "You cannot leave!"

"Why is he laughing?" Jules says, eyes wide. "Shut him up!"

I feel sick. "We had a deal—" I start to say.

"Shhh," Perdu whispers, and places a long thin finger to his lips. "He is close."

Will stiffens. I look over my shoulder at the doors, my heart squeezing up into my throat.

"Who?" I prompt. "Dorf?"

"Non." Perdu wraps his arms around his bony shoulders. He seems to shrink, twisting. And as he turns,

he points down the length of the library to the closed doors, silent behind their cage of furniture. *"L'homme papillon,"* he says, in a guttural, piercing croak. *"L'homme papillon!"*

"What's he saying?" Lilly hisses.

"The butterfly man."

"Who?"

"I don't know."

"Ask him what we're supposed to do!"

"Perdu?" I whisper fiercely, and he jerks upright, jittering. "Perdu, what do you know? Who are you?"

20

Perdu rises slowly, facing us. "I crawl through the dark," he says. "Through forests of gilt and crystal I wander. Friend to the friendless, rescuer of dead and broken things. I am the watcher in the treetops."

I turn to the others. "He's crazy."

"Great," Jules says. "No, really, that's good to know now that we're *locked in here with him.*"

I spin back to Perdu. "You said you would help us," I say in French. "Does this room have another exit? Do you know the way out?"

Perdu's watching me, wheezing. I can't read his gaze. Usually I feel like all those books about deranged folk paid off and I have a really good idea of the depths of people's depravity, but I can't tell with him. I don't know if that gaze is dangerous or imploring.

"If you leave now," he says, and saliva flies between his

lips with each breath, "you will die. You will step through those doors and he will see you. His eyes shall eat you like mouths, and you will lie on the floor, and ants and wasps and nits will crawl from your wounds like drops of night. Four little plums, all chewed up."

He says that last sentence so casually that for a second I swear he's sane. And now his hand swings around, smacking Will right in the temple, and he scuttles away, cramming himself into the space between a chair and the wall, like he's trying to hide. He looks out at me from under the armrest, eyes glinting. "I am the only one you can trust," he hisses.

I look over at Will. "You okay?"

He nods quickly, like he didn't even feel it. "What was he saying?" he asks. "*Prunes mâché*, what does that mean?"

"That if we leave now we die."

"All those words meant 'You're going to die'?" Jules says.

"Basically. Also, he seems to think there's just one person out there now. And it's a he."

Lilly nudges me in the ribs. "He's moving. What's he doing?"

Perdu is out from behind the chair, standing up. Will

is about to dive after him. I grab Will's shoulder. "Wait."

The shadows swallow Perdu. He's just a slight variation now, another shade in the dark-to-black spectrum. It sounds like he's pawing through a drawer. He's coming back toward us, and he's holding something tightly in his fingers. He walks up to me. Opens his fist. It's a compass, the surface scratched and pockmarked in a million places, like a pirate's.

"A token," he says, and his voice is human again, gentle. "A token of my loyalty. I will lead you to safety. There is a secret way. A way they cannot know. Due north as the wren flies, straight as an arrow and straight as string."

I don't take the compass. "Then why are you still down here? You said you don't want to stay, so go. What's stopping you?"

"Everything," he says, looking terrified again. "Fire and blade and bolt and poison. The palace is not easily breached, neither from within nor from without. But my time here is coming to an end. My usefulness is spent. He will kill me soon. But you will help me." His gaze flicks from me to the others, and he smiles that awful, limp-lipped grin. "You will take me with you, *oui*? You will not leave me behind."

"When does he want to go?" Will asks. "If it's up to him, when would we leave the library?"

"Perdu," I say. *"Combien du temps voulez-vous que nous restions ici?"*

He holds out the compass, trying to get me to take it. "In the morning," he whispers. "Tomorrow is a new day, a bright day."

"How do we know when morning is?"

"The hands will tell you. Seven times they will turn, round and round. On the eighth it will be morning."

"You mean in eight hours? We're supposed to stay in here eight hours? What makes you think we'll be safe that long?"

"I will keep you safe," he says. "I will hide you in the shadow of my wings."

That's not comforting at all. Perdu's eyes are alight, fingers squirming along the edges of the compass, leaving a greasy film. I grab it and turn to the others, translating as fast as I can. They listen, their faces getting darker by the word.

"You have got to be kidding me," Jules says. "What if he's lying? What if he just wants to keep us in one spot until the trackers can get here?"

"I don't know," I say. "Look, it's up to us. We can either wait with him, or go and risk whatever's out there. They're both worst-case scenarios, so pick your favorite."

I already know my answer. There's no telling what Perdu would do if we dragged him out there now. We'd have to leave him behind and then we'd be running blind, pushing off into the palace on a teeny-tiny slice of *hey-let's-hope-we-don't-die.* We'll be doing that either way, but the slice seems bigger with Perdu. We *need* to trust him. We need to trust something down here, even if it's just an insane bleeding guy.

"If we wait, someone's going to have to be awake," Lilly says. "The whole time."

"We can take turns keeping watch. Two hours each."

"I'm not sleeping anyway," Jules says.

And so we wait.

21

We've built our own personal bubble of warm light and coziness
in front of the fireplace. Will found a light switch
behind a panel next to the mantel. Jules and Lilly have
constructed a fort—possibly a full-on mansion—out of
chairs, pillows, carpets. It's kind of morbid if you think
about it, setting up camp down here in the palace of your
psycho captors. Like a zombie-murder-sleepover. But
the alternative is cowering in the dark, so we might as
well make the most of it. Also, there's some satisfaction
to be had from using the Sapanis' stuff. I'm assuming
this is their library, if the Sapanis are real people. I'm
also assuming this place is *not* a two-hundred-year-old
archaeological site. It's their house. Their huge, pristine,
underground home, which just so happens to have an
infestation of bleeding men, traps, and general weirdness.
I bet they really don't want their murder-victims-to-be

pawing through their books and using their furs and lounging in their chairs.

I grab a pillow and mush it up behind my neck, leaning against a desk leg.

Will has wandered off to scout out the library. Lilly and Jules are busy with home-improvement matters. Perdu's hiding behind the chair again, eyes pinched shut. His velvet bandages are black and crackly.

"Perdu," I say quietly. His mouth twitches open. Wet, gray teeth flick into view, squeezed together, haphazard and gross. He winces, as if the word hurt him. "Where are you from?"

"Péronne," he breathes.

I'm trying to unstick my pant leg from my ankle. The blood has started to cake where the wire caught it.

"And how did you get down here?"

"C'est ma maison," he whispers. *"Il me garde."*

"This is my home," I translate for Jules, who is looking over at us suspiciously from behind his wall of chairs. "He keeps me."

"Who keeps him?" Jules asks. "Is he like the house pet?"

"Hey," Lilly says, frowning at Jules. "You don't know

what he's been through. He might have been down here way longer than us. It's probably messed with his mind."

"Below," Perdu mumbles, and I raise my hand, signaling Lilly and Jules to shut up. "Down," Perdu says. "Far into the earth. To good luck and safety and everlasting peace, they brought me. But I will be leaving soon. When the war is done, that is what they told me, when the war is done you may go. But it stretches on and on. It never ends."

"What war?" I ask.

"That war." He uncurls a finger toward the ceiling. "Up there. They are cutting off heads in the Rue du Fauconnier. Can you not hear the screaming?"

"There is no war up there," I say. "At least, not one you'd hear down—"

"There is always war," Perdu hisses. He's crying again. I can see the tears, glimmering tracks down his cheeks. "Everywhere. Up there. Down here." He taps the finger against his head. "In here."

"Uh-huh." I glance at Jules and roll my eyes. "How old are you, Perdu?"

His hands come up, fingers splayed like twin fans. He closes his fists, opens them, again and again, and I realize he's showing me—ten fingers, ten years—decade after decade flickering past.

"You're not that old. When were you born? What year?"

"1772."

Will is back. He makes a sound, a soft bark from somewhere in his chest. I think it was supposed to be a laugh. I wouldn't even have known he was there otherwise. Kid moves like a ghost.

Jules glances at Will. "What? What did he say?"

"That he's over two hundred years old," I answer. I lean back against the fireplace. Look up at the ceiling, with its network of lines sketching out the Greek figures. I recognize Andromeda, Cygnus. Someone who I think is Capricorn but looks like a minotaur. That gets me to thinking about the Theseus myth, young people being thrown into a labyrinth to feed a monster. But if they wanted to reenact that one, they got the numbers wrong: there are supposed to be seven of us. And Dorf didn't sound like he wanted us to be food for that thing. He sounded like we were ruining his plans.

I sigh, still staring up at the ceiling. If this were a proper indie movie moment, I'd be doing my stargazing next to a spray-painted van, while on a road trip across Montana. I'd have a guitar and a big old happy dog. I'd stare up at the endless night sky and feel small or something. Since this is my actual life, I'm looking at stipples of white paint on a ceiling, thinking about being eaten alive.

I ease my pant leg back over the cut. Glance up at Will. "Did you find anything?"

"No other doors out," he says. "Lots of books on philosophy. And the chimney's blocked about six feet up. Oh, and I found a clock."

He hands me a little brass wind-up on two miniature clawed feet. It's awesome looking, like it could run away giggling and ringing furiously every time you really didn't want to wake up in the morning. I start winding it up.

Perdu has turned his back on us again, crouching, head pressed into the corner. He's singing softly, under his breath:

> *"Four blind mice, oh, four blind mice.*
> *See how they run, oh, see how they run.*
> *They all ran after the farmer's wife,*

Who cut off their tails with a carving knife,
Did you ever see such a sight in your life, oh
As four . . . blind . . . mice."

"He's singing nursery rhymes now," I say. "Creepy ones. Must be past his bedtime."

Lilly starts to laugh, but she can't quite decide whether I'm hilarious or not. And now Perdu turns suddenly, staring at us.

"Dance around the edge of the pond and you'll fall in," he says, soft and urgent, like he's telling us a secret. "But if you leap in the middle, all will be well. You will still get wet, but you chose to, then, don't you see? It is your own fault."

"Okay, Perdu." He could just come out and say it: I'm not going to tell you anything helpful, because either I want you to die, or I'm just really clueless.

I stand abruptly and walk quietly over the furs. Someone follows me and I think it's Perdu for a second, but it's Will.

He doesn't say anything. Just lopes down the library beside me. We stop in front of the doors.

I gaze up at the furniture mountain, ears straining to

pick up any blip of sound on the other side. The whirring is gone. Every scratch, creak, whisper, hum noise is gone. A solid white silence is crushing against the library doors, so complete it's like the hallway and the Sistine Room and all the other rooms have vanished. I imagine opening the doors and finding nothingness. Blank space. A vacuum, the library floating like a shoe box in the void.

"It's so quiet," I say.

He nods. We're breathing in unison. An itch starts crawling up my arms like a million tiny insect feet. I have the overwhelming urge to shove down the furniture, open the doors, run.

"What if this is our chance?" I say. "We're sitting ducks in here. What if we should be running?"

"We'll be okay," Will says, and rolls his shoulders.

Deep, Will. Logical and well-founded. A layered argument.

We head back to the others.

22

Jules hands me some grapes. He's got his colorful shirtsleeves rolled up to his elbows and is rubbing his arm furiously, except you can't really tell because he has an actual ink sleeve under the cloth one: a Cheshire cat and abstract flowers and the words *Plague of Monkey Lice* in Mandarin on his wrist. I bet the tattoo artist told him it meant *Good Luck* and *Fortune*.

I swallow the grapes. They taste like ash, dry and bitter. It looks like everyone's getting ready to sleep. I wonder how long we were out in the glass cube room. I wonder if it's nighttime up on the surface.

"There's another pillow here if you want it," Lilly says, apparently taking pity on my Spartan sleeping arrangements. I take it and nod at her, which she can interpret as thanks if she wants to.

She nods back. She's curled up on a wing chair,

wrapped in a carpet like a Bedouin lady. Before I went to check the door, she'd been wearing a fluffy fur sewn from the pelts of a thousand small and adorable animals. I guess Jules explained that to her, though, because she dragged it all the way to the other side of the library and pushed it under a table as a form of protest.

I pick up the clock Will brought and look at it. "One hour gone, seven to go." I flick my head in the direction of Perdu. *Watch him*, I mouth. "Every two hours we'll switch, okay? The first one will probably be the easiest, since you won't have to wake up. Who wants it?"

I expect Lilly or Jules to volunteer. They don't. No one does, which is admirable and also completely unhelpful. I hand the clock to Jules. "When the hands hit eight, shake one of us."

Jules takes the clock. Will stretches himself out onto a rug, laying his sword down carefully next to him. "If something happens . . ." Will says. He trails off, gazing down the library.

"If something happens, wake up Will," Lilly finishes. "He'll chop down our enemies. We'll send him supportive thoughts."

Wow, Lilly, was that sarcasm? Will pushes himself up

onto his elbows and blinks at her. He's probably deciding whether she's making fun of him or not. She is, but for some reason she can't bear to let him think that, so she leans off her chair and ruffles his hair. "I'm joking, Will. Hey. I'm joking."

She smiles at him, a huge bright smile, all pink tongue and teeth. Will smiles back. His cheeks dig into dimples, and his eyes take on a wry gleam, all before he can stop himself. It's kind of incredible to watch.

Will's facial transformation makes Jules laugh, which makes me laugh because Jules sounded exactly like Pete the Parrot, croaking farewell to me from his cage in the breakfast kitchen. The fact that I laughed makes Lilly laugh, and pretty soon all three of us are laughing, dry and brittle, like a really terrible trio of beatboxers. None of this is even remotely funny. That just makes me laugh harder.

Will gets his face under control. Raises his eyebrows at us and rolls over. I'm pretty sure he's still smiling, though. Our laughter trails off.

I feel full as I curl up against the table leg. Full and warm, which is ironic because those grapes were crap and the temperature in here is fairly chilly, lights or no. I decide I'd live on laughing if I could. I'd probably starve, but maybe it would be worth it.

I start to doze. Get a crick in my neck and move my pillow to the floor. I'm nearly asleep, my whole body fuzzy and dull. I open my eyes, more of a slow, reverse blink. Will is asleep. Jules is standing by the fireplace, looking nervous, kicking his foot against the marble. Lilly is asleep in her chair. And behind her, just outside the bubble of light, Perdu is standing, watching me, his eyes burning scabs into my skin.

Palais du Papillon—Chambres Jacinthe— 112 feet below, 1790

The servant's name is Jacques. He has come every day since I struck him with the vase and he no longer locks me out upon his arrival. He seems to enjoy the company as much as I do, though he is far more ready to say so. He is altogether too insolent, I think. He smiles when there is nothing to smile at and he does not walk like a gentleman, he *saunters*. Furthermore, he is slow in being useful.

"Why can you not simply unlock the panel and let me out?" I demanded the day we met.

"Mademoiselle, they are *watching*!" he said, cradling his bruised face and staring at me as if I were a wild troll. "What can you not understand? I will already have to spin a pretty tale to explain this face you gave me. 'Oh, yes, I slipped while feather dusting the china and blackened my own eye.' You must understand, we have direct orders from Lord Havriel never to allow anyone into the serving passages, least of all you. And if you *were* to leave, you would be caught. There are other servants running to and fro constantly. You would not get a hundred feet before they raised the alarm."

I shook my head and turned away as if to say: *You do not know me, and you do not know how many feet I would get.*

He carried on. "And once they've caught you, they'll put you somewhere worse and you'll get a warty old hag for a servant, and I assure you she won't speak a word to you, especially if you beat her with a vase. Listen. Please, mademoiselle, listen to me and I will help you."

I turned toward him again, curious. His face was earnest, his eyes the colors of slate. "I know of your plight, mademoiselle," he says. "I know they have locked you away, and revolution or none, it is not right to be caged so. But you must tread carefully. You will have one chance to get your sisters and get back to the surface. You will not get another."

And so we began to talk.

This is what I have learned, six days later. The fact that I can put it all down so briefly vexes me: Jacques follows orders from the head butler, Monsieur Vallé. Jacques's job is to take care of my hyacinth rooms and to provide me with all that I need. He is strictly forbidden to speak to me. He has seen no one else of my family. The last Bessancourt he saw was Mama. She was no longer breathing when he and the old guard carried her down. Jacques would not tell me her wounds, but he has a mother, too, in Péronne, and he said that if she were to die, he would weep for a year. His face was grave when he told me this, and when I cried he did not leave me, but sat at my side until I was exhausted, wrung out like a bit of washing.

Today I am sitting on the floor of the boudoir and he is cleaning, or pretending to.

"Why are you no longer a guard?" I ask him. "When we came down, you were in uniform."

He shakes out a sheet with a snap. "They told me there was no need for guards here. Peace and everlasting safety and suchlike, you know? The palace is invincible. So now I am a chambermaid." He laughs and begins tucking the sheet in at the corners, and I cannot help but notice that when he laughs, his face becomes quite wonderful to see.

"Did you come of your own choice?"

If he says yes I will like him less.

"No." He starts on the pillows. "Well, yes, I suppose, but does a starving thief choose to steal? Does a soldier choose to kill? We do things or else we die." He tries to twinkle at me, but I will have none of it. I saw the shadow cross his face. I watch him sharply, and wait.

"You are a nosy sparrow. Mademoiselle," he adds quickly, "I came here because my father is off at sea, and I have three sisters and four brothers, all living on what coins my mother can scrape together darning socks and patching trousers. My siblings needed bread, and stockings for the winter. So I hopped a cart to the château and begged for work. We don't have choices the way highborn lords and ladies do."

I bristle at that. "Perhaps you have noticed, *Monsieur*, that highborn lords and ladies do not have quite as many choices as you thought. A golden cage is still a cage."

"A cage with no shortage of bread and stockings," he says evenly.

"A cage *alone*." It comes out in a snarl. I see suddenly what he is: his sympathy for me is mixed with disdain. He pities me, is sorry that my mother is dead, but it is the pity of an older sibling patting the younger one crying over a lost toy. He thinks I do not know hardship.

"I have food and clothing, yes," I say, my voice low. "And my mother is dead. There is no difference between pain of the heart and pain of the belly."

"And you think peasants are spared heart's pain? We have both."

"You have a mother!" I shout. "She is alive. She was not shot before your eyes, and your sisters were not torn from you and locked away in some godforsaken palace. But you will not spare a drop of pity because I am rich? We have death in our gilded courts, too. We have disease and cruelty, and not a breath of air or freedom. You cannot say our lives are easy, any more than I can say yours is. They are lives, and so they are *horrid!*"

The last word is a screech. I gasp, forcing the tears to keep from falling.

Neither of us says a word for several moments. Jacques begins to move again, wandering about and straightening the pillows. Finally he turns to me. "I'm sorry, mademoiselle. Let's not fight. Please? Everyone in the kitchens is on knife's edge, every day. There is nothing but bile spewing and bitterness. Let us not fight, at least."

He finishes the bed and sits down across from me, cross-legged. I pretend great interest in a groove in the floorboards. I feel a stab of remorse for shrieking at him. He is poor and I am rich, and we each think ourselves the sadder and the more hurt. But there is no measure for pain. How wonderful it would be if there were no limit to sympathy.

"I'm sorry, too," I say. "And you may call me Aurélie. Please do."

We stay on the floor, neither of us looking at the other, simply lingering, unwilling to part. We are the same in some things: we are both young and lonely. We wish to protect the ones we love. We are both unable to do so.

"Will you come with us when we escape?" I ask after a while.

He looks up, surprised. "Where to?"

"I don't know. Wherever we go. London, I suppose."

I must sound terribly frivolous. I don't care. I can almost feel the sun up there, the wind and the green grasses brushing against my fingertips. I can hear the birds. I feel I could burst these walls, burst the ceiling with my shoulders.

"You would not want me along," Jacques says, and he is looking at the same groove in the floorboard that I was so studiously inspecting. "I am no match for English chambermaids."

"And you have a family here," I say practically.

He stares at me. Nods. "That I have."

A knocking sounds, somewhere in the walls, dull and faraway. He leaves me.

It is almost a week before I see him again. He unlocks the door to the boudoir and grins at me, tries to be light and jolly, but I know at once that he is neither. When he stretches himself long to reach the cornices, I see he has bruises on his hands and peeking, purple and green, from behind his collar. He will not tell me how he got them. I hope he is not being punished for the time he spends here.

"Have you found a way out?" I ask him as soon as I dare.

"No," he says. "But I am closer. The butlers are run ragged with work. They . . . they become angry when the lower servants are slow, but there are fewer of them now and they cannot watch everything. I think some of them are being sent back up. Or perhaps they are escaping." He studies his own hands, opening them across his knees. His fingers are brown and weathered like a farmer's. "They will not let me near the outer chambers of the palace, or in certain wings, but I think it is only a matter of time. It is vast down here, immense. But it feels small. It feels *airless*." His voice becomes soft. "I've been having the oddest dreams."

I wonder if they are like my dreams. I am about to ask him when a sound from beyond the door startles us to our feet. Jacques runs for the panel. I go with him, and as he steps through, my hand brushes his and he squeezes it. Now he is gone.

I sometimes think I like him best when he is gone. I think of all the things I want to ask him, and I remember that if I were not here, if I were not a prisoner, I would not care to speak to him at all.

23

I'm dreaming. Nightmaring. Whatever it's called. My back is flat against the floor. My shoulders stick disgustingly to my shirt.

I'm in a banquet hall—beautiful, hideous, ornate. Everything is black and red. Red light. Black shadows. And everything is upside down. Chandeliers sprout from the floor like trees. A long table hangs from the ceiling. The table is covered with heaps of food, grotesque and unrecognizable in the dark, and somehow it doesn't fall.

I'm sitting at the table, upside down, my shoulder blades digging into a high, carved chair. And now gravity shifts and I'm upright. A plate is in front of me. I can't tell what's on it, but it's piled high, steaming. . . .

I flinch. Someone else is sitting at the table, way at the other end. He's obscured by shadow, but I feel his eyes on me, and they're cold. Sharp. Ice blue.

*A sound, like a knife against a crystal goblet, and the red
lights flare along the table. I see the figure at the other end.
It's a huge man, a silhouette against the ruddy glow. For
some reason I can only see parts of him, a red velvet coat,
lacy cuffs resting on the table in front of him. The lower part
of his face. Warts pressing like boils through the powder. The
man is chewing, smiling, chewing and smiling, faster and
faster, smacking his lips. I get little glimpses of his teeth—red
teeth, stained teeth chewing.*

*"Are you the butterfly man?" I want to ask, but some-
thing is clogging my throat, and I'm coughing, choking,
vomiting bullets onto my plate—*

I wake up gasping.

The sweat is freezing on my back. I shudder, pinch my
eyes closed. Sit up.

What time is it? Lilly is hanging off her chair. Jules
and Will are sprawled every which way on the floor. The
light seems to have changed. It's pale white now, not the
golden glow we went to sleep in.

Something's not right.

The room feels crowded suddenly, stiflingly full. Lilly,
Jules, and Will are next to me, but there are other people
lying across the floor, propped against the fireplace,

draped over tables. Sleeping people, their faces turned away from me, unmoving.

I spin, searching for Perdu. He's in the shadows behind a massive globe, crying, clawing at the painted map. And now he turns to me, and his eyes are red fire.

Run, he spits. *Run while you can. He's seen you.*

I wake with a shout. Shove myself upright. The light is soft and warm. The sleepers are gone. It's just Jules, Will, Lilly, me. Four.

One.

Two.

Three.

Four.

Perdu's gone.

24

I tear across the library.

"Perdu!" I don't even care if anyone hears me. The clock stopped at 2:17. Five hours after I last checked it. There's blood on the floor, dark, stinking of hot metal. My feet are slapping in it.

I reach the doors and stare up at them. All the furniture we had stacked in front of it is lying in a pile. I see soggy stacks of paper, stained red. Broken chair legs. The massive walnut table is on its side. The doors are still closed. The floor peg is out.

No-no-no, how long was it out, how long was the door open—

"Will?" I wail over my shoulder.

I jam the floor peg in again and spin, racing back toward the fireplace. It's not just blood on the floor. There are tufts of dark hair floating in the red, and fatty, pearly strands of white. Like something *ripped* at Perdu.

"Jules!" The others are just starting to stand, gaping at the blood. "Jules, please tell me you didn't fall asleep. Please—"

He jerks around to look at me, his eyes wide.

He fell asleep. We all did.

Will peels away from us, heading for the door. I drop to hands and knees and crawl between the chairs, trying to see if anything is missing. My letter opener is still in my pocket. The compass is on the floor, half hidden under a heap of pillows and carpets. I grab it and clench it in my fist, still crawling. The two swords are lying on the floor. We don't have anything else to steal.

I leap to my feet and run back to the doors. Will's there, one hand hovering over a bloody print on the wood. It's smaller than his hand. Smaller than my hand. It's tiny, almost delicate. *Did Perdu have delicate hands?*

"Nothing's broken," Will says quietly. "The floor peg and the fire poker, it's all fine, which means . . ." He coughs. "Which means the door was opened from this side."

I let out some sort of animal cry and turn in a circle, my fingers going to my hair, digging into my scalp.

"Perdu *let someone in* and we didn't hear? He pulled down a mountain of furniture, was possibly attacked and mauled, and we just slept through it?"

Lilly and Jules race up, carrying the swords. Will grabs his. I drop down and jerk the floor peg out. We thought we were safe in here. We *slept*. As long as we're down here, we're nowhere close to safe.

I stand, and we stare at one another for a second, our eyes popping from our dirty faces like marbles. I nod, knuckles bobbing around the grip of my weapon. I can almost hear our hearts beating, our thoughts screeching in unison.

"It's okay," I say. "We'll be okay."

I open the doors.

25

It's like jumping into a nightmare, some sort of surreal, Dadaesque ballet. The floor is covered with bodies.

They lie splayed over the marble, black suits glistening dully, legs pinned under them at horrific angles. We stand, frozen in the library's doorway, gazing over the carnage. There's no blood. Just helmeted bodies, dripped over the floor like tar.

I'm the first one to move. I step forward and squat next to the closest one. If it's a trap, we're dead anyway—

I nudge it. Its helmeted head rolls, facing me. The red light along the jaw is off, now only a dull, empty strip.

"What did this?" Jules whispers, and Will says, "It doesn't make sense."

No. It doesn't. These were the trackers Dorf sent. They must be. They look exactly like the ones with Miss Sei in the mirror cube, and those things were fast.

They probably could have killed us with one punch and picked their teeth with our swords. But there's no sign of a struggle. Not a scratch on the surface of their glossy black suits. And no way did they stumble into a trap. No way we walked through this hallway unscathed and the actual inhabitants of this place were massacred.

"Should we take off its helmet?" Lilly asks.

That hum is back, turning the air bright and tickling. Will leans down next to one slowly. I watch in horror as he wraps his fingers around its helmet and pulls. It won't come off. He grabs the visor. Slides it up.

Bile rises in my throat. I reach over and slap the visor closed, but it's too late. I saw the face. Everyone saw the face.

It was almost human. Its skin was milky, a gel-like blue fluid making a film over its cheeks. Some kind of tech had been implanted around the lashless eyes. It was definitely dead. Thousands upon thousands of hairline scratches covered its skin, circling the eyes, the mouth, traveling down its neck and into its suit.

"Perdu had scratches like those," Lilly whispers. "All over him."

"You guys?" Jules stands. He's pointing at something on the wall opposite the doors.

We all look.

There's a sentence on it, gouged deep into the splintered wood—six words, chopped into the silk wallpaper and paneling in savage, angular letters:

SEE HOW THE MIGHTY HAVE FALLEN

I stand abruptly.

We exchange looks, the message hanging behind us like a gruesome grin, a jagged row of teeth. "Let's get out of here."

We leave the bodies behind, running for the end of the gallery. Burst through the doors. Slam them and bar them behind us, but it doesn't make me feel safe, not even close.

"They're supposed to be the bad guys," Lilly says, leaning against the wall, pulling frantically at her clothes like she can't breathe, like they're constricting her. "So who killed the bad guys?"

"Perdu—" Jules starts.

"Not Perdu," I say, cutting him off. "Perdu was scared. He was terrified of something down here, and he wanted to escape with us. I think it got him before he could."

"Then why didn't it get us?"

I shake my head. I have no idea. And the thought that there are worse things down here than trackers and Miss Sei and Dorf is not one I want to entertain. "Let's just hope we don't run into it."

I take out the compass and turn, watching the needle. I hear Perdu's voice, high and excited, melding with the static in my head:

A secret way . . . Due north . . . You will help me, won't you? You will not leave me behind?

I stare at the needle. Look up. And head north.

26

Walking in the open feels awful. Like leaving the house in your tiniest, flowiest party dress and realizing your front door opened straight into the tiger enclosure at the Bronx Zoo. Which is possibly something only I've ever worried about, I don't know. We're in a high, narrow gallery lined with doors. The lights are low and the floor is carpeted with an endless, purple-black Persian runner, embroidered with profusions of bronze flowers and satyrs. The carpet gives the space a weird feel, like it's supposed to be homey, but my body knows I'm underground, in a windowless hallway below a trillion tons of soil and rock. It knows I'm trapped. It puts a little itch right in the center of my skull, impossible to scratch. This must be what insanity feels like.

Behind me Lilly and Jules are talking in low voices. "Seriously, there's no reason we, in particular, should have been picked for this. We're obviously not here for our skill sets. We don't come from remotely similar cultural backgrounds. My dad's from Egypt. And we're not even polar opposites, either, like a test group or something. We're just random kids." A pause. "I mean, I'm sorry, but when I saw you guys at JFK, I was regretting signing up."

"And now you're not?" Lilly's voice is scared.

Jules doesn't answer. We get to the end of the gallery. I shift the compass into my other hand, my throat dry.

"Are we just going to hope Perdu was right about the exit?" Jules asks, his voice rising a notch. He's talking to me. "The *secret* exit that we'll totally find on our own?"

"When you have a better plan you can tell us, Jules. No really, I'm on pins and needles."

The next room is a study, a shimmering chamber paneled entirely in polished squares of amber. We cross it in ten steps.

"We could try negotiating," Jules says.

"D'you want to offer yourself up so the rest of us can go free? Yeah, me neither."

"I'm just suggesting maybe—"

"No, Jules, you're being a whiner."

"You guys, stop—" Lilly says nervously.

Jules throws his head back and guffaws. Who laughs that loud when there could be literally *anything* right around the corner listening? But he's got a wounded look to him now, injured pride, and he says: "Who are you calling a whiner, Miss I'm-so-saaaaad-I-have-to-forge-my-parents'-signatures-just-to-get-out-of-the-house?"

Oh, he did *not*. I'm going to slap that kid's face off, little punk hipster with his ink sleeve—

I spin on him. Lilly jams between us. "Stop," she snaps, and Will moves in front of Jules, saying, "Come on, bro," really softly.

I try to get Lilly out of the way.

"Seriously, stop it," she hisses. She braces herself against me. The top of her head barely reaches my collarbone, but she's strong. "Us fighting each other is the last thing that's going to help us get out of here. Okay? You need to quit."

Jules and I glare at each other. And now Jules is getting awkward and apologetic, and I hate that. It's like cheating. You can't punch someone in the throat and say you're sorry and think that's all it takes.

But Lilly's right. Fighting each other is straight-up stupid. I raise an eyebrow in what I hope is a devastatingly condescending gesture and head down a gallery.

Jules comes after me. "Look, I'm sorry," he says, but I don't want placating. I'm tired and thirsty, and we have bigger problems. "I'm just saying, maybe there are other options. We're walking around hoping some insane person was telling the truth, and in the meantime they're chasing us—"

"*Who* is chasing us?" I slam into the next set of rooms. "Not those trackers anymore. And why us? Why fly U.S. citizens to a different continent to murder them? And why are we all teenagers?"

"Maybe they have preferences."

"For *what*? Stupid spoiled brats?"

Everyone stares at me.

"Sorry." I look down at my shoes. "What I'm trying to say is, I'm pretty sure stabbing people with gas nozzles has the same effect whether you're American or French. You don't need to import your victims. You definitely don't need to invent a complex ruse and send a Brazilian rain forest's worth of paperwork, while literally prepping them for the ordeal."

We walk in silence for a minute. Pass under an archway and into a dim, grotto-like room with drifts of embroidered pillows and a tiled fountain in the middle. It looks like one of the courtyards at the Alhambra in Granada. We all check for traps, moving slowly across the floor. When we get to the fountain, we practically dive into it, drinking greedily. The water tastes cool and liquid and that's all we care about at this point. I look up after a few gulps, and realize that there's no door in the north wall. We're going to have to turn west.

As soon as we start moving again, Will clears his throat. "I have a theory," he says, and it's like we even try to walk quieter just so we don't miss anything he says. Apparently not talking often has the awesome side effect that when you *do* decide to talk, people actually listen.

"Not about why we're here, just . . . you know, about the palace. We're running from two different things." His voice is low, and he looks at us one at a time, earnestly. "It's like a triangle. Here's us at the base on one corner. And Dorf and the trackers on the other corner. And at the tip is something else."

I blink. That was a lot of sentences at once.

"What's at the tip?" Lilly asks. "What's your theory there?"

"I don't know." He starts rubbing his thumb furiously along the leather hilt of his sword, as if the fact that he hasn't figured this whole place out yet is mildly embarrassing. "The thing that got Perdu. The thing that killed those trackers and wrote on the wall. I don't know." He looks away, and his voice becomes even quieter. "But whatever it is, it's bad enough that the Sapanis are afraid of it. And they keep it locked underground behind traps and blast doors. It's out of their control."

"And they threw us into the middle of this, because why?" Jules asks. "Just for kicks?"

"No," Will says. "They brought us down for something, but it wasn't so that we'd lock ourselves in their palace and end up as food for whatever they keep down here. I think we screwed up their plans. A lot."

A chill runs down my spine. I glance up at the ceiling, plaster moldings, arched like the top of a pale, sickly mouth.

"Well, the enemy of our enemy is our friend, right?" Jules asks.

"No, Jules," I say. "Something that can kill a room full of superhuman soldiers without making a sound: not our friend."

I'm suddenly afraid to look back, to look anywhere except straight ahead. I think of Perdu cowering behind the chair in the library, his trembling finger extended toward the doors. *L'homme papillon.*

"The butterfly man," I say quietly. No one hears me. The gallery seems to lick up the words and swallow them whole.

27

We're climbing a wide marble staircase. I'm thrilled, because anything leading upward is good. Means we're getting closer to the surface, Wi-Fi, police stations, sanity. . . . We reach a landing. The stone balustrade is carved with writhing, white marble sea creatures, twisting around one another like they're in the process of devouring themselves. I glance back over the huge hall we just crossed, an empty expanse of diamond-shaped tile, dozens of square yards of fresco paintings. The staircase splits in two after the landing, jutting out at right angles. We take the left one, and I get this irrational hope that there will be doors at the top, maybe the exit Perdu was talking about—

Nope. We reach the top and we're looking down an exhibition hall. Glass cases stand in rows down either side. Hundreds of feet away, at the end, a pair of double doors, flung wide. I can see more rooms through them, gold and paintings and decadence, stretching away. The palace just keeps going.

"How many floors d'you think this place has?" Jules asks Lilly.

She shrugs. "Will?" He doesn't answer. "Will?" Nope. "Wi-ill!"

At the third "Will," he finally looks over, like she'd just rudely woken him up from a nap.

"You study architecture," Lilly says, the way dumb people say "You're American" when wondering about hamburger recipes or how to do a rodeo. "D'you have any idea how this place is designed?"

Will shakes his head. "I thought maybe it was based on Versailles, but . . . it's not. It's like they just kept building in every direction. If the folder was right about this place being inside natural caverns, they probably just built until they ran out of space."

I watch the needle jiggling inside the compass. Listen to Jules and Lilly murmuring behind me. We've slowed down a lot.

"Maybe this whole thing is an experiment," Lilly says. "Like, maybe they're total GMO pushers, and they're testing a virus on us. We had to send in medical documents and get checked for Ebola. That could have been part of the requirements. Maybe they shot us up with something." She pauses, says thoughtfully: "Or there's something else, something we don't know about."

"Could be psychological," I say, turning and walking backward a few steps. "They do it all the time with rats. Get control groups with animals from different environments. Put them in a labyrinth and see what happens."

"I'm not an animal," Jules says.

"Could have fooled me. Look, maybe Perdu was from a previous group. And maybe we all come from terrible families and they're seeing how we react to trauma, who survives and who goes insane."

Crickets. Jules looks like he's about to laugh. Lilly is peering at me curiously. It sounded reasonable in my head.

"I have an awesome family," Lilly says.

I turn quickly and keep walking. "Oh. Cool." *Awkward.*

"It could also be hallucinogens," Jules says, and his

voice is quiet, because he's only talking to Lilly now. The conversation moves on to zombies. The apocalypse. Time travel and aliens and elaborate retreats for wealthy serial killers. I liked my theory better. I glance around at the gallery.

Behind the display cases, the wallpaper shimmers royal blue, studded every few yards with silver wall sconces. Dark, heavily carved wooden beams rise to the ceiling, twining overhead like branches. Between them, in alcoves or hanging on the walls are sculptures, portraits, still lifes.

I pause, leaning down next to one of the displays. Inside is an antique pendulum clock. The face is alabaster, the color of bad teeth, cut so thin I can see the tangle of gears and sprockets behind it. It looks ancient. Seventeenth century at least. The next case holds a wire-spewing device that I think is a telegram machine. Then an old telephone. I get excited for a second, wonder if we could use it to call someone. Nope. The cable snaking out of its base is rolled up and zip-tied. I highly doubt we'll find a hookup to a landline down here.

The displays seem to be organized chronologically, by type. I'm in front of weapons now. Some weird, medieval-looking stone cannon. Now flintlocks. Revolvers. I stop in front of an ammunition shell. Blunt, dark metal with a brassy tip—the kind they shot in the First World War when the whole "noble heroes" illusion broke down and it was all bloody tussles in trenches, corpses stuck in the mud, and gas masks.

I squint at the little brass plaque below the box.

First mass-produced shrapnel shell, 1912, by H. B.

Like it's a work of art. Like it's something beautiful, not something that eviscerated people in bursts of fire, something some human designed to destroy other humans.

I turn and stare down the row of glass cases. My heart does a clumsy, reverberating beat. From here on it's all weapons. Grenades. Missiles. Guns poised on tripods, like spiny black insects.

Seriously?

Lilly's ahead of me, inspecting an exhibit of bright red canisters stamped with biohazard symbols. "By H.B.," she reads out loud, and cuts her eyes toward me.

"This one's marked with insignias," Jules says from the other side of the hall. "Red Army, Khmer."

I start walking again. The guns stare out, lifeless

but still somehow watchful. I imagine one of those black-eyed barrels winking suddenly, a bullet ripping through me—

"This is their stuff," I say. "Their hall of fame or something. Maybe they invented all this."

"That would explain why they're so rich," Lilly says, crossing to the other side of the gallery. "If they're weapons manufacturers. I mean, you're never going to go out of business."

I pass Will standing in front of a case containing the black carapace-like armor of a tracker. He's frowning at it.

"You know what's funny?" Jules calls over his shoulder. He's in front of what looks like a giant iron sea urchin. "Those blue folders we got. All that stuff about parts of the palace maybe being underwater, that we might have to dive, that they had no clue how big this place was, yadda yadda. They knew exactly what was down here. We were never supposed to live long enough to see any of it."

"And we believed them," I say as I pass him. "That's the funniest part."

We barely even questioned anything until it was too

late. We saw their snazzy names, looked up their snazzy websites. It was all just paper and internet stuff, stuff that's so easy to fake and lie about.

Selective Perception n.—The tendency to disregard or more quickly forget stimuli that causes emotional discomfort or contradicts prior beliefs.

Aka, if you don't want to see it you won't.

I can't even fathom myself from twenty-four hours ago. I was so busy following my rotten little heart, Disney princess–style. I did end up in a palace, so that's cool.

I slow down, because the others are still milling around the weapons. I wish they'd hurry up. "If we get out of here, these people are done for," Lilly's saying. "Can you imagine the court cases? I mean, even if we *don't* get out, something's going to happen. Our parents will go to the cops."

Something about Lilly's words gives me a sinking feeling. She's still banking on her parents, still thinks they might rescue us. And it's not just because I'm bitter and my parents don't have a clue where I am that I'm worried. (Also, if they knew, they would probably be planning a celebratory lobster brunch right now.) Down here, in this huge, fake, beautiful alternate universe, words like *cops* and *court cases* sound ridiculous. The Sapanis flew us on a private jet out of JFK. They marched us over international borders without us ever showing our passports. I doubt they care at all about cops and court cases.

I'm passing more modern weapons now. Mortars and shells morph into high-tech warheads, night-vision helmets, body armor. Body armor like the trackers wore. Sleek and angular. A helmet stands on a display arm like a severed head.

I focus on the pictures on the walls. At least they're gorgeous. The one nearest me shows a woodland clearing full of people having a country lunch. The sky is almost completely blocked out by leaves, but the light's finding a way through anyway, dappling everything in mottled gold. The people in the painting are draped artfully over a blanket, plucking things from a woven basket. They're dressed in late eighteenth-century costumes, obviously wealthy, but with little hints of carefully tailored farmer chic. A straw hat here. A striped apron there. It looks like a family. A really beautiful, happy family.

I take a step toward it and I feel something like

nostalgia, which is strange because God knows I've never been on a picnic like that. I catch details: the wine, glossy red inside crystal goblets. A spot of sunlight on a silver fork, almost hidden inside a fold in the blanket. The smiling lips of the woman holding the cake. There's a glow to her, like the painter wanted to make her look even more beautiful than she already was—

Her teeth are bloody red, her smile stained.

I blink.

No. Her teeth are normal. White and small and delicate, like chips of bone.

I tear myself away from the painting. *What is wrong with you, Ooky?* The others are ahead of me now. I hurry to catch up. They've congregated around a painting of a rabbit. We should be moving, running, not hanging around, browsing art. I reach them. Jules is right in front of the painting, staring up.

"Are you sure?" Lilly's saying, incredulous. "It could be a copy."

"It's not a copy; look at the brushstrokes," Jules says. He's doing some sort of indignant, expressive hand gestures up at the canvas. "You can't copy that kind of motion. I know this one. I know it!"

I look up at the painting. It's not even that interesting. Definitely doesn't grab me and shake my brain around like the meadow scene did. The rabbit is standing against a brown background, draped silk, I think. Its back is to the viewer, its head turned over its shoulder. It's looking at me.

Okay, maybe it's a little bit interesting. Something about the rabbit's gaze is heartbreaking, a sort of reproach in its almond eyes, maybe inevitability, like the rabbit is going to a horrible fate and it's partially my fault.

"What is it?" I ask. It's awkward that I don't know.

"It's *lost* is what it is." He looks over his shoulder at us, eyes wide. "Or it should be. It's by Kanachev. The Russian master? They only have black-and-white photographs of it, and his pictures were stolen during the siege of Leningrad. He disappeared during World War II, died in a concentration camp or something. This was his masterpiece."

"So what's it doing here?" Lilly asks.

What is *it doing here?* I don't even want to know. I don't want any more revelations and I don't want to know who these people are, because every time we get another inkling, they get more nightmarishly awful. I start walking toward the doors at the end of the exhibit hall, fast.

"Oh wow," Lilly whispers behind me. "Anouk, wait. Look."

I glance back. She's pointing up at another painting, a small gilt frame high on the wall. I stop dead in my tracks.

The painting is of a girl. She's wearing a gray silk gown with a blue sash, and she's standing, one arm resting on a marble bust. Her fingers are curled around a key and a sprig of something, a daisy maybe. A gauzy shawl hangs from her bare shoulders. Her hair is dark. Her eyes are piercing blue. Her face is sharp, angry.

It's a portrait of me.

28

I hear the others congregating behind me, rustling like birds. I feel my face rearranging itself into an expression of abject horror. "What's that?" I squeak. "What—?"

Jules breathes out: "Whoa."

My knuckles go white. I want to hold my skull, squeeze it like a lemon and feel the craziness drip out, bitter and golden between my fingers. *I'm hallucinating again. Microbes. Bad air. It's been happening a lot lately.*

I drop my head, breathe.

I look back at the portrait. Still me. Still my thin arms protruding from the dress, snaking around the bust. Still my angular, closed-up face, looking miffed even when I'm not. My eyes are narrowed, a spark of rebellion in them, as if I was angry at the person painting me, and now I'm angry at the person watching me, I'm angry at *me*—

I shake my head violently. Turn away. We're in the underground palace of a criminal, weapons-dealer family. There's a portrait of me on their wall. It didn't make sense before, it doesn't have to now—

I start running. *But what if it does make sense?* A sick, guilty feeling slithers into my stomach, the one that comes every time I win an award and no one cares, every time I learn a language and I don't have anyone to speak it with, the one that was there when I was standing in the airport and my mom was chewing gum and Penny was hiding her scarred face behind her hair and they wouldn't look at me; they didn't want to. *You're hanging on that wall like a prize buck because that's where you belong, Anouk. You're a bad kid. A bad person.*

I hear the others coming after me. Lilly tries to grab my arm. I shove her off. She grabs me again and jerks me around. "Hey," she says. "Anouk, *stop.*"

I can't look at her.

She keeps walking with me toward the doors, but she doesn't let go. I have a flash of fear that she's going to turn on me now. They all are. They're going to bash my head in and leave me for dead, a psycho daughter, bleeding out on a psycho's floor. I would if I were them. If it were Jules or Will or Lilly inside that gilt frame, I would go ballistic.

I feel something welling up inside me, rage at myself, but also hurt and fear, and I feel like I'm slipping—losing control.

Lilly pushes open the double doors at the end of the gallery. Jules closes them behind us.

You're not going to cry, Ooky. You've gone eight years without crying. It was just a picture, and you have to think—

I let out a long, grating sob. The sensation is so bizarre I kind of wonder if it came from someone else. I spin away from Lilly, try to hide my face. She's staring at me. "Go away," I say, stupidly. I want to make them all turn their backs, but they don't, and I'm crying now. And for some reason the others don't look like they want to bash my head in.

They look worried. They're huddling around me, and now Lilly grabs my hand and knots her fingers through mine. "It's okay, Anouk. It's okay."

How is this okay? I want to shriek. *How is any of this okay?*

But I feel Lilly's hand in mine, and Jules and Will—
the warmth of them and the weight of them beside me—
and I hear myself wail, loud and long like a newborn
baby.

Palais du Papillon—Chambres Jacinthe— 112 feet below, 1790

"Aurélie? Aurélie, I must speak with you!"

Jacques comes tearing into the boudoir. I leap to my feet, smiling, straightening my sleeves—his visits are becoming ever more seldom—but now I see him and the smile drops from my face. He is gasping, his shirt drenched with sweat. His eyes are wild.

"Jacques, what's wrong?"

"I don't know. Perhaps nothing. I don't know!" He begins pacing, his hands raking through his hair.

I grip his arm, guiding him quickly toward a chair. "Jacques, stop this. What has happened?"

He collapses into the chair and stares at me, and something odd and fearful passes behind his eyes. Now he blinks, and he is himself again. "I have seen something, I—"

"What. Tell me." I say it as gently as I can, but I want to scream and shake him.

"One of the cooks," Jacques says, and his breathing begins to slow, his posture dropping deep into the chair. "Madame Boucheron. She was a saucier in the château's kitchen, Parisian, very good and well paid. But they do not need sauces here. The marquis eats only biscuits and boiled mutton, day in and day out, and she is left stirring bouillon for the servants—"

"I do not see how this is so alarming."

"Aurélie, listen! The servants are all discontented. Everyone is. There are no parties to cook for, nothing to look forward to. And she was saying so. She was demanding to be let back up, to be allowed to return to Paris. And now . . ."

"Now what?"

He turns his head away, his eyes pinched shut.

"Jacques, tell me! What is it?"

"I will not go down there," I hear Mama whisper, framed in the open window to the park. *"Do not ask me to."*

"I found her today," Jacques says. "I was cleaning the marquis's private apartments above the *salle de Jupiter.* The marquis did not know, he was busy elsewhere, but Monsieur Vallé gave me the key and told me to hurry. I went in with brushes and buckets. There was something on a table. I thought it was an animal at first, I thought—"

His hands go to his face.

I stare at him, uncomprehending.

"They had been working on her," Jacques says. "They had opened the skin of her arms, and . . . there were diagrams everywhere, and books and papers and cisterns filled with water, large enough to hold a human body, and vials of blood, and in the corner was a man. At least, I think it was a man. I do not know. He was seated like a sculpture, and he was marble white, and his face, his *face*, Aurélie."

He grips my hands and peers at me beseechingly, searching my countenance as if it holds some secret he is desperate to know. "He spoke to me," Jacques whispers. "He asked me to come closer and sit with him awhile. He asked me if I was afraid. He said everyone else was afraid of him—his parents, and the servants—and that all he wanted to do was to make them happy. I ran from there, but I can still smell the blood and the stench of decay. It was like a charnel house. They have been murdering us, Aurélie! Your father and that thing they killed, the servants that went away, the ones we thought had been released— they have been butchering them."

I tear my hands out of Jacques's grasp. "I refuse to believe this. My father is mad, but he is no murderer. What would he have to gain from this? He is a man of reason, a philosopher and a scientist—"

"I am afraid to return to the kitchens," Jacques says, as if he did not hear me at all. "I am afraid to speak to anyone. What if the marquis were to find out what I saw? What if that thing tells him—?"

.I cannot breathe. It is too warm in this chamber. The air feels thick and silky, like hot steam.

"What if they kill me?" Jacques's voice is pitiful, a little boy's keen, and it pierces my heart to its core, because I know it is not fear of pain or death that drives him. He fears what will become of the ones who depend on him. His siblings and his mother, my sisters and me.

I grip my skirts in my fists, so tightly it hurts. "There is a logical explanation to this. I know there is. Ask the head butler to come to me. Better yet, tell him I *demand* to speak to Father. Tell anyone. Tell them I left a note for you. They have nothing to gain from murder. Perhaps it was the carcass of an animal you saw, or perhaps Madame Boucheron was already dead. It is not unheard of, the study of corpses for medicine and the betterment of human knowledge; it is not impossible—"

"And what if he tells you the truth? What if he says he is killing us?"

I go very still and release the skirts from my hands. "Have you found the way out?"

"I'm close, I—"

"Then bring me a key, Jacques. Bring me a pistol, bring me *something!*" I feel the tears pricking behind my eyes, a hot, painful pressure. "If they catch you, I will have nothing, do you understand? My sisters are lost!"

And suddenly we collapse into each other, and his arms are tight and fierce around me. We cling to each other like drowning people, part in fear, part in desperation.

"I will come back, Aurélie. I promise. They will not kill me, not before I've found a way. I will return as soon as I possibly can, and when I do, we are leaving. We will go back to the surface. Home."

When he is gone, and I am alone again in the beautiful room, I lay my head against the wall and weep.

Come back, I pray. *Come back before it is too late.*

29

The announcements start about twenty minutes after my feelings-vomit outside Rabbit Gallery. We're moving through a suite of warm-toned, curlicue-filled rooms, all idyllic landscape paintings and satin wall coverings glittering like insect wings. Jules is ripping a strand of thread from the frayed edge of his pocket. I'm feeling like a car ran over me. And now Lilly freezes, one hand raised.

"Guys?" she says.

"What?" Jules pauses, looking back at her.

"D'you hear that?"

Will and Jules hurry over to her. I don't. I don't hear anything. Honestly, I can't even bring myself to care right now. All I can think about is the picture hanging in the gallery and me bawling. I try to listen for whatever Lilly is talking about. All I hear are the lights. Maybe the whirr of an air vent—

"*. . . is being transmitted . . .*"

There it is. A single spike of sound, and now it's faded back into a distant, indistinct line. Deep in the palace, a voice is droning.

"Trackers?" Jules asks.

"I don't think trackers talk," Will says.

I don't think so, either. Those things were massacred right outside the library doors and we didn't hear a sound. Something tells me they weren't made to vocalize their feelings.

"I think it's a recording," Lilly says. "I think it's Dorf."

On some unspoken command, the others break into a jog. I follow, making a point to run a little behind them. I know this is pathetic junior high–type behavior, but I'm emotionally stunted and this is how I deal, okay? We're heading north like Perdu told us to. The voice seems to be on a loop, sometimes closer, sometimes farther away. The cut in my foot starts to throb again. I want to eat everything—painted fruit, stone grapes, the wallpaper. I want to hide behind my hair.

I swipe it out of my face so I can't. *I cried. I got it out of my system. It's done.*

But it doesn't feel done. Once people see you cry, it's

like they own part of you. It's like you ripped a hole in yourself, and they saw through whatever armor you had on, got a good long view of all the screaming alien goop underneath. I definitely think Will and Jules are being quieter now. Like they're worried the crying might become a regular thing.

Lilly notices I'm not jogging with the rest of them. She slows down until she's right beside me. Will and Jules do, too.

"I'm not an invalid," I snap, but Lilly just keeps jogging next to me, and it makes me feel worse, because it means she knows I'm full of crap.

We're passing through a room that looks like the residence of an upper-class goldfish: aquamarine silks, the chandelier dripping with silver-plated seashells and crystal. Behind us the voice is echoing, fading into the distance. I'm guessing it will be piped into where we are, eventually. The fact that it hasn't yet might be a good sign. Maybe it means the Sapanis don't know where we are.

Except we don't know where we are, either. We slow down.

"What if we die down here?" Jules mutters. He's breathing hard.

No one answers.

"I'm serious, what if we don't get out? Hayden didn't make it. We knew him for exactly twenty-four hours and then he was dead, and we didn't even . . . we didn't even *like* him. I don't want to be—"

The doorways stretch ahead of us like a fun-house infinity mirror. Our feet are loud on the parquet, rubber soles squeaking. I wonder what Jules was going to say: *I don't want to be forgotten. I don't want to die surrounded by people who hate me.*

"We're not going to die," I say, and I make sure it comes out loud and clear.

"Says who?" Jules says, slightly surprised that I'm speaking again. "If we run into those trackers again, I'm the first to go. Shouldn't we . . . shouldn't we know something about each other?"

"No," I say. "Because, what if we all survive? Then we know things about each other."

"So?" Jules says.

"So no." I flip out the compass again.

"I think we should," Lilly says.

Oh great. I don't know what it is with Lilly. I remember the sharp look she gave me on the airplane, her lifting that chair in Razor Hall even though she's tiny, and stopping Jules and me from fighting, and I have a hunch that under those blond ringlets and hippie vibes, she's something else entirely. Possibly an annoyingly determined boss.

Will glances over his shoulder at us. "We need to keep it down," he says in that mellow voice of his, when really he should be snapping: *Shut up, or we will be murdered.* "Sound carries down here."

Jules ignores him. "You want to start?" he says to Lilly.

She looks worried for a second. Starts playing with her hair feathers again. "Okay," she says. "Okay. I want you guys to know that I lied." We step through the last doorway of the corridor, into a room like a checkerboard. Black furniture, white marble walls, onyx-framed mirrors, blinding-white sheepskin rugs. "About my aunt in Wisconsin and the tattoos. About a lot of things. I don't actually have any tattoos and there is no town called Flemings in Wisconsin, and I'm not actually nice. I act nice because I don't want people to hate me, but . . . Also, I'm not really smart. I don't know how I got on this trip. It took me two years to repeat eighth grade and I have dyslexia pretty bad, and when I got the letter that said I made it onto the expedition, I was super proud because I thought I was actually good at something besides being a weirdo. But I'm not."

Nobody says anything for a full ten seconds. We've all stopped, pooling in the black-and-white room. I think Lilly's joking. Until she starts crying.

"You're not a weirdo," Jules says quietly. "You had the idea with the chair. Jamming the wires? That was smart. That was awesome."

What is this, therapy round? But Lilly doesn't stop crying. So maybe she has a limited vocabulary and bad taste in fashion, but I don't know whether she should be crying like that, like she's a terrible person. I could count all the genuinely nice people I know on one hand. Actually I could count them without any hands, and Lilly's definitely one of them.

"You should stop," I say. "Stop crying. You're nice. Not that many people are actually nice."

Stunned silence.

Was that the wrong thing to say?

And now Jules smacks both hands to his cheeks and says: "Awwwww! Nukey!" muted and whispery, and in my mind I tip him into a brush cutter and watch stoically as his shoes disappear down the chute.

He sees my expression. Laughs. Lilly laughs, too, a little shakily.

"I'm serious, Lilly, it doesn't matter why you're here; they clearly didn't invite us for our brain power anyway. It just matters that we get out. So let's keep going."

We start walking again and Will smiles at me, quick and cautious. I see it, but I keep my gaze fixed straight ahead.

The next chamber looks like a children's playroom. Rocking horses. Painted wooden blocks arranged in precarious towers across the carpet. There's even a miniature stone castle built into one wall, complete with kid-sized portcullis and glass windows. Jules starts telling his story. Something about growing up in small-town Nebraska and being picked on all the way through middle school for being the only kid in town with a Middle Eastern dad, and then being picked on all the way through high school because kids didn't like kids who stuck out like gangly scarecrows, who had purple hair and weren't interested in football. He starts talking about how he got expelled for breaking someone's nose, even though it was seven to one and the person he punched had just pulled a knife. How he ran away to San Diego to art school two years early because if he stayed, he'd end up exactly like his tormentors, flipping burgers at Benny-O's for all of eternity in his own personal minimum-wage hell. He tries to make it sound funny, like he's recounting a vignette from a hilarious coming-of-age movie, but it's not funny. It's awkward to listen to, and I want someone to take him away and pat his hand or something.

He delivers his clincher in a bitter, irony-dripping newscaster's voice: "But look at me now, Stainfield, Nebraska. Chilling in a French palace. More gold than I know what to do with. Living the dream."

He swings around to me. "Anouk. Your turn."

"I'm not telling you anything. This is stupid."

"Just talk to us! Tell us why you came to the airport dressed like a bag lady."

"No."

It would be cool to hear Will speak. I would like to listen to his drawly accent, figure out if his house is nice, if his parents do dishes together while listening to *Greatest Country Hits of the '70s*, whether he likes William Makepeace Thackeray's *Vanity Fair* or if he's more of a

Joyce kind of guy. Except maybe he likes neither. Maybe he likes loud baseball games and corn dogs, in which case he should just continue not-speaking forever and let me live in my delusion.

"Why?" Jules asks.

"Because. I don't need to give you reasons."

There aren't any doors in the north wall. We're still heading east, and I feel like we're getting more off track by the second.

"Come on, Anouk. Maybe I won't be next. Maybe you'll be."

"Psh. Please . . ." My voice is caustic enough to burn metal. "I'm the Final Girl. Gaze upon my wholesome innocence and despair."

Will has maneuvered to the front of the pack, either completely oblivious to the jabber or pointedly ignoring it. I hurry after him. I think of the little smile he gave me. Maybe I can talk to him alone, without doing this awful group storytelling thing. He's moving pretty fast.

"Will?"

He stops in the doorway three steps ahead of me, shoulders tense. I scuffle up behind him.

I freeze. We're looking into a vestibule. An alabaster

vase of red roses, petals thick and velvety, stands on a table in the center.

"Uh-oh," Will says.

The buzzing is back—a high whine, shimmering in the air. I put my hands to my head.

I think I hear the announcements, only it's a new voice now, a thin, indistinct whisper, murmuring in French, almost like another frequency overlapping with the first. And in the background, barely, barely audible, someone is singing.

"Four blind mice. Four blind mice. See how they run, oh . . .

. . . see how they run."

The buzzing spikes suddenly, piercing, sliding red-hot into my ear—

30

Everything stops. Sound. Time. Will, Jules, and Lilly seem to be floating mid-stride a few feet ahead of me. I'm paralyzed, one hand raised.

I see the figure out of the corner of my eye. About ten feet to my left. A woman.

Fear slams my veins, a ten-milligram morphine drip shutting me down. My eyes swivel. The woman is standing, staring at me. She's wearing an elaborate gown, deep red. Makes me think of slaughterhouses in dim light, raw carcasses hanging in the shadows. The skirts seem to be drenched, dripping dark water onto the floor. Her hair is powdered gray, piled up on her head, but her face is young. Flawless. Beautiful. Creamy white, no wrinkles. Her eyes are wet black.

"Fuyez," she says to me, and the word is like the tinkle of a bell, pure and dainty. *"Enfuyez-vous d'ici."* She

extends a hand toward me. She has something on her wrist, a knobble of veins, pulsing under her skin. She opens her mouth and I don't know what it is—a smile, a grimace?—but the teeth behind those delicate lips are crazy, every which way. *"Enfuyez-vous d'ici!"*

Flee from here.

"Anouk?"

I spin. Jules is beside me. I feel like I've just been electrocuted, like I grabbed an exposed wire. Will and Lilly are turning to me, wondering what's going on.

"You okay?" Lilly asks.

I look back over my shoulder. The woman is gone. The floor where she was standing is gleaming, spotless.

"I'm fine." I move past Jules. My brain is breaking. Cracking up like a mirror.

The announcements are coming closer.

Palais du Papillon—Chambres Jacinthe—
112 feet below, 1790

We went on a journey once, to visit an old duke, a relative of Father's from the Bordeaux region. It is the custom with noble children, once they have been born, to send them away. An aristocratic child's life is a parade of wet nurses, governesses, maiden aunts, and gloomy tutors, children's apartments in the high floors of the family château if you were fortunate, convent schools and distant relations if you were not. I was packed off at seven years old. Father accompanied me, though he rode in a different carriage, hiding behind his scented handkerchiefs and that tin mask full of herbs for fear of the plague, or fevers, or whatever diseases were crawling through the towns and byways that year. When we stopped at inns for dinner or to exchange the horses, he always looked at me nervously when my governess brought me too close, as if I were a feral little lapdog contemplating opportunities to gnaw on his leg.

My memory of the duke's house is dim. It was a drafty old fortress, a precarious and ancient heap rising from the middle of a great forest, like a castle from a fairy tale. The duke's children and the servant's children were indistinguishable from one another and seemed terribly frightening to me, scarecrow creatures drinking ale in the kitchens and playing wild gambling games with the guards. But there is one scene that stands out clearly: I am kneeling next to a great bed, surrounded by many people, and I am peering at the cankerous old duke. He died only days after Father and I arrived at his house. His body lay curiously solid and forsaken, his belly a vast snowy hill beneath the sheets. His face was covered in sores, and his wife and children, even the guards, were all weeping quietly into their sleeves and beards and lace handkerchiefs.

Father had not yet begun the return journey. He was in the chamber, too, and I remember his expression as he looked upon the figure in the bed. It was an expression of animal terror, a condemned man looking upon the black mask of his executioner. And I could not understand why, for to me the duke's silent, oozing face looked perfectly at peace.

31

The announcement finally reaches us in a room that looks like a candy box. Pillows in powdery pink and mint and blue, fat as marshmallows. White furniture. Everything soft and pastel. Everything except Dorf's voice, which comes scratching through the ceiling like the rusty prongs of a fork.

"Anouk. Will. Jules. Lilly. I hope you're doing well."

We stop dead in the middle of the room.

You hope we're doing well? What are you, a holiday card? It's like shooting someone in the chest and then asking if they're hurt. *No, we're not doing well, FREAKHEAD, thanks for asking.*

Dorf doesn't miss a beat. *"I'm sure you've noticed you're not alone down there."* His voice was probably icy smooth when they recorded it, but it pipes in tinny, the flow interrupted by a steady sequence of ticks and fizzes. *"You've* caused quite a bit of trouble. Clever of you to cut the camera feed."

"What?" Jules says. Looks over at me. I stare back, shoulders raised in a shrug.

We didn't cut the camera feed. We smashed a few lenses in that big hall with the razor wires. That's it.

"I want to inform you that your continued movement through the palace is an exercise in futility. It is a house divided, a war zone. You cannot survive it. Even if you were to reach the surface, you will find the world closed to you. Your parents have already been informed of the unfortunate circumstances in which all of you were killed in a plane crash over the Atlantic. The media is running the story. Debris has been found. Your families will be paid a generous settlement."

"Are they serious?" Lilly whispers.

"So you see, it might be best to accept the circumstances as they are. We'd like to make a deal with you. It is of the utmost importance to us that you not be injured. There is another in the depths who would prefer you never reach us. If you are getting this message, if you are still alive—and we're fairly sure you are—come to the salle des glaces. *The hall of mirrors. We'll meet you there."*

"Our parents think we're dead?" Lilly says, full-on panicking now. "They actually think we're dead?"

She looks like she's about to cry, and I feel sorry for her. She loves her parents. They probably love her, too. How awful must that be, knowing they think you're gone forever when really you're just lost and trapped and all you want is to get back home?

Will and Jules have gone really quiet.

We hurry through the candy-box room's cloud-blue doors.

They slam behind us. We're in an antechamber of some sort, a cloakroom judging by the hundreds of polished oak drawers and cupboards lining the walls. The little desk in one corner. The voice comes on in here.

"Anouk. Will. Lilly. Jules. I hope you're doing well—"

The message repeats itself. I can hear it on the other side of the next set of doors, too. We throw them wide.

Behind me I hear: *"Oh, and to be clear . . ."*

We missed a part.

". . . this is not a request."

Will closes the doors behind us. We're standing in a vast, pale hall, almost as big as Razor Hall. A ballroom.

"These messages are being transmitted in a staggered pattern throughout the palace. If it's a trap room, we have programmed it to trigger within twenty seconds of this message's transmission. That should give you enough time and encouragement to move. You'll have only one safe direction to travel. Toward the salle des glaces. *We will be waiting."*

I pivot. The floor is a checkerboard, white and black.

Every black panel has a butterfly etched into it.

Every white one a glaring, angry eye.

"Trap room," I say stupidly. "Trap room—"

We start running, pelting toward the opposite end, but the speakers are off now. The clock is ticking. *Twenty seconds.* We can do this. The tall double doors are eighty feet away.

My legs pump. I throw myself forward and the air rushes in my ears, streaking my hair back from my face.

We reach the doors with ten seconds to spare. They're locked.

No. No way.

A shudder flies through the hall. I can feel it in my entire body, an arthritic clicking, skittering behind the walls. And now every butterfly panel in the floor flips up.

"Back!" Jules screams. "Back!"

We whirl, sprinting for the other end. One panel opens right in front of me. I leap. Skid to the side to avoid another.

Jules is shoving himself to his feet. Running again, limping.

This isn't happening. We're not dying here, right when we were making progress.

My lungs burn. I run faster, barely manage to dance around one of the holes in the floor. Something's rising out of it. Glass globules, floating on thin wires, like delicate balloons. They shimmer coldly, poison blue.

"They're not going to kill us," I whisper to myself. "They need us for something; they're not going to kill us—"

The glass balloons are drifting up by the dozens. Some reach hip height; others rise higher, diffusing the light and throwing it down like iridescent jellyfish. They begin to sway, ringing softly, piercingly.

The one nearest to Will bursts with a musical *pling*! A cloud hangs where the glass was. Blue, spreading. Will swerves to the side. Whatever is in that globe got on his arm. His sleeve is smoking.

The hall is full of the balloons now, hundreds upon hundreds, swaying gently. They're so close together, almost touching. I can't run anymore. I've slowed to a walk, slithering between them. They're shifting against my thighs, bubbling around my shoulders. *Pling!* I hear, somewhere close by. *Pling!*

Fifteen feet to the door. Only fifteen feet.

"It's burning me," Will mutters, somewhere to my left. *"It's burning me!"*

A globe brushes my cheek. I feel like I'm choking, drowning in a clinking glass sea. Something pops close to my ear. I feel a prickle. The sudden itch of a million tiny crystals, and now wetness. *Blood?*

No-no-no, NO, it's going to burn me, burn my face. I gasp, clamp my mouth closed, and breathe through my nose. High above, the lights begin to flicker. Or maybe it's me. Maybe my eyes are dissolving. The itch on my ear has turned into a screeching pain, burrowing under skin and into bone.

"Keep moving, Ooky," I say to myself. "You can make it."

I fall. I'm crushing them under me. Blue powder is everywhere, and I hear Lilly screaming. Will grunting in pain.

I roll onto my back, my arms clamped over my face,

glass bulbs popping and hissing under me. I look up. The blue is closing over me, an ocean of glass and creeping fumes. My eyes are tearing up, my throat closing. I think I hear something, far away, beyond the shimmering whine of the globes—

"Anouk!"

I shove myself to my hands and knees. I'm coughing, a deep chesty hack. I feel it ripping out of me, but the sound is far away. My eyes are burning, tears streaming down my cheeks. Through the blur I see a figure. It's running toward me, almost flying, a shadowy shape against the lights.

It's not Will. Not Jules or Lilly.

I think of the laughing woman in her red gown. Perdu in his loose, bloodied shirt.

I sway, tip forward. See crushed glass and whole glass rising to meet me. The wind-chime plink of the globes is suddenly deafening. Someone is coming toward me. Throwing something—*a rope?*

Shouting, yelling for me to grab hold. The lights are still flickering, chopping out. I raise my head. And I see . . .

It's Hayden. He's standing at the edge of the field of

glass bulbs. His hair is matted, plastered to his scalp. Grime and blood slick his skin. He's yelling at me.

I grab the rope. It's thick and tasseled.

I'm out from among the poison bulbs in one pull, squeaking over the floor.

"Hey, Anouk," Hayden says, and that jerk-face grin is on at a thousand watts as he drags me to my feet and shoves me toward the doors. "Better run."

Palais du Papillon—Chambres Jacinthe— 112 feet below, 1790

On the seventy-fourth day of my entombment, a visitor arrives.

I am still in bed, half asleep, and in that foggy valley between waking and dreaming I dare hope my visitor is Jacques and we are leaving now, finding my sisters, returning to the sunlight. . . .

I hear the rasp of a coat, heavy velvet, the whisper of lace.

"Aurélie? Wake. I have a surprise for you."

My eyes crack open. Father is bustling toward me like a great swollen blood fly. The white lead paint that clings in flakes and patches to his face cannot hide how old he has become. Skin hangs in swags off his skull. His eyes are sunken, his wig is askew, and his red coat is stained and wrinkled, as if he has not changed in many days.

I sit bolt upright. "Father? Father, what is the meaning of this—"

He ignores me. He begins to pace along the side of the bed, his hands tight around the head of his cane. "A surprise," he says, impatient and wheedling. "Dress quickly, and let us be on our way. It was a success!"

I slide out of bed opposite from where Father paces and hurry behind a painted silk screen. *What was a success? What does he mean, and what am I to do?*

I have been waiting for someone to come—Father or Havriel or the head butler, Monsieur Vallé—someone to explain to me this horrible aloneness. But now Father is here and I am caught like a maid in the wine cellar, drowsy and foolish. This is both too sudden and too late.

"Hurry," I hear Father muttering, his heavy step as he wanders through the room, the rattle and clink of objects he touches. "Hurry, hurry."

I feel in the dark for my clothing. I will wear it all today—stockings, petticoats, hoops, more petticoats, and damask skirts. I begin to wriggle into the cold things. When I feel suitably well armored, I step from behind the panels and fix Father with a cold stare.

"Father," I say, and my voice is vinegar. "Good health to you. It is wonderful to see you again. I'm sure you have been very busy, but I must confess, I have found the explanations for my imprisonment, for my separation from my sisters and our complete isolation, to be rather slow in revealing themselves."

Father looks straight through me, his piggish eyes fixed on a point on the wall behind me. "A success," he says, and flutters his great hands. "Come! Come!"

My skin crawls. "Father," I say again. My voice shivers. "You will speak to me, please. I am your daughter. I am kept here as a prisoner, without human company, without a word of justification. Our mother is dead, my sisters are alone, and we cannot mourn her, or comfort each other; we—"

Father's eyes are on me now, twitching, making a diagram of my face. Then the stupidness and the dullness return and he throws back his head. "Havriel?" he cries in his high, quavering voice. "Havriel, she is being a goat!"

Instinctively, I take a step back behind the screen, as if it will protect me. Havriel opens the door to my bedchamber. He is holding a blindfold.

I cry out at the sight of it. I scream, and my hand closes around the nearest thing, a china figure of a dog. I hurl it with all my strength. "Get out!" I shriek. "Get out! I will not be kept this way!"

The dog shatters a full yard from where Father stands.

The two men stare at me, and I feel such a fury toward their great, slow selves. Havriel starts toward me again. I cower behind the screen, my skirts pooling. He pulls me upright and slips the blindfold partway over my eyes. I struggle. It is no use. His hands are as large as my head. He could crush my skull with nothing but his fingers.

"Aurélie," he says, and there is a warning in his voice. "Do not."

And now the blindfold is in place, and I see only darkness.

"Come, come," I hear Father mumbling. "Come and see."

Havriel pulls me through the chamber. I am trembling, anger and hate twisting inside me. *I am not your puppet! I am not your dog; you cannot treat me this way!*

But they do.

We step out into the hallway. The doors click shut behind me and we walk in silence. I do not cry. Father would not notice. Havriel would, and perhaps he would pity me, but he does not deserve to act the good man. He is as guilty as anyone in this pit.

I try to focus on the number of steps I am taking, try to remember where we turn, how many doors we pass through, how the floor changes beneath my feet. *Parquet, marble, carpet, parquet.* But we walk for so long and pass through so many chambers that after a time it becomes impossible to remember the sequence. I can recall the length of the first passage and three of the ensuing rooms, the fragrant, jumbled scent of potpourri and dried rose petals in the first, a crackling fire in the third, and then it all becomes tangled together and I am lost.

We are descending stairs now. *Stairs? Are there more levels than one in this palace?* The air turns dank. My shoes scuff against stone. We are in a close space for a brief moment, and with my vision snuffed out, it seems my nose seeks to make up for it, capturing every nuance and shade of scent around me: Father's perfumes, matting the air like fur—cloves and freesia and rich ointments. The slightly mildewed smell of clothing, sweat and silk and wool. Something flat and dull from Havriel, like salt and stone. A key is inserted into a lock, followed by the soft grind of many prongs sliding back.

Huge metal hinges yawn open. I am pushed forward. The blindfold loosens from my head. I blink.

I am standing in a banquet hall. The colors here are entirely red and black, a disconcerting, flickering panorama, deep shadows and black wood and ruddy brocade. Even the light seems red, a murky, bloody glow.

Behind me Father is snuffling with excitement. Havriel

remains impassive as a mountain. I turn and see the door we came through. It is like none I have ever seen before, low and built of iron—thick as a wall, its surface a labyrinth of bolts and complex gear systems.

"Look," says Father. "Look, Aurélie!"

My gaze darts around the hall, adjusting to the red light.

I see a long table, many chairs, dim, low-hanging chandeliers, tongues of red flame smoldering behind the crystals.

"I do not know what I should be seeing," I say coldly.

Havriel goes to a brass knob beside the door and turns it with a soft squeak. The red lights flare, not brighter, but hotter.

"We are so close," Father says. "So close to achieving what we have been seeking."

I peer into the blaze. Someone is seated in the shadows at the end of the table. It is a woman. She wears a towering gray wig, ornamented with jewels and a small boat. Her neck is slender, her shoulders delicate. Her great skirts are so wide they spill around the corners of the table, a watery foam of white and blue.

I see her face.

My skin seems to detach from me, loosening from bone and muscle as if it seeks to escape. Father is speaking, but his voice rings hollow, echoing up from the bottom of a well. The red lights reduce to pinpricks.

It is Mama. She is lovely, her mouth a glimmering crimson bow. I see her bust rising and falling beneath a necklace of sapphires. She is breathing. Alive.

She catches sight of me and raises her hand, waving. "Aurélie, my sweet!" she calls out, and her voice is high and soft. I see a bullet, bursting slowly from the mouth of a gun, blood creeping over cloth, a pretty face, dripping tears—

It cannot be.

32

We collapse just inside the doors. I can't feel my legs. I can't feel anything but pain, like a swarm of microscopic insects burrowing into my flesh.

"Hayden," I mumble. Something bitter and chalky is coating my tongue. "Hayden?"

There's no way it's him. I saw him die.

I'm looking along the floor at the others. My vision is blurry, all flickering shadows and sudden, poisonous bursts of color when someone moves.

I see Lilly and Jules. They're scratching between their fingers, spitting on them, tears streaming down their faces. At least they *have* fingers. Will is next to them. His right hand is half gone, three of his digits burned to nubs. He's hunched over, eyes closed, teeth gritted.

I try to sit up. I feel my cheek knock against the floor, and I realize my sitting-up attempt has failed. I have absolutely no sense of balance. The chandeliers are out, replaced by a murky green glow. Emergency lighting. Dorf's voice is droning somewhere in the distance. Muffled. Thumping.

And Hayden's still here. He hasn't turned into a hallucination and disappeared. He's kneeling next to Will, trying to pry his arm away from his chest.

I get myself into a semi-upright position. Immediately I feel like I'm going to vomit. My skin is stiff and dry, like the outside layer has hardened into a shell. My legs are still attached. That's cool. They feel like deadweights, prickly stumps, but at least they're there.

I rub the side of my face. Flakes of skin come off on my fingertips. A tuft of hair.

"Hayden," I rasp, and I sound like a wicked witch, a million years old. "I saw them kill you."

Hayden turns. His face flickers oddly in the shadows and the green light. He leaves Will. I catch a whiff of him as he approaches. *Oh, gross.* He smells rank. Worse than us, and I doubt we smell like roses, either, after this many hours down here. It's a blood smell, but also dirt and damp, sweaty clothes, and something dark, hot, tarry.

"Yeah, well, I *felt* them kill me. Stop scratching; you'll

spread the poison. Wave your arms to get the particles off and don't put your fingers near your mouth."

I stare at him. Blink. Behind my eyelids I see: *Hayden, lying on the floor of the cube room. Miss Sei, trailing a thumb along his brow. The nozzle driving in—*

"How do you know?" I ask quietly. "What happened to you?"

He ignores me, gives my ear a cursory inspection, and apparently doesn't deem it problematic because he's heading over to Jules and Lilly now. "We can't stay here," he says over his shoulder. "This room isn't rigged, but there're some traps between here and where we need to be."

"Oh, and where do we need to be, Hayden?" I say, spiteful, because if he's a hallucination he's a stupid know-it-all one. I wave my arms anyway, sitting on the ground and swinging them in circles like some sort of demented flightless bird.

"I found a panic room," Hayden says. "About six rooms that way." He jabs a finger toward a door in what I think is the western wall.

I drop my arms. "A panic room?"

Someone, I think Jules, mumbles, "I thought this whole palace was their panic room."

I drag myself to my feet. The painful swarming feeling is subsiding, dulling to a prickly, sandpapery itch. "Show me your neck," I say.

"Anouk, we don't have time—"

I stagger toward him and grab at his arm. *"Show me."*

Hayden stares at me. I think I see disdain somewhere under all that grime, and I wonder if he's going to throw me across the room. I don't let go of his arm. He rips free and turns, dropping his chin to his chest.

The wound on the back of his neck is raw. Deep. It looks like he tried to clean it—the edges have been wiped—but it's still exposed, a glimmering dark-red hole driving right into his spinal column.

"Happy?" he says, facing me again. "Look, I want explanations as much as anyone, but right now we need to move." His voice explodes. "Get up, people!"

I want to barf again. I bend over, gasping. "I saw you die, Hayden. I saw you stop breathing, how are you—" *Alive? Anouk, what is your problem? He didn't die. He's standing right in front of you. This is a good thing!*

"Anouk?" Lilly manages.

I go to her and help her up. We totter a few steps over to Jules. Hayden hoists Will up, and the three of us follow them, half jogging, half dragging each other into a bedroom.

The chandeliers are off here, too, the furnishings just spiny shapes in the gloom. I really need some water. We get to a bathroom, the scallop-shaped marble tub in the center straight out of Botticelli's *Birth of Venus*. It's dry as a bone.

In the next room, even the emergency lighting is gone. It's pitch-black. And now a flashlight clicks on, a searing white beam.

"Move it," Hayden says, gesturing us forward. He sweeps the light over the wall. Stops it on a point low to the ground. He ducks down. I see a panel clicking out, sliding to the side on invisible tracks. Behind it is a square metal hatch. He jerks it open.

"In here."

Seriously? *Hansel and Gretel*, the tatty old paperback, upside down on the couch in the playroom: *"Creep inside," said the wicked witch. "And see if the oven is hot enough."*

"What's in there?" I ask, but Lilly is already pushing Will through, and Jules is following. I watch them go, look to Hayden holding the hatch open.

"Idiot, it's the panic room!" he says, and his eyes are wide, scared. "Get in!"

I hear Jules's voice, tinny, somewhere inside the wall: "Anouk, come on!"

I drop onto all fours and crawl through the hatch. Stale, metallic air envelopes me. The panic room is tube shaped, a gray metal capsule like a storm shelter. Six feet wide, five feet high. Maybe fifteen feet long. A strip of dim, flickering light runs along the ceiling, barely illuminating the space. An unmade bunk folds out of one wall. Sleek plastic containers fill a shelf on the other.

I'm thinking: *Who built this panic room and what exactly is it for?* And now I hear Dorf's voice outside, sharp, so loud it sounds like he's standing a foot away. "Anouk. Will. Jules. Lilly. I hope you're doing well—"

Hayden clangs the hatch shut.

33

The light buzzes.

The only other sound is our breathing, fast, getting slower. Slower—

Will lets out a muffled groan. I snap out of it. Push past Jules and start scooting along the shelves, picking up boxes, clicking them open and upending them.

"How did you survive?" I snap at Hayden. I wriggle around him. The capsule is way too tight. The light is so weak, barely enough to see by, and the shadows in the corners are pitch-black.

Hayden makes an angry noise and dives after me, grabbing at scissors, a reflective blanket, a bunch of little bottles that go rolling and bouncing off the shelf.

I find a box with a Red Cross symbol on it and rip it open. Bandages. A syringe. Penicillin. A round tin of salve—blue label with a blocky, '70s font on it, even though it looks brand-new. *For burns and swelling.*

I grab it. Go over to Will. Lilly and Jules are on their knees next to him, making futile attempts to comfort him. I start dabbing some of the gray goop onto a cotton swab. "This'll probably hurt, but it should help." I hand the swab to Lilly. Look back over my shoulder at Hayden. "Hayden, talk. What happened?"

Hayden leans back against the end of the capsule and crosses his arms over his chest. His blue eyes are flinty. This was clearly not how he envisioned his heroic rescue efforts turning out. We're hijacking his space. And I realize now that we don't really know Hayden. At all.

"No idea," Hayden says. "Last thing I remember is you having a hissy fit in the dining room. When I woke up, I was lying on the floor of this really huge hall, and I had a hole in my neck."

"What, they just dumped you?"

"Who?"

"Miss Sei. The trackers."

"I don't know what you're talking about." He glowers at me, like I just insulted him. Lilly is daubing the salve onto Will's wounds. Will has his teeth clenched, and Lilly flinches every time he sucks his breath in. Jules is sitting really still, looking dazed.

Hayden uncrosses his arms and squats. "I walked around. Kind of guessed I must be underground in the Palais du Papillon, since I saw the butterfly coat of arms everywhere. I assumed there had been an accident and it knocked out my short-term memory."

"So you don't know why we're here," Lilly says. "You don't know what's going on."

"Not a clue."

I squint at him. He's definitely jittery. Thinner. I can see his clavicles jutting through his shirt. And there's a twitch in one of his eyes, a constant blink.

"How did you find us?" I ask.

"Dumb luck," Hayden says. "I'd been hearing the messages from Dorf for a few hours, but I could never make them out. So I decided to head in the direction they were coming from. Then I heard you screaming."

"I don't think I screamed," I say, still sorting through the supplies, making a heap of the things I think might come in handy. "And why did you have rope with you? You just happened to be toting curtain ropes with you because that's the fashionable accessory for traversing underground palaces?"

Hayden throws up his hands. "What do you want, an admission of guilt? You're welcome, I saved you!"

He stares at me, his eye still twitching, arms crossed like a pouty kid having a bad birthday party.

I look down at Will. Hand Lilly another cotton swab. "Sorry," I say. I shouldn't be the one apologizing—suspicion is kind of necessary at this point—but someone has to, or we're not going to get anywhere. I scoot back to the first-aid kit. "We've seen a lot of bizarre stuff and we're paranoid. I'm sorry, Hayden."

He's still staring at me reproachfully. Now he's grabbing some clear plastic bottles from the shelf and filling them with water from a spigot in the wall.

"Forget it." He screws the top onto one of the bottles. "I heard someone screaming and I came running. I tore the ropes off that four-poster we passed. You can check if you want. Otherwise I would have gotten there faster." He tosses the bottle to me. I want to guzzle it down—my tongue feels like it's going to crack—but I stoop and hold it for Will while he drinks.

"Now you tell me something." Hayden's eyes dart between Will and me. "What have you found out?"

"Not much," I say. Will stops drinking. I empty the

rest of the bottle in three gulps. "We think the people who kidnapped us are a centuries-old, weapons-dealing, art-stealing crime family. We also think they're not in complete control of what goes on down here. They keep talking about a rogue party, and it's like it's toying with us, and toying with the Sapanis, too, and they're in some kind of unhealthy symbiosis with each other." I pause, thinking. "The transmissions were only for us. That means either Dorf thinks you're dead, or he's deliberately leaving you out of the equation. Have you seen anyone down here? Like, for example, a creepy pale guy bleeding all over the place or a dripping Frenchwoman?"

"What?"

"Nothing. Have you seen anyone?"

"I saw some guys in black gear run past once. I hid behind a table, thought I was done for. They didn't see me. They didn't even look anywhere but straight ahead. I haven't seen anyone since. They haven't come back."

"That's because they're dead. They were probably trackers. Something killed a bunch outside the room we were hiding in."

"*Something* killed them? What's that supposed to mean?"

"Or someone. The rogue party. Perdu was talking about an *homme papillon*."

Hayden glances up at me. "Who's Perdu?"

"The creepy pale guy."

Hayden cackles. Full-on throws back his head and natters like a chainsaw. I think of the wound on the back of his neck, squeezing open. Wince.

"What kind of name is *Perdu*?" Hayden says. His eyes are bright, almost fevered.

"He said he was lost and we needed to call him something," I snap. "Perdu equals 'lost' in French. So we called him Perdu. Shut up."

"Right," Hayden says. He returns to bottle filling, but he's shaking his head. "So where's Perdu now?"

I look at the others for help.

"He left," Lilly says quietly.

Hayden glances between us, trying to figure out what's going on. "Well, did you talk to him? Did you figure out what he was doing down here? Gah, you could have had all of this figured out by now!"

"We did talk to him," Jules says. It's the first time he's said anything to Hayden, and he sounds annoyed. "He said there was a secret exit due north. He also thought he was born in 1772, and when we were hiding from the trackers he unlocked the doors on us while we were sleeping." Jules giggles, a surreal sound, not even remotely happy. "Something got him."

"There's that word again. Something. *Something* got him."

"Yes, Hayden, *something* got him," I say, turning away. I go back to picking through the shelves. "There was blood all over the floor. Pieces of— Look, that's what animals do, okay? Not people."

I find a flashlight. Two more flashlights. Four chunky black batteries.

"You said he was a creepy pale guy bleeding everywhere. Was he hurt when you found him?"

"Yeah."

"So who says there *was* anyone else? Who says he didn't open those doors and kill all the trackers himself?"

"Because of a lot of reasons. We think they were killed right after we hid in there. Perdu was *hurt*. He was terrified—"

"Or he was a really good liar." Hayden finishes filling another bottle and throws it hard and fast to Lilly. She catches it. Barely.

"He could have been hit by a trap room."

I glare at him. "You weren't there, Hayden. You don't—"

"On second thought, maybe I do know something you don't," he interrupts. "We're on the eastern edge of the palace. There's only one route that heads north from here: that hall that's now filled with poisonous blue fumes. We'd have to backtrack through trap rooms and head west at least a thousand feet before we get to the next gallery heading north. If the exit *is* that way, and you're claiming it is, we can go now, look for another route, and risk capture. Or we can do something they won't expect. We stay here and go through the rigged hall."

"And you have five hazmat suits where exactly?"

"We won't need hazmat suits. I passed another trap room a while back. Same type of blue poison gas. Something had activated it, fumes all over the place. When I ran past four hours later, it was clear. No fumes. I could walk right into it, totally safe. If we assume it was activated within two hours of me first passing it, that means at some point after the six-hour mark, there's a window of safety where the fumes have cleared and the trap room hasn't reset itself yet. Here's what I'm suggesting: we lie low. Wait for that hall to clear. Then in six hours we haul out of here and make a run for it."

"A run for what?"

"The exit, Nancy Drew."

"That's a lot of assumptions. We tried waiting before. It didn't end well. Also, we won't be moving. They might think we're all dead."

"Good."

I stare at him. I still can't believe he's real. He's right here, skin slick, unhealthy looking, in the wan light of the ceiling. Eye twitching. That bloody smear on his neck.

He crawls over with the last of the bottles and hands one to me, and I reach out and touch his wrist just below the sleeve of his sweatshirt. That would have been weird a few days ago, but nothing seems that weird anymore. I feel his skin, slightly greasy and clammy, but warm. Alive.

He jerks away. "It's me, Anouk," he says, right eye going *twitch-twitch* like a camera lens. "I'm not dead."

34

Six hours is way too long to spend in a six-by-fifteen-foot space.
It feels even longer when you have to share that space
with four other people. Time basically stands still to
taunt you. We've eaten gross, vacuum-packed MRE food,
scraped cold out of the packaging. We all went through
the ordeal of using the toilet. The panic room has a flush-
able one that folds out of one wall, like on a boat. Thank
heavens for the little air vent up near the ceiling or we'd
all have suffocated.

Right now everyone's crouched against the walls,
exhausted, staring at nothing. Jules is humming a pop
song, off-key, the same bars over and over. After a while
he pushes himself onto his elbows and says, "Will. It's
your turn. Tell us your story."

I groan. "Jules, stop. Will just got his hand maimed.
Could we please pretend this is a serious situation?"

Jules just looks at me dully. "We don't need to pretend. But we're all in one piece and we're going to be in here for hours. Why not? Come on, Will."

I want to stuff Jules's mouth with all of the remaining gauze bandages before this escalates. Too late.

"You're telling each other stories?" Hayden is on his cot, hands knotted behind his head. He glances at us like we're dumb kindergartners. "How adorable. I'll do 'The Three Little Pigs.'"

"Not fairy tales, idiot," Jules says, and the word *idiot* comes out so violently I glance at him in surprise. Hayden sits up a bit. Jules is glowering at him, unflinching.

"We're telling each other things about us," Lilly says quickly. She's been super quiet ever since the announcement that our parents think we're dead. But she's not zoning out. She's still helping, still dealing. "So that we all know. In case something happens."

I edge over to her. "Are you okay?" I ask, and she looks up briefly. Smiles a quick, pained little smile. "Yeah," she says. "I'm fine."

"You should do it, too, Hayden," Jules says, still glaring. "Now that you're alive again. After Will."

"Jules." I toss a kernel of rice at him. "Stop."

"And after Anouk."

"You wish."

"Come on, Will," Jules says, slinging an arm across his forehead. "Give us something."

"There's not a lot to tell," Will says. "I don't have an interesting life, really."

"I'd believe it," Hayden says under his breath.

Will doesn't even acknowledge him. "I grew up in a little town on the South Carolina coast," he says, fiddling with his wounded hand, turning it slowly at the wrist. "It's called Beaufort. My parents run a gift shop. I'm interested in bridges and how they're constructed. I have a little sister. I like sailboats, but I don't own one. That's pretty much it."

Jules peers at him curiously, as if gauging whether he's withholding any juicy bits of information. He might be. He might not be. He might just like sailboats and not own one, and that's the end of it.

"Is your hand okay?" I ask, trying to end this as soon as possible.

Will nods, lifts his bandaged fist in a slow salute. Lilly went a bit crazy with the gauze, three full rolls, wrapping it up sloppily.

"You can say you sacrificed it for a noble cause," Jules

says. "Or tell people it was eaten by a shark. That's what I'd do."

"People?" I pick up more kernels of rice from the bottom of the plastic dish it came in. Bite them slowly. "What people?"

"You know." Jules drops his gaze. "People. When we get out . . ."

I glance at him. Smile. I can't stop myself. It's nice to hear him say it—*When we get out*—like it's a foregone conclusion. Like just because that's where we've set our sights, it's going to happen and nothing will be able to stop us.

I try to imagine it: me, creaking off the plane at JFK in a wheelchair. Apparently my subconscious has given me a broken leg. Extra pity points. My parents are waiting for me at the top of the skywalk. They're smiling. *We thought we'd never see you again!* they're saying. *We're so proud of you. We always knew you could do it.*

But for some reason, I can't quite get Dad's face straight in my head, or Mom's clunky rings, the ones she wears every single day, and I don't care all that much when they start congratulating me, telling me how I'm good enough after all, good enough to be their daughter. They start to blur, like figures behind glass, water flowing down a car window. Now they're gone. I wheel away into the airport. Pass newsstands with my face plastered everywhere. It's my picture on the papers, but it's like somebody cloned me and put that sour, pinch-faced version of me out for everyone to see. I don't see any similarities. I keep wheeling, out of the airport and across the parking lot, and I think someone's waiting for me up ahead, people who don't care about newspapers or anything I've done—

"Ooh. Someone is having secret thoughts." Hayden's watching me, and he has a weird expression on his face, part challenge, part slinking envy.

I plunk myself against the wall, bending my neck to fit the curve of the metal. *Stop daydreaming, Ooky. You're still trapped.*

35

Lilly, Jules, and Will are lined up like sardines at the far end of the capsule, huddled together under the reflective thermal blankets. I set down a bottle of water quietly. Watch them. The light buzzes overhead. I've just finished counting every food packet, battery, and medicine bottle on the supply shelves. I separated them into five equal piles. This way, if we have to make a run for it, we'll each have stuff to grab. It only took twenty minutes. We have hours to go.

I stare down the length of the panic room with half-lidded eyes. Hayden's not asleep, either. He's sitting on the cot, staring at the hatch. His knees are drawn up to his chest, oddly vulnerable.

I sit up and scoot toward him. He doesn't say anything when I settle next to him.

"When you were out there," I say, staring at the hatch,

too, trying to see what Hayden's seeing, "did you find anything about a butterfly man?"

"Is that your boogeyman?" Hayden asks. "Is that who you're blaming all this on? Because you should stop. It's people doing this. People like you and me."

"They're not like us. We're not that insane."

"Aren't we?"

I smell that overpowering stench again, sickening sweet and rotten. And I stare at my brogues, gleaming black against the wrinkled landscape of the sheets.

"Hayden, did you cut the camera feed?" I ask suddenly.

"What?" Hayden glances at me. "No. Why?"

"I dunno, I just—I was hoping you had."

We're silent for a second. A wave of sleepiness washes over me. We've been down here at least forty-eight hours now. No sunlight, no way to tell whether it's night or day. My internal clock is seriously messed up. I think my brain has started filtering out that buzzing, like it does with birdcalls and passing cars.

"Four hours till we head for the exit," Hayden says. I look into his eyes. They're so weird, flat and coin dull at first glance, but deep, deep down, something is moving, struggling—

"We don't really know where the exit is," I say.

"We'll find it."

I don't like how he's looking at me. I can't handle the smell. I nod and crawl back to the others. Curl up next to Jules. When I think it's safe, I crack open one eye.

Hayden's watching us. He's so still on the cot, like he's in a frozen movie frame. He has that same slightly wondering, longing look Perdu had. It's like he's thinking: *Friends. You guys are friends now. Must be nice.*

I blink. His face is blank again. Cold. I close my eyes and hope he didn't notice me in the dimness.

36

Someone's outside the hatch.

I sit bolt upright. The strip of light is still on, dull and buzzing. Lilly, Jules, and Will have piled into a crinkly silver heap behind me. Hayden is asleep on the cot, his face to the wall.

I hear it again: the gentle *snick-snick* of wires and metal prongs shifting. Someone's outside the hatch, trying to get in.

"Hayden?" I crawl quickly down the capsule and grab his shoulder. "Hayden!"

He jerks awake. I nod toward the door. He scrambles off the cot. "How long?" he whispers.

"Don't know. Just heard it."

Outside, the clicking stops.

We stare at each other. A million horrible possibilities jumble together in my mind. Helmeted figures. Miss Sei on hands and knees, a gun clenched in those thin white fingers. A huge spiny butterfly, dragging itself through the shadows, its wings rustling behind it.

I shudder and crawl as fast as I can back to the others. "Get up," I say, quiet and urgent. "Get up, now!"

"What?" Lilly rolls onto her back, rubbing her eyes. Jules is trying to swat me away. I grab his hand and slap him with it.

"Get up!" I whisper.

The *snick-snick* has started again. Not faster. Not slower. Patient, like a dentist.

Lilly sits straight up and stares. "What was that?"

Again the sound pauses. Again it starts up.

Lilly and Jules crawl toward Hayden. Will follows. His wounded hand is still clutched to his chest, but his face looks better, the glazed look gone from his eyes. I watch them, disconnected for a second. My head feels fuzzy, numb. We must not have been asleep for more than an hour or two.

"They can't get in, can they?" Lilly whispers. "Not from outside—?"

Hayden slips a hand under his cot, pulls out a serrated hunting knife. He leans against the tiny hatch, knife in one hand, gripping the bolt in the other. "There's no way. It's made for this."

The bolt rattles. He drops the knife and dives for it. Jules makes a tiny noise in his throat.

"Don't let them in, Hayden, please—"

"How can they open it from outside, it's a freaking *panic room*—"

"I don't know, but they are!"

Hayden wraps both hands around the bolt. His face goes red, a ligament popping in his neck. He's straining, holding the bolt back with all his strength. The handle rips from his grasp. The bolt slides an inch.

Hayden pulls away, swearing, his fingers warped white from the pressure. "They slipped the lock." He's turning, grabbing knives, flashlights, throwing them to us. "They're coming in!"

Will scrambles for his sword. Hayden is snapping open a black box, pulling something out, a handgun.

And now the hatch is opening and we're all yelling, pressing forward like moles, lights strobing into the darkness beyond.

"Who's there? *Who's there?*"

37

"Aurélie," a voice whispers in the darkness. It's Perdu. He's backed away from the hatch, crawling through the ruins of the room, eyes white and fishy in the flashlight beams. It looks like someone ransacked the place. Drapes hang in slashed tatters over the faux windows. Chunks of crystal glitter across the floor. Perdu doesn't blink, doesn't stop.

Hayden bursts from the hatch. Reaches Perdu in three strides and kicks him savagely backward. Perdu goes flying into a chair, crashes to the floor.

"There you are!" Hayden yells. He's got the gun in one hand, steel knife in the other. The knife comes up in an arc.

I shove myself to my feet. "Hayden, wait!"

He kicks the chair aside. It goes spinning away, even though it's massive.

I catch Hayden's knife hand. He pivots.

"Stop," I hiss. Hayden's eyes are wild. Sweat glimmers on his upper lip. His arm is still straining downward, like he doesn't realize the knife is pointed at me now. "Hayden, it's him, it's the guy from the library. We think he knows the way out of here—"

Hayden wrenches away from me. Perdu screeches, cowering inside a shattered nest of furniture legs and broken wood. The velvet bandages I tied around his arm are gone. It's hard to tell in the wobbling light, but I can't see the wound anymore, either. I get between Hayden and Perdu.

Hayden shoves me out of the way so hard my head snaps sideways.

Will launches himself past me. He catches Hayden's arm, and even left-handed he's strong. His fingers dig in, and Hayden's hand opens like a claw. The knife clatters to the floor.

Will stoops slowly. Picks it up. Offers it to Hayden, hilt first, not once moving his gaze from Hayden's face. "She said wait," Will says.

Hayden grabs the knife. "You don't know anything about him," he spits at me. "If he killed those trackers, he could kill every one of us here."

"Five minutes," I say. "Give me five minutes to talk to him."

I kneel next to Perdu. His head starts bobbing. He's bowing, being grateful. "Aurélie," he whispers again, and I pull the letter opener from my pocket and place it against his throat.

Something flickers across Perdu's gaze. Shock. Terror. He stares at me, his neck pulsing against the blade.

"Listen to me," I say in French. "You're going to tell us how we get out of this palace. I want to know *exactly* how we'll find the exit, and if you lie to us again I'm not going to stop anyone from hurting you."

"Aurélie?" Perdu whispers. "You are angry with me. Because of the library. I had no choice; he came for me! I led him away from you. I am on your side. I was only ever on your side." He's crying, eyes dripping. "Let me in with you." He gestures toward the hatch. "Please, I will tell you everything. Do not leave me out here alone." He throws a furtive look at Hayden and the others, then into the darkness over his shoulder. The room beyond the glare of the flashlight is a pitch black so thick it's solid.

My heart blunders wildly in my ears. I think of the trackers, liquid black, dripped like ink on the floor outside the library. The hatch's bolt being ripped from Hayden's grip. *He could kill every one of us here.* "I can't do that, Perdu; just *answer the question!*"

Will starts translating softly for the others.

"Please!" Perdu wails. "Please, it is not safe! I can feel him. He is near. *He hates me.*"

"Perdu, stop!" I jab the tip of the letter opener into his neck. It's an accident. A reflex. Perdu gurgles, but there's no blood. Just a dry cleft in his skin, like birch bark, splitting. "Stop lying," I say through my teeth. *"Arrêtez de mentir!* How do we get out of here? Who is the butterfly man?"

Perdu freezes mid-sob. His head is turned away from me. Slowly his eyes swivel and he's looking at me, sidelong. He's not crying anymore. His face is full of hate, sharp as a spade.

"He is poison," Perdu says, and his lips twitch into a smile. "He is death."

He inches toward me. I try to keep the blade in place, but my hand is shaking. His eyes are piercing, infinite layers of gray and blue and darkness.

"He is an angel," he whispers. "Fallen from the skies. Cast down from the stars."

I pinch my eyes shut. "Perdu, we *need* to know what we're up against, tell us—"

"*I AM TELLING YOU!*" He rises, unfolding to a full six feet of bony limbs and pale skin, and for an instant I catch a flicker of something beyond that ravaged body. A proud man, strong and handsome. Hayden's knife is raised, poised to cut Perdu down, but Perdu doesn't seem to notice. He keeps talking, muttering away like he's in a trance.

"They formed him from skin and blood and wisdom," Perdu says, and his voice is a deep, ragged growl. "Without fault and with knowledge beyond any man, and they sought his favor. *L'homme papillon*, they called him, their butterfly man. They built him a house far underground and they told him it was a gift, but they lied. It is a prison. And you are in it. He is moving you across the board like chess pieces, and if they do not catch you, he will, and he will tear you *limb from limb*—"

Perdu leaps at me, teeth bared. Hayden knocks him out of the air like a fly, the hilt of his knife connecting with the back of Perdu's head. Perdu drops to the floor, wailing.

"You will die!" he shrieks. "*Vous allez mourir*, you wretched children of darkness!"

Lilly, Will, Jules, Hayden, me: we all stand stock-still, gaping at each other.

"What did he say?" Jules asks.

"He wants to come into the panic room," I say. "He says it's not safe out here, but he's not making any sense, he's—"

"He said the butterfly man hates him," Will says quietly, turning to me. "And he's moving *us* around like chess pieces. Perdu might be working for the butterfly man, but I don't think it's voluntary. He wants to get out of here."

"We're not taking him in with us," Jules interrupts. "Not in a million years. We need to get rid of him and we need to get back inside—"

"We're no safer in there," I say, and Jules snaps right back: "We are. We're definitely safer than out in the open."

"We can't let him go," Lilly says. "It doesn't even matter whose side he's on. He knows where we are, and he can tell on us."

"Lilly, do you *want* him in there with us?" Jules says, exasperated. "He almost got us killed! We have no idea where he's been these last twelve hours."

Hayden's chewing the inside of his lip, head down. He

looks up sharply. "This is how it's going to be," he says. "Anouk, you said he knows where the exit is? So he'll lead us out of here. If he tries anything he's dead; until then, we've got a guide. Keep your friends close and your enemies closer, didn't Confucius say that?"

No, Hayden. Sun Tzu said that. In The Art of War. But Hayden's already dragging Perdu roughly across the floor. "Somebody help me. Rope and two carabiners, I need them now."

Lilly runs for the hatch.

"We're taking him in with us?" Jules asks, disbelieving. "We're doing this?"

Lilly reappears out of the panic room, a heavy coil of fluorescent-orange climbing rope looped over her shoulder. Perdu watches her pass the rope to Hayden, and I see the exact instant the realization hits him.

A spasm races down his cheek. He shrieks, high and birdlike, tries to wriggle away. Hayden places his foot at the small of Perdu's back and pins him to the floor. *"Aurélie!"* Perdu coughs. *"Aurélie!"*

"Don't hurt him," Lilly says, and I watch as Hayden ties his wrists, his legs. I try to force my thudding heart back into its designated cavity.

"Don't look at me like that," Hayden says to Jules, knotting the rope through the carabiners. "It's either this or we shoot him in the head, and something tells me you wouldn't approve of that, either."

Perdu's tied up in so much orange rope he looks cocooned. Hayden shoves him through the hatch. Lilly nods at Jules reassuringly, and they crawl in after Hayden.

It's just Will and me now, standing in the darkness. He's right next to me, his wounded hand resting against his stomach, his face slightly illuminated by the light from the hatch.

"It'll only be for a few more hours," he says quietly. "We'll be okay."

"You say that every time we're in imminent danger of being killed."

"I haven't been wrong yet," Will says, and somehow he manages a smile. His eyes spark warm and blue as he looks at me.

"Get in!" Hayden barks, and we both move for the hatch.

"Three more hours," Hayden says as we squeeze past him into the panic room. "Three hours and we're walking straight out of this hellhole."

38

Forty-five minutes to go. Will, Jules, and Lilly are sleeping again.
I don't know how they can. Perdu's tied up at the end of
the panic room like a psychotic freaking Sméagol. His
wrists are knotted to two hooks in the wall, his arms
stretched wide, hands limp. He doesn't talk. Doesn't
move. He's just glaring, his eyes dark and glittering.

The light strip on the ceiling has started cutting out.
Flash-flash-flicker, the panic room going black for seconds
at a time. The oppressive heat is gone, replaced by a damp
airlessness. A warm sheen has settled clammily against
my skin. I'm curled into a ball right next to Will, his body
so close I can feel the warmth coming off his back. I hold
my face, sweet-talking myself into a calm that won't
come.

*You're safe, Ooky. They're all right beside you, Will and
Lilly and Jules and Hayden, they're right here—*

I open my eyes. Perdu is watching me from the far end of the capsule. I can feel the hatred gathered around him like a cloud of insects. Images fly into my mind: The picture of me hanging in Rabbit Gallery, only someone's scratched out my face; a bunch of veiny purple grapes, tiny black bugs floating inside them like embryos; six gleaming wires carving me up neatly—

Don't look at him, Anouk. Don't think about him.

But something in those eyes makes me want to hide, to apologize or beg forgiveness. Something in those eyes is accusing me.

39

I wake to find Perdu leaning over me, blood and spit glistening down his chin. He exhales—a short, sharp gasp. And slumps forward, right on top of me.

I scream. Shove him off. Hayden is behind him, holding the serrated hunting knife. The blade glints ruby in the light. His shirt is covered in blood. "Anouk?" he whispers. His eyes are wide.

I scrabble backward, falling into Lilly's sleeping form. *"What did you do?"*

Hayden drops the knife and it slides across the floor, leaving a red smear. "He got free, I don't know how, he charged you!" His voice is scared.

Blood is starting to pool under Perdu—dark, dark red. He's still breathing, gurgling softly. Lilly's sitting up, pushing me away.

"What happened?" Jules says. "What's going on?"

"I heard him when he started crawling or you would be dead, too," Hayden says. "We need to go."

Lilly sees Perdu and lets out a shriek that quickly devolves into a tired, defeated moan. Hayden squeezes past us, starts grabbing things off the shelves, toppling my five careful piles. Food packets and batteries go spinning, falling to the floor. He's got the flashlights. The batteries.

"Everybody up!" he bellows over his shoulder. "We're getting out of here."

"He's bleeding," Lilly says. "He's dying!" She crawls to him, rolls him over. She's trying to staunch the flow of blood from the wound in his back with her bare hands, but there's too much of it, and there's something weird about: it's thick and gloopy, and something is swimming in it, strands of darkness—

Hayden shoves her away. "Don't get close to him," he growls, but she shoves him back, crying.

"Hayden, he's going to *die*." She slides around him. Starts looping the leftover gauze from Will's bandages over Perdu's wound. It's soaked through instantly.

I don't know what to do. I feel sick. Will is sitting perfectly still, staring at the knife on the floor.

The buzz is back, dark and low, pulsating in the air. Everything is pandemonium, everyone crawling over everyone else.

"We should never have let him in here," Jules says. "This was your *stupid idea*, Hayden!"

Hayden practically throws the three flashlights at us. Now he's snapping open the black, oblong box again. Inside is the handgun, encased in black foam. He takes it out and shoves it into his waistband.

"What about Perdu?" Jules asks, and Lilly starts smacking the metal arch of the wall, her eyes squeezed shut.

Hayden is unbarring the hatch, crawling out. "Leave him," he says over his shoulder. "We're not coming back."

Lilly looks at me, her face streaked with tears. I meet her gaze for a fraction of a second. Shake my head and scramble out after Hayden.

Flashlights click on. The floor creaks under our feet. I catch one last glimpse of Perdu in the panic room. His head is tipped back, eyes wide as he watches us go. Hayden slams the hatch shut. Now it's just us, the dark, our flashlight beams swooping along the walls.

We hurry east, the way we came, darting through the doors as quietly as we can. Hayden's up front, then me, Will, Lilly, Jules. We're drawn out in a line.

Will taps my shoulder with his good hand. I glance back at him. "Anouk?" he says under his breath.

"Yeah?"

"Can I talk to you for a second?"

"Sure."

He starts talking, fast. "It's Perdu. I don't know if I was imagining things or what, but when he was in the panic room, he—"

Hayden doubles back. "Stay close," he mutters.

I recognize the bedroom we're in. The ornate four-poster, tasseled ropes missing from the canopy. Somewhere up ahead I hear a dull rushing, crackling sound, like a distant waterfall.

I look over at Will, waiting for him to continue, hoping he'll save it for later.

He sees my expression. "I don't know what I saw," he says, moving away from me again. "I'm going crazy."

Join the club. We're back in the antechamber to Jellyfish Hall, the cloakroom with its dozens of small drawers and cupboards. It seems smaller somehow.

Our light beams bounce on something. Something that definitely wasn't there before.

"What the—" Jules starts to say. My stomach drops.

A roiling mass hangs in the darkness. The doors to Jellyfish Hall are half gone. Blue fumes are creeping toward us in a hissing, bitter wall.

40

"Get out!" Will yells. *"Out!"*

We stumble backward, turn, run. Hayden's screaming, raging, like the whole universe has conspired against him. We back into the bedroom, try the set of doors in the eastern wall. They lead into a room buzzing with magnets. It's a billiards room, but the orbs are shimmering steel, floating above the table, ready to smash anyone who enters. Hayden is almost jerked in, the gun in his pants dragging him through the door. We all pull him back, clawing at his shoulders, trying to get him into the bedroom. Will slams the doors shut. We pile up against the side of the bed, gasping.

"Now what?" Lilly whispers.

Now what, indeed. We can't go back to the panic room. It's Perdu's tomb now. I think of him shut up in there, wheezing, almost dead, maybe all the way dead.

Hayden has his head in his hands, fingers working his scalp. "I want *out*," he says, his voice awful, deep and grating. "I hate this. I hate *them*."

"We can get around," Lilly says. "We can backtrack and keep heading north a different way, like we were going to do in the first place. It's—it's not the worst thing that could happen."

But it is. We waited six hours for nothing. We banked on getting through Jellyfish Hall and getting out, not running back into the middle of the palace.

I tuck my flashlight under my arm. My head aches. "Perdu told us something about this. At least, he tried to. He said if you go along the edge of the pond you'll fall in, and if you jump in the middle you'll be all right. He meant the traps. That the traps go along the perimeter of the palace. And if Dorf wants us in the hall of mirrors, it's probably going to be somewhere at the center. Which means there's no other way to go. The traps are always on. I don't know if Hayden just stumbled on a broken one, but the rest of them are trigger-ready, to keep everything down here in. We'll have no *choice* but to go find them."

"We're dead," Jules says. "We're just done, over, terminated—"

"You guys made it this far," Hayden interrupts. His face is greasy, sweating. "How hard can it be to get through a couple of trap rooms?"

I laugh bitterly. I don't care if he's angry; so am I. "We made it this far because we had help. Something saved us in Razor Hall, then you rescued us from Jellyfish Hall. The Sapanis don't want us mangled, but now I think they're done being patient. They need us for something and we're not cooperating, so either they're going to scrape our pulverized corpses out of their trap rooms, or catch us. I wouldn't be expecting any merciful treatment anymore if I were you."

"Merciful treatment?" Hayden snaps. "I'm suggesting we run. I'm suggesting we force our way out at all costs. What are *you* suggesting? Nobody hold your breath; she's not that great at being helpful."

I sit up. "I could try kicking your teeth in, Hayden. I think that might be really helpful."

Hayden looks like he's about to go ape, pummel everything, me included. I press my thumbnail into the grid of lines on my flashlight's grip, until I no longer want to smack him with it. "We can fight," I say.

Hayden snorts. "I'd take you out in two seconds."

"Not us, idiot, we can fight the Sapanis. We can go to the hall of mirrors. Dorf thinks he can bag us when we get there and that'll be the end of it, but what if we're not that easy? What if we stop freaking out and actually *do* something instead of just running around screaming?"

"I think running around and screaming has been really acceptable behavior under the circumstances," Jules says.

I shake my head. "They're fighting something, too. They already lost a bunch of trackers. Their camera feed is down. We have a gun." I point at Hayden.

"They probably have more guns," Will says.

"We have the element of surprise," I say. "They think we'll be terrified and panicked—"

"We *are* terrified and panicked," Lilly says.

"But we don't have to be!" It comes out angrier than I wanted it to. "What's the worst that could happen? We die. But we could die sitting around here, too. At least we died trying to *do* something, at least we tried to show those people we're not—" *We're not weak.* I'm not. I'm not some brainless little pawn waiting around to be stomped on, manipulated. I've been that before, and I'm done with it. "They'll be expecting us to stumble in there all bloody and desperate and give ourselves up, maybe betray each other for a chance to get out of here alive. What they won't expect is us coming in guns blazing."

Okay, that was cheesy. This isn't a pep rally, Ooky, and you're not Lara Croft.

But everyone's listening. Not agreeing, but definitely listening.

Hayden is smirking. "I like it," he says. "We'll call them out. Duel at twenty paces."

"I can't shoot," Jules says nervously. "I don't believe in guns—"

Hayden reaches over and digs his thumb into Jules's collarbone, giving his shoulder a decidedly unfriendly squeeze. "You'll learn to." He trains his eyes on us. "I think we should do it."

Will's got his one good hand spread across his knee in his thoughtful pose, his eyebrows knit. In the beam of my flashlight I see the door to the magnetized billiards room. The wood is barnacled with metal trinkets—a snuffbox, a small clock. I watch a long hairpin turning slowly, floating toward the door as if through water.

"Maybe we can do a decoy or an ambush," I say. "Plan out as much as possible in advance. And we'll need more weapons."

"And when they're all dead?" Lilly asks. "Like, hypothetically, we're standing on a mountain of corpses; but then what? We're still stuck down here."

"Hostage," Will says. "If Dorf is there, or Miss Sei, we could take one of them alive. We would have a bargaining chip."

"So are we doing this?" Lilly asks. She doesn't look opposed. She looks like she's bracing herself for the answer, armoring herself, battening down the hatches. "We're fighting?"

"Looks like it," Hayden says. His arm is limp at his side, but his fingers are tapping a nervous beat against the floor. "If we're going to die, let's do it splattering Dorf all over a wall in the process."

Lilly throws Hayden a concerned look. I turn to Jules. "Jules?"

"Well, we're not finding the exit without Perdu—" Jules starts.

Hayden pounds his hands together. "Unanimous." He stands, and faces the dark. "And now we need a new base camp. Pronto. Check out the chandelier."

I glance up. The chandelier is turning slowly, rotating down its chain with a soft creaking sound. Its arms are blades, folding outward in elegant swoops, reaching almost to the corners of the room.

41

We crawl out of the chandelier room, pick ourselves up, and run six rooms farther. Will swings us to a stop in front of a pair of ornate doors carved with golden petals. I peer up through the gloom, squinting at the scroll above them. "'Chambre de la Rose,'" I read out loud. "'For my darling, my heart, my treasure, Madame Célestine.'"

"Sounds like a safe bet," Will says, and we push in, light beams swinging through the space. It's a bedroom. Beautiful. Everything is small, not quite child-small, but like it was built for a very short person. The wallpaper shows massive blooms, huge, abundant leaves, no thorns, makes you feel like you're a tiny bug right inside the rosebush. Pale wood tables and flowery upholstered chairs look like they're sprouting right up out of the floor.

This does seem like a safe bet. No one wants My

Darling, My Heart, My Treasure tripping a wire and blowing herself up, right?

Hayden slams a dainty white writing desk against the door, and we congregate around the bed. I drop onto it, dragging my legs up. Jules kicks off the pillows, hurling them at the wall.

"Hall of mirrors," I say. "We need to get there. We need to get in. And then we need to take it over."

Will hangs his flashlight from a tassel and gets on the bed, too. Lilly follows. Hayden throws himself into one of the tiny chairs. It creaks under him, the dainty legs bending.

"How are we going to find it?" Lilly asks. "It might be miles from here."

"I don't think so. It's obviously not to the north. They said we'd have one safe direction to travel. They're basically rolling out a carpet for us."

"What about weapons?" Jules says. "I'm sorry, but if we're hacking at the trackers with swords, this is not going to be a successful endeavor. It's just not."

"Wait." Lilly sits straight up. "Rabbit Gallery."

"What?"

"It's full of weapons. It's like a weapons buffet."

"That hall is at *least* a mile back, and there were trap

rooms between here and there. Remember the room Will got all excited about?"

Will does that barking non-laugh thing and looks at the ceiling.

"We'll take a different route," Lilly says. "We can go six or seven rooms west. That should be far enough from the perimeter. Hopefully. And then we can head south. We'll be fine."

"What's Rabbit Gallery?" Hayden asks. He's tugging at something at the bottom of his leg, like he's got an uncomfortable wrinkle in his sock.

"It's an exhibition hall full of weapons and stolen art somewhere south of here," I say. "But I'm not sure if we can make it that far." I glance at the others.

Lilly nods. "We can. It's either that or we find swords and letter openers and, like, joke them to death."

Hayden grimaces. I look over at him. He's still pulling at something inside his shoe. When his hand comes up, it's holding a waxy yellowed strip of skin.

Jules's eyes widen in disgust. "Leprosy much?" he says.

Lilly swallows loudly. "Hayden, are you okay?"

"Yeah," he says, but he looks confused. "Yeah, I'm fine."

We stare at him a second. I shake my head. "We make a run for it, then? All in favor?"

Nodding all around. We grab our flashlights.

"Leave the food and anything we don't need," Will says, dragging the desk away from the door with his good hand. "We'll come back here."

I dig the compass from my sweater. Lilly shines her light at it. We head out.

We're going west this time, away from Jellyfish Hall and toward what we assume is the center of the palace. At the very first door we all stop. Listen. No sound. We open the door and step over the threshold, and it feels like walking toward an oncoming truck, staring down those glaring headlights and sixteen growling wheels, and being like: *Psh. I got this.* We're heading straight for Dorf, straight for the trackers and whatever it is we were brought here for. It feels like tempting fate. So, about 30 percent exhilarating, 70 percent stupid.

After five rooms we turn south again, through the dark, echoing halls. No traps so far. Dorf was telling us the only safe way to go was toward the palace's center, but I don't think he counted on us backtracking. We start to run, lights flashing, our feet quiet on the polished floor.

42

It's possible we're lost. We're heading south, and no one's been decapitated yet, both good things, but we had to go up a steep, narrow staircase about five rooms back, and now we're someplace I don't recognize at all: a suite of small, luxurious rooms, tucked above the huger halls and ballrooms below. Little windows are embedded in the paneling, low, near the floor. The panes are angled downward, and through them I see chandeliers, marble floors about thirty feet below. These rooms are small, paneled in dark cherry wood. The ceilings are so low. It's like running through a dollhouse. The air is warm. The lamps are lit, glistening on coffee-colored leather and brass-riveted wing chairs.

And now we get to the last room. It's a complete dead end. One door in, one door out.

"Whoa," Jules says, drawing up short. "Wrong way—"

We all spin, jostling one another. I throw a glance back over my shoulder, glimpse a desk, shelves. *An operating table?* I pause. Jules runs into my back.

It is an operating table. It's standing in one corner of the room. The surface is covered in ancient, tightly stretched leather. It's spattered in places, marked with dark rings and stains.

"Is that blood?" Will has stopped, too, now, peering around.

"Coffee stains," Jules says. "Let's go."

But all of us have stopped now. It's like a little laboratory. Not a creepy, Frankenstein one with pig brains on the shelves. A neat, organized study, almost cheery. Glass ampoules line the shelves, stoppered with cork. Stacks of books, some of them marked with feathers and silver pins. Old paper everywhere, crinkly heaps of it.

I look again at the desk. My skin goes cold. A glass of red wine is standing next to the pen stand, still half full. The rim is stained a little, like someone just drank from it.

"We need to go," I whisper. "Someone was here. Like, minutes ago."

If they come in, we're stuck. Done for.

Will has gone over to the operating table. He's leaning over it, and I see there's an enormous leather-bound book lying open on top of it, cracked bindings, the paper old and yellowed, wavy with moisture and age. Will places a hand on it, brushing a finger down the page.

"Will, we need to get to Rabbit Gallery," Lilly says. "You heard Anouk; someone was here—"

"Look," Will says. "You guys, look at this."

I walk to the table and peer over his shoulder, but Lilly's right. We need to get out of here. This room feels tiny, claustrophobic, like any second the walls will collapse and the ceiling will fall and we'll be crushed under the weight of the soil and stone. What if someone walks in? The others are gathering at my back, shifting nervously.

I see the page Will is pointing at. Three columns— lists of names, numbers, then a wider column of notes. The handwriting is spidery, a little bit shaky.

Jean Leclair. Age 67. Failed.

Monsieur Mascarille. Age unknown. Failed.

Eleanor McCreery. Age circa 27. Failed.

"Stonemasons," Will mutters. "Maids. Painters."

"What is it?" Lilly asks. Words pop out at me from the scribbled notes. *Se détériore. Le sang souillé. Manqué. Manqué.*

"Failed," I translate quietly. "All of these are failed."

But what does that mean exactly?

Will starts flipping through the pages. He reaches the beginning of the book. Taps a name with two fingers. "These are scientific notes, surgical procedures. It says they started in 1760."

He starts reading aloud: "'Guillaume Battiste, Age thirty to thirty-five. Beggar. We . . .'" He swallows. "'We caught him on the roadside. He was stronger than he looked. Struggled, much blood. Frédéric brought him back to the château. He had the pox. Failed.'"

Will looks over at me. "There are hundreds of names in here." His eyes run up and down the columns. "Hundreds of experiments."

I see an entry about halfway down the page, circled in a thread of bright red ink. I grab Will's hand, stopping him from turning the page. Let go again quickly and squint down at the writing.

July 7, 1788. L'homme papillon. Success.

The butterfly man.

There are more words after it, hurried French, blotted with ink.

He has awakened. We took him from his glass cistern yesterday. He has already begun to walk and imitate us. He learns swiftly, quicker than any child. What will he be tomorrow, in a week's time, in a month?

The lists continue. One success. Hundreds of failures. They didn't stop after whatever it was they had created. They kept trying for something, for . . . what?

Monsieur Vallé, head butler. Experimented on by l'homme papillon. Failed.

Aimée Boucheron, saucier. Failed.

Célestine Bessancourt— Whatever's been written after her name has been scratched out violently, but I'm pretty sure it says "Failed," too.

Behind me, Jules sucks breath in through his teeth. "Are we in there? Are we one of their experiments?"

Will flips forward again. Nods slowly.

"Here," he says, and we're all looking now, staring at our names listed on the last written page of this ancient book.

Anouk Peerenboom–17. NYC

Jules Makra–16. San Diego

Will Park–17. Charleston

Hayden Maiburgh–17. Boston

Lilly Watts–16. Sun Prairie

No notes. No explanations.

Something is nagging at the back of my mind, some connection I feel I should be making but can't quite grasp—

"We need to go," Hayden says. He's practically bounding from foot to foot, his gun out. "Come on, move it!"

We slip out of the room and run for the stairs. My lungs are heaving, scraping me hollow. We don't stop until we're back in the palace and the study feels miles above us.

43

We get to Rabbit Gallery about twenty minutes after leaving the study. I recognize the blue wallpaper in the circle of my flashlight beam, the dark wood arching overhead like trees. I see the doors where I had my emotional breakdown, the paintings lining the walls.

"Hayden," I say quietly. "This is it."

I'm not thinking about the cracked leather volume on the operating table, the lists of names, and what it was they did with all those hundreds of dead people, the Carolines and Aimées and Guillaumes. I don't want to know. I just want to get out of here.

Our lights flick along the rows of glass cases, illuminating the displays inside for an instant before plunging them back into darkness. Hayden goes straight to the nearest one. Smashes it with his gun. The whole case breaks at once, glass raining over the pedestal.

I feel the sound in every cell of my being. Brace myself for the wail of a siren, traps to trigger and splatter us all over the walls like gruesome Jackson Pollock pieces. Nothing happens. No siren, no blades. They didn't rig anything this deep in the palace. Probably nobody ever got this far.

Hayden's face is tense, his eyes glittering with excitement. He doesn't stop to grab the weapon inside. He runs on to the next case. Smashes it. Now the next. The rest of us pick through the glass as fast as we can. A nervous hush falls, punctuated only by the explosive shattering of the display cases.

I find a handgun, a lightweight polymer throwing knife, a small brushed-steel orb that I'm hoping is a tiny bomb. Most of the weapons are too huge to be used by a single person. Others look too complicated. I study the handgun in the light from my flashlight. Figure out how to click out the cartridge. Feel brilliant for a second. The gun's loaded.

Will comes over with more ammunition. I show him what I found. He holds up a Taser.

"You can have it if you want," he says, and I actually melt a little, because what's more adorable than someone offering you a Taser before going into battle?

I grab it. Give him a half smile. We join the others.

The hall is covered in chunks of glass now, like the ceiling rained ice. Lilly and Jules have an entire arsenal of weapons lying in a heap by the door. We sort through them, tossing aside the ones that are too big or heavy, slinging the rest onto our backs, attaching them to belts, clutching them in our hands.

I keep thinking someone might hear us—maybe trackers, or Dorf in his camel trench coat and neat little beard—and this whole desperate operation will be over before we even start. But no one comes. The palace feels dead around us. Hollow. Waiting.

We hurry out, leaving Rabbit Gallery in ruins behind us.

I'm almost giddy heading back to the rose room. We're not talking. We don't need to. This must be like the parade-and-bugles part of war, the run-up when everything's still bright waving flags and heroism. You don't think about the bad things. You focus on nebulous notions of victory and let that float you. A part of me knows it won't last. But I'll take it while it does. I'd rather be pumped than terrified.

As soon as we're back, the writing desk barring the

doors, everyone starts talking at once.

"I don't even know what this does," Lilly says, picking up weapon after weapon and rattling it next to her ear.

Jules starts lining up explosives on the embroidered seat of a chair, eyeing them mistrustfully.

I sit down cross-legged on the floor and spread a snowy white pillowcase in front of me.

"You got a plan now, Nukey?" Hayden asks, and he's being a jerk, but the thing is, I *do* have a plan. At least, part of one.

"Yep!" I jump up, start rummaging around inside the desk. Find some ink, still liquid, and a long curved quill. I start scribbling a hypothetical floor plan of the hall of mirrors onto the pillowcase, guiding the quill's nub as smoothly as I can across the cloth. The others gather around.

"They obviously don't know where we are," I say, and the nub snags, splattering ink. "Which means they probably don't know how many of us are left. And they're going to try to trick us. That's a given. So we're going to trick them back." I look up at their faces, pale and glowing around me. "We're going to need a volunteer."

44

We've gone over the plan four times. We've gone over our weapons, discussed how we're going to use them. We're ready to go. But we're waiting, hanging back. It's like being at the top of the highest drop of a rickety, sure-to-collapse roller coaster, and you—you, in the wagon—get to decide when to take the plunge, freak out, die. No one's super excited about that part.

"Your turn, Anouk," Jules says after a while. "Tell us your story."

He's not expecting an answer. He's waiting for me to tell him to shut up, and I almost do, just out of habit. But I change my mind. What difference does it make if somebody knows? What difference does it make if *everyone* knows? Maybe in forty minutes I'll be gone. Wiped off the face of the earth. I'd like to tell someone before then.

"What d'you want to know?" I say.

"Whoa, really?" Jules sits up. "Everything! Why do you hate people? Why did you have to forge your parents' signatures? Why are you angry all the time?"

"Jules, don't," Lilly says, but I wave it off.

"No, it's okay. I'll tell you. I'll have to lobotomize all of you afterward so you can't tell anyone my secrets, but you're okay with that, right?"

"Definitely," Jules says.

"Okay," I say. My voice cracks. I feel self-conscious all of a sudden. I brace myself. There's nothing left to do but let go, talk. "Okay. My parents adopted me when I was four."

I stare at the wall, at the roses. They don't look that great suddenly. Whoever stayed in here would have realized that really fast. The huge leaves and forced perspective: it's like it was engineered to keep you feeling small. "My biological mom left me at a shelter in Pennsylvania. I don't even know what her name was."

Lilly makes a consoling sound, like that was the punch line of my story. Not even close.

I pick at the pillowcase plan, the black arrows and scribbles bleeding into the fibers. I think about my biological mom sometimes. Who doesn't? But she's not the one who makes me angry. She's not the one who made me want to run away to foreign continents or break Japanese porcelain with a baseball bat, or sit under the dining room table for three hours ripping my straight-A report card into smaller and smaller pieces, because no one had even asked, no one had cared at all what it said—

"Usually if you're in an orphanage past the toddler stage, it means you're going to foster care. People don't want messed-up babies, or ones with druggy parents. So when this couple came in and said they would adopt me, it was amazing. I was the weirdest kid. I never smiled. I hardly ever spoke. I just watched people. But for some reason they didn't mind. They were rich. They really wanted me. At least, I thought they wanted me." My lungs feel tight. I can still remember the first time I saw them, coming across the parking lot, all honey-colored lighting and flowing hair like they had stepped straight out of an insurance commercial. I bet there are all sorts of great adoptive parents out there. Waiting lists of people who can hardly wait to give some random kid a great life.

Mine were not those parents. It was like they were shopping for a purse or a new car, something to complete their idyllic image of familyhood.

Step 5: Adopt a small child. Great for holiday pictures and also to shut up all your annoying, judgmental friends who think you're self-absorbed.

"They could have been monkeys and I would have loved them," I say. "I *did* love them. And then when I was six, they had a real baby."

The shadowy roses look monstrous now, writhing across the walls. The others are sitting stock-still, waiting, and that old, hot anger is creeping back into my stomach. I see fourteen-year-old-me snipping my hair short in the bathroom, calling myself names for being a whiner, for being needy, for being a typical spoiled brat with no real problems, even though they *felt* like real problems. They felt like the biggest problems in the world.

"My parents got the news and it was, like, from one day to the next, I was extra. They didn't need me anymore. It's like they blamed *me*, like I had somehow tricked them into adopting me. I was this imposter they had let into their home and pretended was theirs, and now they didn't need to pretend anymore. You know how that hurt? Do you have any idea how it *hurts* when you're six years old and you don't have anyone in the universe, because some people came along and said they'd take care of you and . . . and they *lied?* They tossed you aside after five minutes, like you're not even a person; you're just a photogenic accessory and now you're done, *who even cares about you anyway, Anouk.*"

I'm crying. It started somewhere between *hurt* and *take care of you* and now it won't stop. Jules and Will are staring at me, wide-eyed. Hayden's leaning over a pump-action shotgun, fiddling with it. I want one of the roses to detach from the wall. Swallow me down whole.

"You wanted all the gory details, right, Jules?" I say. "Well, here you go: my parents hardly even talked to me after my sister was born. They talked *about* me. I overheard them all the time, being, like, 'What about *her?* What are we going to do with *her,* what if she exhibits emotional *problems* and influences our *daughter?*' And yeah, I had emotional problems after that. I thought my parents were aliens. I started getting paranoid delusions and I couldn't trust anyone and I watched them playing with Penny and how they loved her a million times more than me, and one morning I took her out of her crib and carried her down the driveway to the street. I was barely big enough to lift her, and she was crying and I was crying, too, and I was telling her we were leaving, and I hated her, and we were never going back, our parents would never see us again . . . I didn't know what I was doing, okay? I was a dumb little kid and I took her out into the street. A food truck hit us. Larry's Brasserie Chickens, how ridiculous is that? I broke four bones in my arm. Penny flew fourteen feet. She almost died."

"You were six," Jules says. "It's not your fault, you—"

"It is my fault!" I say, and it comes out vicious, jagged. "I wanted her gone, okay? And even after she survived, I wanted my parents to see her ugly, scarred face and love me instead, and think I was special, and think I was talented and awesome, because I never was; I was never enough for them." I hiccup, and wipe a hand angrily across my eyes, mashing the tears into my skin. "Penny never did anything. She was never angry at me. She just existed, and now she's going to live with that for the rest of her life, and yeah, I'm sorry. I'm sorry she was born with a mentally unhinged adopted sister and awful parents. I'm sorry for everything, but being sorry doesn't change jack."

I'm still crying, and I can't read the expressions of

the others through the dark and the blur of tears, but I bet they're horrified. I bet they're finally realizing what a god-awful excuse for a human being I am. It's about time. I want to leave now. I want to run out there into the hall of mirrors and spray fire and death around me until there's nothing left, until this whole palace is ashes at my feet. And then I'll lie down in the ruins and die, too—

"Hey," Lilly says. She grabs my hand. She sounds way too calm. "I'm sorry about your sister. I am, that's really terrible what happened to her, but you were six years old and your parents sound like complete . . . complete *poop*, honestly, excuse my French. They were supposed to be your parents and they weren't, and people do bad things when they feel alone." She pauses and looks at me earnestly. "But you're not alone anymore," she says. "You're not. You have us now. Right, Jules? Will? Hayden?"

You're not my parents! I want to scream. *You're not my family!*

And Jules looks straight at me and says: "Right."

"Right," Will says.

Hayden's watching us. "Righty-o," he says, and his eyes glimmer, sharp and scornful.

"We're alive," Lilly says, and she's squeezing my

fingers so hard it hurts. "We're here, and we're together, and that's what we've got. I mean, we're in a stupid palace full of psychos trying to kill us, but . . ." She trails off.

I feel the pain in my chest spreading down into my fingertips and sparking away, like Lilly's a lightning rod. And now it's gone, and Will's hand is on my shoulder, and Jules is patting me awkwardly on the back.

"Are we ready?" Hayden says. He's putting the shotgun to his shoulder, looking down the barrel, pointing it around the room.

"We're ready," Lilly says, and I am.

45

We're out of the rose bedroom, moving in single file into the heart of the palace. No one's talking. We've said all we needed to say. Our plan's in motion.

We start to run, our feet thumping softly against the marble. We keep our lights pointed downward, the beams skimming the floor.

Ten minutes later we reach a wide, low staircase. At the top is a pair of mirrored doors. We jog up the steps. I open one of the doors, just a crack, as quietly as I can.

"Guys?" I look back over my shoulder.

"What?"

"I think we're here."

The others peek in. Nod.

This hall of mirrors is not at all like the one in Versailles. I saw the original on a humid day in August, jammed in along with all the other fourth graders whose parents felt Paris would be more enriching than the binge-watching nanny all summer long. I remember thinking the hall of mirrors didn't really have that many mirrors in it. It was mostly gold. Huge windows, parquet floor, a bunch of chandeliers hanging from the ceiling. On the other wall were some big mirrors, but overall it seemed like a misnomer.

The Palais du Papillon has an *actual* hall of mirrors. It's like a huge version of the glass corridor through which we entered the palace. A kaleidoscope, a fractured prism, high and narrow, glittering faintly blue. Only ten feet wide. Maybe a hundred feet long. Everything—floor, ceiling, walls—is made up of massive panels of reflective glass.

At the far end, another doorway stands open. Golden light shines out of it, radiating in sharp lines down the hallway.

Slowly, I ease the door closed again.

"Ready?" We're all staring at each other, wide-eyed. I feel like I should say something, give a stirring speech and send us off to death or glory, but my heart's thudding, deafening. My mouth feels dry suddenly. I can't think of anything.

"Ready," Will says.

I nod. I feel someone's hand on my arm and I realize we're grabbing at one another, gripping hands, sweaty and dirty and alive. And now Lilly pulls away from us and steps through the doors, into the hall of mirrors.

Here goes.

She starts down the hall, feet tapping quietly. She looks like a little lost deer. She's not. She's got a gun tucked under the bulky sweatshirt Will lent her. She's got a small bomb and two knives. About halfway down the hall, she slows.

Don't turn around, Lilly.

Adrenaline burns through me. She doesn't stop. Doesn't turn.

I feel every muscle in my body, every tendon and ligament straining, as if I'm keeping Lilly alive by sheer force of will—

"Hello?" Lilly calls out. Her voice echoes down the glassy expanse. "Dorf? Is anyone here?"

Bam. A tracker shoots out of the doors at the other end of the hall, sprinting straight for Lilly, the red light thrumming along its jaw. Lilly doesn't make a sound. She lifts the gun and fires, and the tracker goes flipping backward, its body squeaking over the mirrored floor.

Jules throws me a panicked look. I don't move, don't look anywhere but down the hall of mirrors.

Lilly keeps walking.

And now the ambush starts.

Halfway between us and Lilly, one of the mirrors flips open soundlessly. Two more trackers step out and move toward her. She doesn't see them. She doesn't need to.

The trackers whirl, but Will and I are already on them. I zap one with the Taser. The second hits the floor, Will's knife protruding from its leg. A second later it's knocked out, too, twitching against the glass.

Lilly's reached the end. She waves, once, the signal that she's coming back.

Jules steps into the hall.

There's no way this is it. I draw out my own gun. *Come out, come out, whatever you are.*

Lilly reaches us. She's soaked, her hair sticking to her forehead. We start back toward Jules.

Hayden has stepped into the hall. Maybe it's the light, but he looks sick. He's moving over the mirrored floor like it's thin ice. He passes Jules and heads toward the open panel and the trackers on the floor. Kneels next to one. Grabs it by the neck and rips open its visor. Slimy skin glimmers in the blue light.

"Tell us the way out," he says through his teeth. "Tell us!"

The tracker gurgles, its eyes rolling back in its head. Hayden goes for the knife already in its leg, and he twists, slowly.

That was not part of the plan. I run for him. Will's half a step behind me. "Hayden, stop—"

He slides out the knife and thrusts it in again. I grab his shoulder. He whirls, inhumanly fast, and smacks me so hard my ears ring. I stumble back. Lilly catches me. My vision blurs, but through the neon flashes inside my skull, I see Hayden stand.

He's shuddering. His whole body is jerking, twitching back and forth like a bad frame of celluloid film. He pauses, motionless, slouched between the mirrors, head lowered, eyes turned up. His reflections extend away behind him, into infinity. They grin and he grins, lips stretching, eyes dull and fevered.

He drops the tracker. It's dead now. Will charges toward him. Hayden's faster. One second he's standing, hands empty, and the next he has a gun, and the barrel is jammed against Will's head. Jules makes a cracked, frightened sound, tries to do something, maybe run. Hayden flicks a long steel blade to Jules's throat, stopping him in his tracks.

"Hayden?" I whisper.

Will dives, tries to slash at Hayden's stomach. Hayden twitches again. His arm sails down, up, so fast I can barely see it, and the grip of the handgun connects with the back of Will's head.

"Hayden!"

"Give the Bessancourts my warmest regards," Hayden says, and his voice is dead in his throat, thin and metallic. He's holding Will up by his neck now, one arm snaked around him. "Tell them I win this round."

A rattling echoes through the hall. The mirrors begin to move, sliding around.

I get one last glimpse of Jules and Hayden and Will, frozen in a horrible triptych. Now the mirrors slam into place, and it's just Lilly and me, and rank upon rank of trackers.

Palais du Papillon—Salle du Sang Rouge— 116 feet below, 1790

"What have you done?" I breathe. "Father, what have you done?"

He stands behind me, one hand resting awkwardly on the back of a chair as if he is proud, as if he waits to be carved into monuments and painted on a great canvas. Little tears glisten in the corners of his eyes. He does not answer me.

I step toward Mother. It is some trickery—strings and mirrors. It must be. I saw her die. I heard the bullet and saw the blood, and Jacques carried down her lifeless body.

But it is Mama. These are her eyes, blue as cornflowers, with the little scar under one of them like a scratch of moonlight. This is her smile, shy and beautiful, as though she never saw any ill in the world, as though Father and the palace and her brief, sad life were all some strange play, and if she pretended diligently enough the curtain would fall, and the actors would vanish, the lavish sets, too, and she could leave the stage behind her and wander into the fields and the sun. "Aurélie," she says again. I cannot stop myself: I hurry to her and kneel by her chair. "Mama?"

She gazes down at me, her face full of tenderness.

"Mama, how—?"

"How what, my darling?" She laughs. "Why are you making these silly faces?"

I am close to laughing, myself, close to leaping up and embracing her and smothering her in kisses. I feel her hand on my cheek. It is cold, colder than ice and marble. I look back at Father.

"Do my sisters know? Delphine and Bernadette and Charlotte, have they seen her?"

"No," Father says, licking his lips. "You are my eldest. I wanted you to be the first to see. Is she not sublime?"

"They must know! She is their mother and they think she is dead; can you not understand how they must have wept—"

I look back at Mama. She reaches out to touch my cheek again, but this time she misses and her hand drops to the armrest, a deadweight. She does not attempt to raise it again. She continues to sit, slumped in the chair, smiling.

"Mama?" I say, and now to Father: "What did you do to

her? Father, she is not the same." Panic is gripping me. I blink away the tears, but they are forming too quickly, flooding their dams. "Father, she died, I saw it, she was *dead.*"

Father looks on, his mouth twitching into a smile, his gaze crawling over my face.

I crouch next to Mama and grip her arm. "Mama," I say. "Do you remember the château, Mama? The tree we used to eat under in the arbor, what sort of tree was it? Mama, what was it?"

She continues to smile. "Aurélie," she says, and her voice is low, a thread of wind in the shrubs, in the rosebushes. "My beautiful, beautiful daughter . . ."

It is as if she is asleep. She sees me, but it is as if I am a dream to her, a wisp of thought somewhere deep in the vaults of her mind. I clench her poor, cold arm. "Mama, do you remember the tree? Please remember!"

And all at once, she twitches, like an animal with its back broken.

"Mama, what's the matter?"

Havriel takes a step toward us.

"Mama?"

Her eyes begin to change. I see veins in them, strands of black, spreading through the blue. She seems to realize something is wrong, and it is as if she is surfacing, her head coming up out of a deep inky pool. It is my real mother, Mama, awake. Alive. She looks directly at me, and she sees me.

"Aurélie?" she says. Her voice is panicked. I smell smoke and flames, see her pale hand coated in her own blood, wearing it like a gory ornament. "Aurélie, my daughter, *do not leave me behind.*"

Now the veins spread like a wild thicket, unstoppable, and her eyes flood black.

I jerk to my feet, backing away. Mama writhes, contorting in her chair. "Father, what did you do? *What did you do to her?*" I scream.

Father is shaking, crying. "We brought her back," he says. "We found the key, hidden in the branches, and we gave her life. . . ." He stops shaking. His gaze drifts far away. "We made her eternal."

A cold hand clamps my wrist, and I spin to face the thing that was my mother. It is staring at me. It is still smiling, but there is no kindness left there. Only hunger.

Its head tilts oddly. It opens its mouth. A long tongue slides out, purple and mottled. "Aurélie," it whispers. *"Aurélieeeeeee."*

Havriel pushes past me. He grips Mama, and she shrieks, slashing at him with hands that are suddenly clawlike, white skin stretched tight over bone. She struggles. Havriel is stronger. He is strapping her to the chair, and the chair has wheels, and he is leaning it back, pushing it away, and she is thrashing, her head whipping like a snake, smiling eyes, smiling lips, and that great purple tongue.

The doors slam behind her, and I still hear her screams, echoing through the palace.

"It was an apple tree," I whisper, when she is gone and it is only Father and I, standing in the red glow and the shadows. "We used to eat under the apple tree."

46

Click. The lights in their helmets ignite. Another *click.* The trackers start toward us, fast.

I bring up my gun in an arc, my finger on the trigger. A split second before I shoot, the mirrors swing around. The whole space rearranges itself, revealing the trackers, obscuring them. The spindly gilt poles aren't supports. They're hinges, and what used to be one long hallway is now dozens of tiny blocks—passages, corners, dead ends.

A maze.

"Move, Lilly," I whisper. "Anywhere, just move."

We start for the nearest opening, my hand scrabbling across the glass. I glance over, see my reflection hurrying next to me, a whole row of *me*s. I hear the trackers, I think, on the other side. Pounding boots and the soft creak of bodysuits. I can't hear Jules or Hayden or Will. No voices.

We turn a corner and almost collide with a pair of trackers. Before I can even react, one of them lashes out, tarry fingers pinching into my throat. I try to bring my gun up. The tracker catches my wrist with its other arm. I kick out desperately. My foot connects with its shin. Pain explodes in my jaw, fear and shock—*it's trying to lift me by my head*—and I hear a gunshot, so close it's like a punch to the ear. The hand around my neck loosens. I drop, start crawling over the floor. A second gunshot.

"Lilly?"

She's next to me, staring at her gun like it's some kind of disgusting metal slug. I stagger to my feet, and we're running again, dodging around the mirrors. Footsteps seem to be approaching from all directions. Everywhere I turn I see helmets, red lights, slicing black legs, and I don't know if they're reflections or if they're right there, inches away from me.

Another three trackers burst out diagonally in front of us. They spot us. Whirl. We skid to the right, dart down a short passage, left, left again, deeper into the maze. And now we're at a dead end, hemmed in on three sides by mirrors.

I spin, feeling for an opening. I see something skim

past. I run for it. And slam against solid glass. I reel back, hot blood trickling from my nose and into my mouth.

"Whoa," I say shakily, turning to Lilly. "Whoa, that was—"

Lilly gasps.

"I'm fine," I say. "I'm fine, we—"

Three trackers are standing at the entrance to the dead end. Another one approaches. Four, five-six-seven, silent and glittering.

What are they waiting for?

My eyes flick to the left. We're trapped. I see Lilly and myself in the glass, desperate, frozen.

Wait.

One of the reflections isn't Lilly.

About four reflections in is a shape. It's matching its pose to Lilly's, head down, arms limp at its sides. But it's not Lilly. It's the woman in the dripping red dress. And suddenly she skips a mirror as easily as stepping through a doorway and starts toward us.

Oh please no. I reach out to touch the glass. It isn't glass. It's air. The woman picks up speed, coils into a crouch, and launches herself upward. The trackers leap toward us.

I grab the first thing I can get out of my pocket: the steel globe with a button at the top. I jam the button and hurl it. The globe cracks against the first tracker's helmet. Rolls away. *Seriously?*

The woman rams into the trackers, and she's like a tiny vicious hurricane. She swings through them, sinuous and savage, a whirl of red, her arms wrapping necks and legs, breaking them. I catch a glimpse of teeth, long and spiny.

Lilly and I dive through the opening between the mirrors and feel our way down a passageway. I glance back over my shoulder. I can still see her. She's corpse white and hunched, and her dress is in tatters, whirling around her like a cloud. She hurls a tracker into a mirror and turns, looking toward us. She's not breathing hard. She's not breathing at all. Her eyes are dead black.

A tracker strikes her aside and heads our way. It never gets a chance to run. The woman catches it by the neck. I spin forward again, but I hear the sound it makes, the bite.

That thing is not human.

None of them are.

Slam, slam.

The mirrors keep shifting. Something's coming after us.

We're in another compartment, three walls of glass. Another dead end. I hear something running. I hear someone muttering close by, right next to me, then veering away.

Lilly, I mouth. Gesture toward a gap in the mirrors. We're going to have to backtrack.

Snick—soft as a fingernail paring. And there's the woman, her head emerging between the mirrors.

I freeze. White skin, glossy and hard like stone. No hair. Not even eyelashes. Her wig's gone. She blinks once, translucent lids over black. She slides into the compartment, lithe as a cat.

"Stay back," I hiss, pulling a knife out of my belt. "Stop, do *not* come any closer!"

She lets out an ear-shattering shriek.

I lash out, and she dodges. Skitters to the side. Now she leaps forward, catching me behind the knees. My legs fold. I fall and my head slams into glass.

She vaults onto my stomach. Liquid like dirty water is flowing from her dark eyes. She's sniffling, crying.

"Aurélie?" she says. One of her hands flies up, and

the hand has claws, spiny thin like a cat's—

Over her left shoulder, a harsh zapping sound.

The thing falls in a heap on my chest.

Lilly's standing behind her, an expression of sheer horror on her face. She's holding my Taser. We stare at each other. I push the woman off and scramble to my feet. The woman has a smile on her face even though she's stunned, convulsing on the floor. Her eyes are open, flipping back and forth between us, and there's a little scar under one of them, like a scratch of moonlight.

47

We follow the glow of reflected light, three turns, straight ahead. Now we're out of the maze, in a music room with a gilt spinet. A tropical jungle mural is painted on all four walls, lush and colorful, bright birds peeking through the brushstroke undergrowth. There's a door in each wall. We head for the one straight ahead.

The lights are on. Finally, finally, the lights are on again.

"We'll get them," I whisper. We're clinging to each other, stumble-running like a couple of drunks. "We'll find them; it'll be okay."

But I don't know that. *When we get out,* Jules said, like it's a foregone conclusion. It's not. It's wishful thinking.

A voice, soft and singsong, drifts after us out of the hall of mirrors.

"Aurélieeee."

I let go of Lilly and surge ahead. Rip open the doors of the music room. Step into a gallery. It runs perpendicular to the music room, like the crossbar on a T. There's another door straight across from me. And about thirty feet away, at the end of the gallery: people. Way too many people.

It's a triangle formation of trackers, waiting like inky statues.

Dorf and Miss Sei are next to them, sitting at a table in high-backed gilt chairs, like they're posing for a portrait. Miss Sei's legs are crossed elegantly. Dorf's hand is resting on the marble tabletop. They both have guns.

I freeze. Right in the middle of the gallery, like a deer caught in headlights. Behind me, still in the music room, Lilly does, too.

"Anouk," Dorf calls out, and his voice echoes, deep and final, like a funeral bell.

The trackers start toward me. Three steps and they've accelerated to full speed. They're flashing past Dorf and Miss Sei, straight for me.

They haven't seen Lilly. She's still in the music room. I have a split second to make a decision.

"Lilly?" I keep my voice low, without turning. "Get back, *go, RUN!*"

And I throw myself forward across the gallery. I burst through the doors opposite, spin, start closing them. I see Lilly through the narrowing crack. She's running back through the music room toward the hall of mirrors—

I slam my doors, kick in the floor peg. Something massive crashes against them, rattling the hinges. I run blindly into the next room, the next, not even trying to lock anything after me. *This was your idea, Anouk. This whole thing, it was your stupid plan, and now we're separated, waiting to be picked off like ducks on a carnival conveyor belt.*

The doors to the gallery crash open. They're catching up. I dive behind a sofa, coughing, gasping.

Four trackers burst in. I empty my clip into them. When I stand, there are four bodies on the floor. My hands are shaking

"Lilly?" I whisper to the empty room. But Lilly's gone. I'm on my own.

Palais du Papillon—112 feet below, 1790

A serving woman, huge as an ogress, leads me back to my chambers. Her face is a weary mask, her apron filthy. She smells of onions and dirt and sour milk, and yet I feel a strange sort of companionship with her as we trudge up staircases, through chamber after opulent chamber, these treasure rooms of ruby, jet, and emerald. She held a blindfold when she came for me, and perhaps she meant to use it, but she took one look at my reddened eyes and twisted it into her fist. I suppose I should be grateful for this kindness. Or perhaps *she* should be grateful, for had she tried to bind my eyes, I might have scratched out hers.

A cold, iron numbness has taken hold of me and settled into my bones. Somewhere deep inside I feel rage, hot enough to melt glass, but I cannot reach it. I stare straight ahead of me, and I try to keep my feet moving, try to forget the cracking of my heart, Mama's face when she cried out to me.

We arrive at my chambers. The serving woman unlocks the door and stands aside. She is so still, a great brooding mountain, delicate and hulking both at once. I turn to face her, my eyes pleading.

"Madam," I say quickly. "Madam, I beg of you, let me—"

But she will not look at me. She lowers her head and pushes me hurriedly through the doors. I hear them slam shut, the wrench of the lock sliding home.

I slide to the floor and lie in a heap. Still I do not cry. I feel as though I could, feel a strained cord of muscle in my chest, fit to snap, but no tears will fall. All I can think is: *We must get away from here. Delphine, Bernadette, Charlotte, Jacques, me. We must escape.*

Jacques finds me this way and pulls me upright, crushing me to him. "They are mad here," I whisper, and bury my face in his collar. Only now do the tears come, hot and endless, wetting the linen of his shirt.

"I know," he says, but he doesn't. He cannot know the depths of their madness. I try to explain to him what I saw, what has become of Mama.

He holds me more tightly with every word, and when I am finished there is no shock or outrage from him. Only grim, weary determination. "It is not just *la marchioness* Célestine," he says, and I stiffen. "We found Marie-Clair in a chamber near the edge of the palace. She was barely sixteen, one of the youngest. They had emptied her of blood, taken parts of her, and that pale thing in the room . . . Monsieur Vallé saw it walking today in the western wing, free as you like. He said it turned to look at him, and its face opened like a wound. They are *keeping it*—"

I push away from him, straightening. "You are here," I say, steadying my voice and steadying my chin. "That is what matters. I trust your arrival in my chambers means you know the way out?"

Jacques almost smiles at that. Through the grime and the tiredness, his eyes become merry and warm. "Always straight to business goes Aurélie du Bessancourt. You should be a shopkeeper." His gaze darkens again. "I have found your sisters, yes. They are safe and as well as can be hoped. And I have found a way out. We will go today. Now, if you will allow it."

"If I allow it?" I am laughing now, though my tears have not yet dried. "You tell me this now, when you might have told me the moment you stepped inside? Of course I will allow it, you great oaf! Havriel and Father will be distracted. They will not expect an escape. We must hurry!"

Jacques nods, but he remains where he is. He disentangles himself from me and says, "I have something for you," and ducks his head. "Before we go."

I pause, peering at him. I see us both in the mirrored window, a tall boy and a tall girl, and I see him open his hand. In it is a flower, dried and pressed. A daisy. He lays it gently in my palm. "It was left behind by another servant—" Jacques twists his hands together, stumbling over his words. "I know it is not the time, but I wanted you to have it. There is a good woman, a tavern keeper on the outskirts of Péronne, a friend of my mother's. I thought you might hide there until transportation can be arranged. Her inn stands in a field, off the Rue de Maismont. By the millpond, do you know the place? There are many more daisies there. Well . . . I thought . . . Let this one be a promise."

The flower rests in my palm, dry and delicate. I can smell the warm tinge of straw from it. A memory blooms in my mind of Mama and my sisters and me, lying in a meadow, sunlight falling through the apple trees and dappling our faces. I do know the millpond. We went there once, in better days, with a picnic and silver forks and a painter with a great easel and a hundred daubs of vivid color.

I tuck the flower into my sash. I clasp Jacques's hands,

and I smile at him, and he does not smile back, but grins, his face folding like an accordion. And though we both know the worst is still ahead—there is running to do now, and fighting—a flame kindles under my tired heart, and in the light of it, all the ills of the world seem suddenly small and far away.

Together we move toward the panel in the wall

"Are you with me?" Jacques says.

"I am with you," I answer, and we step into the servants' passageway and begin to run.

48

You're dumb, Anouk. You're dumb, and now you're alone.

I slide around a door into a bare, unpainted antechamber and slam in the floor peg. Up ahead is another double door. I burst through them. Close them behind me as quietly as I can. I scan for a way to lock them. There isn't one. From this side they're just panels of pale-green brocade, two brass rings for handles.

I spin. I'm in another one of these people's pointless ballrooms. The floor is ivory-hued marble, veined with black like dirty snow. The ceiling soars forty feet above me, the chandeliers glowing bright. The walls are a mass of stone carvings and alcoves full of animal sculptures. A row of tall golden candelabras extends down both sides of the gallery.

I run for the nearest candelabra and grab it. Wedge it into the brass rings on the door. Jiggle it once to make sure it'll hold. Whirl and start sprinting for the opposite end.

I don't know if I'm close to the perimeter of the palace, if this is a trap room, but it's too late to worry about that now. I'm halfway down it, running like a crazy person.

A sharp crack sounds behind me as the floor peg in the antechamber breaks.

Something's been following me. Don't know what, don't know who, but it might be Miss Sei, it might be Dorf. They're probably already at the door I came through. I go up on my tiptoes, trying to quiet the squeak of my shoes on the marble. The ballroom is way too long. That candelabra won't hold forever. If they have a gun, I'll be dead before I'm three-fourths of the way down it.

Whatever's outside begins banging hard and fast. The candelabra groans.

I slip to the side of the ballroom, looking around frantically for a side door.

With a ringing *snap*, one of the prongs on the candelabra breaks, spinning into the air.

I won't make it to the end. There's no other way out. Soft and quick I shimmy up onto a ledge in the wall. My toes find the curling gilt. My fingers grip the moldings.

I pull myself up silently. I'm a moderately good climber with harnesses and carabiners and a climbing partner waiting to rope me down when I slip. I'm an even better climber when running for my life.

My lungs heave. Every few feet along the wall are pillars, holding up the corners of the vaults. Each pillar is topped with a plinth. Each plinth has a tiny overhang. Maybe six inches of space. I make for the one closest to me, climbing spread-eagled along the wall. I'm high up now. If I fall, I'll break bones.

I hear the candelabra snapping again. I brace myself. Muscles tense. I leap.

For a millisecond I'm suspended in the air, high up in that hallway of gold and marble. Now my hand catches on the overhang and I swing. My fingers almost wrench out of their sockets. I smack my other hand onto the ledge and lift myself up. Gasp for breath. There's not enough space to rest. Sweat is dripping down my forehead, stinging my eyes.

Without another thought, I launch myself off the plinth.

I'm going for the chandelier. The huge rack of gold and crystal balloons in front of me. I slam into it, and the chandelier swings dangerously. I realize too late that it's set up like a shell, hollow on the inside. I'm slipping through strands of crystal, falling into the center of the chandelier—

I flail, reaching for anything I can hold on to. My fingers wrap around the golden frame. My foot finds one of the tines, and my fall jerks to a halt. I hear the doors to the ballroom burst open. I see the floor bobbing below. Nausea sweeps over me. *Don't be sick. You don't have time to be sick.*

The woman in the red dress is hurtling down the ballroom. I see her through the tinkling crystal beads, her gown swirling across the marble.

Did she see me jump? I glance around. My toes are fitted on either side of the lower bubble of beads. The woman's directly below me, sweeping away the fallen bits of crystal, murmuring.

"Aurélie?" Her voice echoes up to me. *"Aurélie, ne me quitte pas. . . ."*

I feel like I might sneeze. I remember watching a YouTube clip once where a bowler-wearing guy explained how you could stop yourself from sneezing by licking the top of your mouth, so I do that, running my tongue frantically over the arch of my mouth.

Below me, the woman throws back her head. Lets loose a series of hawking, raptor-like cries:

"Aurélie! Aurélie!"

She's looking straight up at my chandelier. The ropes of crystal cut the scene below into ribbons. I hear running. Pounding. The woman stiffens. Now she leaps away, racing for the far end of the ballroom like some sort of red gazelle. She skitters through the doors. I stay where I am, trying to steady my breathing, the shivering beads.

Trackers are filing into the ballroom through the green doors. A swarm of them, glistening black and tiny red lights. They're passing under me—

The gilt prong I'm standing on is bending. I feel the chandelier shiver around me.

"No," I whisper. "No!"

The prong snaps. I'm sliding through the crystal threads. They're breaking against my back. I'm falling, tumbling through the air.

I slam against the floor so hard, it's like a white spark exploding in the center of my skull. My brain goes out before my eyes do. I see a pair of velvet shoes approaching between all those black boots—old-fashioned block heels, bows red as poppies. And now a second pair arrives, plain and dark, standing next to the first.

"Welcome home, Anouk."

Palais du Papillon—
112 feet below, 1790

The servants' passages are mirrored, floor, wall, ceiling. It is an odd sensation, like running down the neck of a lengthy glass bottle. The ceiling is low, the walls uncomfortably close.

"They are in the western wing," Jacques says, breathless, and we turn a corner, my skirts billowing behind me. "The exit is at the northernmost point of the palace, in the *salle d'opéra*. Your sisters are very nearby."

"Why did they ever separate us?" I whisper. "What was the point?"

He looks at me over his shoulder, a wry smile on his lips. "No doubt to avoid this happening. You all conspiring together to escape. Little good it did them."

He says it lightly, but there is tenseness to his face, and fear, and I do not understand it, for I feel nothing but excitement.

We leave the servants' passages behind us, stepping through the false back of an armoire into a room like a

Parisian sweet box. The pillows are colored like petits fours, soft and lovely, the sofas fat as winter rabbits. We hurry to the doors. Jacques presses his ear to the wood. I wait impatiently. Now he nods quickly, and we slip out into a gallery, hurrying down it.

The palace feels frighteningly empty around us, dead and lovely. Candles flicker in the chandeliers overhead, thousands upon thousands of them. I think I hear something in the air, a distant thrum, like a single buzzing note.

"Jacques, do you hear that?" I whisper, and I almost cough, I have so little breath to spare.

"What?" he asks, and together we slow.

"That sound?"

"The air is strange down here. Hurry."

We reach the end of the hall and wriggle into another hidden passage. It ends in a servants' quarters, a warren of dank little rooms, lit only with the occasional guttering lamp. We pass rows of empty shelves, a basket of vegetables, rotting into puddles of dark liquid, a kitchen, a blackened oven with no fire inside. No one is here. It feels as though no one has been here for some time, though surely that cannot be.

My legs begin to ache from running. I have hardly done more than pace and brood for months, and now my body rebels. Jacques's gaze is fixed ahead, as if he is following some thread only he can see. He pauses from time to time and flattens his back against the mirrored wall. There is no sound but our own breathing. Even the hideous, waspish buzz is gone, and in its wake is less than silence, an absolute, deadening void.

We leave the serving passageway through a hinged portrait and step out directly in front of a blue-and-black lacquered door.

"It will be locked—" I start, but Jacques draws a key from his pocket, ornate and toothy. The head is a butterfly, made of iron.

"One of the master keys," he says, and I want to ask him where he got it, but he is already inserting it, the lock clicking back, the door yawning open. And there are my sisters, sprawled across the furniture of a gloomy boudoir. They are rather unkempt. Charlotte has overturned a chair, and is poking her head from under it like a mouse from its hole. Bernadette lies on the bed and does not move. Delphine stands huddled against a small rocking horse. Her little gown is ripped at the sleeve. It has been stitched up with a caterpillar of bad sewing, as if one of the girls tried to mend it herself.

I run to her and drag her to her feet.

"Delphine," I say, crying and hugging her neck. "Delphine, are you well? Come to me, all of you, come! We are going now! We are leaving!"

They approach me cautiously, and I gather them up, and the four of us clutch each other, kneeling on the floor like a swaying, many-armed beast. They make hardly a sound as I embrace them, simply cling to me. Even Bernadette, who before would not have embraced me for all the jewels of Spain, does so now, weeping quietly into my shoulder.

"We are going, my sisters, *oui?*" I murmur. "Upstairs."

I look at Jacques. He stands by the door, smiling.

I pull my sisters to their feet and turn them toward him. "This is Jacques," I say, lifting Delphine to my hip. "He is our friend. Put on your shoes and let us go. Quickly, and not a word, yes?"

Delphine tries to say something I cannot hear. She repeats herself, twice, a third time, her voice oddly stretched and cooing, as if she has forgotten how to speak. "Where is Mama?"

"Mama is not here," I say, and I look up at the ceiling, because I cannot bear to look at Delphine. "She has gone up ahead of us, she—"

A sound behind me stops my lying tongue: a light step, deeper in the chambers.

I clutch Delphine to me and look over my shoulder. "Bernadette?" I say, and my insides twist. "Bernadette, are you alone here?"

The hum is back, that twitching, intoxicating whine, the sound of a thousand nervous bees, boiling within their hive.

"Bernadette?" I whisper frantically.

She turns to me, her eyes wide. Her back is to the door into the boudoir, and one of her hands is clutching at something, a fine toy that seems to be made of bone: a butterfly. The buzzing rises, crawling into my ears. I take hold of Delphine's hand—"Bernadette, take your sister. Follow Jacques, quickly!"

Someone is there. In the doorway behind Bernadette, someone is standing, a small figure in livery, red and gold, and his face, oh heavens, *his face.* . . .

49

I wake up in an enormous bed. Cupids stare down at me from the corners of the canopy, blank eyed and creepy, like they want to eat my face. Red velvet curtains are drawn around the bed, dimming the light on the other side. A thick, embroidered comforter lies heavily across my chest. And I'm clean. So clean my skin feels like a peeled egg. All that sweat, blood, and grime—all gone.

I lie for a second, reveling. My bones feel weird, like they've started to gel, like they haven't moved in ages.

I blink a few times. Wrinkle my nose.

I fell out of a chandelier.

The thought comes to me slowly. Now the next one: the bed smells awful. Like dust, and locked-up sheets, and the time I had to render my own soap out of cow fat during summer camp in Wyoming. It wasn't fun. I didn't stay long. I don't want to stay here long, either. I hear the hiss of gas lamps. The flat, no-sound air.

I'm still underground. They caught me. But why haven't they killed me yet?

My eyes flick from side to side. I hear the tick of a clock somewhere beyond the drawn curtains. I imagine someone sitting in a chair right next to the bed, waiting. Waiting for me.

I sit up slowly, soundlessly, pushing back the comforter. I'm wearing an old-fashioned nightgown. Frills and white cotton and persimmon-seed buttons. My hair's been washed. The cut on my ankle is still exposed, an ugly scab. That's disturbing. Someone washed my hair and dressed me up like a pilgrim, but they didn't bandage my ankle?

I glance around quickly. The curtains are open slightly on either side, letting in a sliver of light and air. I see the corner of a carpet. The leg of a chair.

In one smooth motion I slide out through the curtains. My bare feet hit the floor. I spin, staring around the room. I need to find 1) Something to use as a weapon. 2) Someone to use it on. There's plenty of the first. None of the second. I like that arrangement.

I grab a candlestick from the mantel and pull the gnarled stump of wax off it. There's a long, mean spike where the candle was skewered. I heft the candlestick and pad across the carpet to the other side of the bed. I see a big old armoire, a double door in the far wall, a mirror.

I move toward the mirror, staring at myself. My hair's been pushed up under a white cap. My eyes are huge and ghostly in my face. I feel like I can see every vein in my irises, every strand of dark blue and light blue and gray—

"Aurélie?"

Something behind me moves.

I whirl, raise the candlestick. A man is standing in the corner of the room. He's been there all along. He's huge, face painted chalk white, wearing a red brocade coat and poppy-red shoes.

"Aurélie?" he says softly. "Aurélie, *retourné de l'autre coté de la mer?*"

I run at him like a freaking psycho. Slash out with the candlestick. The spike snips at his waistcoat. He jerks back, fast for someone so large.

"Who are you?" It hurts to talk. My lungs heave, and

a sharp pain like nothing I've ever felt before spreads across my chest. I might have cracked a rib.

The man stares at me. His eyes are weird. Quivering, watery, but under it is a sharpness. A watchfulness.

I slash out again, and this time the spike catches him and rips a ragged gash down his waistcoat. He shrinks, cowering against the wall. He's crazy. Everyone here is crazy.

"Stay back," I say in French, moving. I keep the spike pointed at his chest. "There's another girl down here. Lilly Watts. And three boys. One of them's crazy. Have you caught them?"

The man's eyes are tiny in his powdered face. It's like they don't even belong to him, like there's a small animal looking out from behind the folds of human flesh. He's breathing hard.

"Answer me!" I yell. "Why are you doing this? Is this some kind of sick game? Throw a bunch of kids in with some bionic men and deformed monsters and enjoy the spectacle?"

His breathing slows. His eyes fix on mine. And now the quivering is gone, replaced by the tiniest slither of derision. "Game?" he says. "My dear, this is not a game."

His hand comes up. There's a bottle in it, a tiny vial. It snaps between his fingers, and a rich, sharp tang hits my nose. Hits my brain. I'm tipping, falling. The candlestick is ripped from my grasp.

The man is leaning over me, screaming: "Havriel? Havriel, quickly!"

This can't be happening. I'm on the floor. My hand finds a chair leg and I pull myself up.

I hear running footsteps. I heave myself onto the chair, my head lolling, my muscles suddenly useless. The doors to the bedroom fly open.

The man who enters is dressed in black. Black velvet knee breeches, black stockings, a long black frock coat. I recognize his calm gray eyes. The way he drifts along, great as a giant, but elegant. Like a dancer.

"Anouk," Dorf says. He bows slightly. "Lovely to see you again."

The accent I couldn't place before comes into sharp focus. French. Oddly curled and old-fashioned, but definitely French.

I feel sick. I feel like I need to crawl back into the bed and pull the covers over my head and sleep until it's all over and done. "Dorf," I whisper. "Dorf, why are you doing this? Why are we here?" I stand, wobbly. *Why do you want to kill us? Why did Hayden come back from the dead? Why-why-why* . . .

He's watching me, his gaze hooded, like I'm some exotic display behind glass. Now he turns to the other man and murmurs something. I catch the words *"fille"* and *"parcourt."*

He wheels around again. "Anouk. Where are your friends?"

Well, that answers my first question. They don't know where the others are. They think I do. That's why I'm still alive.

"Dorf—" I start.

"I am not Dorf," he snaps. "Dorf does not exist. I am Havriel du Bessancourt."

"Who?"

"And this . . ." he says, motioning to the other man, "is the Marquis Frédéric du Bessancourt. My brother."

I stare at them. At their centuries-old clothing, their weird hair and stockings.

"There are no Bessancourts anymore," I mumble. "It's an obsolete title, and Frédéric du Bessancourt is *dead*. He's been dead for centuries."

"Has he? Did you hear that, brother? You are dead. Anouk has spoken, and she knows all."

What is going on? I see the shattered displays in Rabbit Gallery again, the white chunks of glass covering the floor. The brass plaques, gleaming.

H. B.

Death by H. B.

Bombs by H. B.

Poison by H. B.

And the lists of names in the cracked, leather-bound volume in the study. That's what was bugging me: the handwriting was the same. From 1760 up until now. More than two hundred fifty years, and the handwriting never changed.

This is impossible.

Dorf, Havriel, whoever he is, breathes in deeply. "Now, my dear . . ."

He goes to a panel in the wall and folds out a glossy metal case, dark sharp corners incongruous with the décor of the room. He snaps it open. A barbed nozzle slides into view, the sharp tip glinting silver. "Won't you sit down? I think it's time we had a little chat."

Palais du Papillon—Chambres du Morelle Noir—
112 feet below, 1790

The figure stands in the doorway, motionless. He is small as a child, but his skin is pale and hard, as if he wears a mask of marble veneer. He is dressed in a frock coat, sharply cleaved at the back into two crimson prongs, a velvet swallow's tale. His hands are at his sides, tiny like a doll's hands, and in one of them he carries a little case, dark wood with many locks.

"Jacques?" The word escapes me in a strangled whisper.

Jacques remains stock-still. "All will be well," he says, but I hear the tremble in his voice, the coursing fear. "He is our ally. He knows of our predicament. He has promised to help you escape."

The whine in the air becomes deafening, wave after wave crashing over me. It seems to be peeling apart the strands of my brain, sifting through my thoughts and fears like they are berries in a basket. It comes from the figure in the doorway. Slowly, long red slits open down his cheeks and across his neck. They are not wounds. They are surgically precise, as if he was made this way, as if the human head was too foolish and this is better.

"It was the only way," Jacques says. "The only way I knew—"

The figure is still in the doorway, watching us, and I seem to detect amusement in those bottomless black eyes, a spark of malice.

"Who are you?" I say to him, and I turn Delphine's head away, shielding her with my arms. "What are you?"

50

"I'm not telling." The smell from the tiny bottle is still in my nose, rich and oily, like blood oranges and musk. We're sitting across from each other, me in a wing chair, him perched on a hard wooden stool, languid but somehow tense at the same time, like a cat waiting to pounce. "I'm not telling you where the others are. You can kill me if you want to, but I'm not snitching."

Havriel turns the nozzle over in his hands. His rain-cloud eyes are fixed on me, measuring me up, tallying every twitch and sign of weakness in my face. "You may not know where they are."

"Oh, I know." I don't know. I don't have a clue.

"Have they been captured?"

"Nope. Still running free."

Havriel turns on the stool, pressing a finger to his ear and gesturing to the marquis, who is still standing, hovering nervously. *"Trois,"* he whispers.

Three. So they don't have Lilly yet. They don't have anyone, except that one genius who climbed into a chandelier. But this doesn't at all guarantee that the others are still alive.

"Let's make a deal," he says. "You tell me *exactly* where the others are, and I will tell you everything you wish to know."

"I won't," I say. "What's the point of knowing everything and then dying two seconds later?"

Havriel turns again to his brother. Says something I don't catch. They titter. They're laughing at me, heads together, like a couple of freakish, waistcoated clowns.

"You still hope to escape," Havriel says, and his eyes dance. He taps the nozzle thoughtfully against his knee.

I stare at its needlelike tip and try to swallow. "Yes?" I say.

"Very well," he says. "I will answer all your questions *and* I will let you go, and you can run away back to New York City and live happily ever after."

He flips a small switch on the nozzle's handle. A red light blinks on. He's going to kill me. He knows it, and I know it, and he's grinning at me like: *You're not this stupid, Anouk. We don't need to play this game.*

But I can play stupid as well as anyone if it buys me time. I don't know where the others are. I have nothing to lose by agreeing, except for maybe some metaphorical points in selfless nobility, but I'm not super attached to those anyway. If he talks long enough, maybe I can think up a way to get out of this room.

"Okay," I say. "You first."

He blinks at me. Studies the instrument in his hand as if he's considering using it right this very instant. When he looks back at me, his expression is infinitely less sympathetic. "You say you wish to know the truth. The reasons behind everything. But you will not understand. You will find it difficult."

"You think?" Fury, blistering hot, scalds my throat. "Yes, I find it hard to understand why you think you can drag us down here and kill us, yes, that's HARD TO UNDERSTAND."

Dorf clicks his tongue. "So angry," he says. "Whenever people fail to understand things they always become so *livid*. You must realize that just because you are too foolish to understand something does not mean it makes no sense. You are not here for nothing. And you are not dying for nothing. You are dying so we can live."

"What are you, the Countess of Báthory, bathing in the blood of virgins for eternal youth? I hate to break it to you, but that's not—"

"Anouk, be quiet," Havriel snaps, and there's a razor edge to his voice. "Listen for once, and keep your clever bits of skepticism to yourself. All five of you carry in your veins a priceless genetic code. It has no outward effects on you. If not extracted and activated, it will pass into dormancy between the eighteenth and twentieth years of your life. These genes have the ability to regenerate human cells. In essence, biological immortality."

Okay, that was a lot. I don't have any clever bits of skepticism. At all.

Havriel isn't finished. "The genes were stolen from us. Injected into the bloodstreams of your ancestors and allowed to escape. The one who invented it refuses to cooperate. Entire labs of scientists cannot replicate the genes. So we find the carriers still in existence, just a few at a time, and we harvest them. Every fifty to seventy years, we require more. Fresh blood. We, the brothers du Bessancourt, have lived nearly five hundred years combined, and I'm afraid the only way we can keep living is by carving up your pretty young bodies and extracting every drop of the precious cargo inside you."

I stand perfectly still. I feel like the room is tipping around me, or maybe I'm tipping, falling. "Who?" I say. "Who allowed the carriers to escape?"

"Don't act like you don't know." Dorf's eyes pin me to the chair. "The same one who cut the camera feed, helped you escape the trap rooms, holed you up somewhere we couldn't find, massacred our teams. He has been helping you from the moment he realized you had breached the palace."

The butterfly man. He's talking about the butterfly man. "We haven't seen him," I say. "I swear, we never met him once."

"No?" Havriel seems to calm down again. His gaze softens. "He was always a shy creature. Self-conscious. He hates us, you know. He is our crowning achievement, and yet he is a great danger. A liability and a blessing, in one. My brother became obsessed with immortality long ago. He was terrified of disease and revolted by death and dying. And when he realized it was beyond his grasp to find a cure for this most human ailment, that eighteenth-century science could never hope to unlock life's secrets, he created something that could. An artificial human. Perfect and logical, unfettered by the physical and mental limitations of man."

Perfect? The thing that clawed the walls outside the library, killed the trackers in complete silence, burned Perdu's arm open? That was perfection?

Havriel keeps talking: "Our butterfly man, we called him. We grew him in a glass cocoon, *killed* to make him. His skin is as delicate as an insect's wing, fragile as paper, but he is more powerful than any man. He can calculate possibilities and variables into infinity, invent technological wonders. He made us rich beyond measure.

"When the Lady Célestine was killed, he began to develop this serum for eternal life. But the serum was not ready, and even if it had been, its effects on those already dead was incalculable. Lady Célestine became something else, neither living nor dead. And now the butterfly man keeps her—to taunt Frédéric, and he keeps his other pet alive, too, but he shares not a drop of his serum with us. So you see, he is the reason for this great ruse and the cause of this bloodshed. If you are angry at your fate, blame him."

"None of this works." I feel pathetic, but I say it

anyway. "Artificial people, fine, whatever, but you can't live that long, okay? The body breaks down; it's called cellular senescence. The second law of thermodynamics. It doesn't *work*, and even if it did, you can't just kill other people so you can live. You can't go around kidnapping and murdering just because you feel like it—" I'm rubbing frantically at the side of my nightgown, my skin burning. "None of this is possible, okay? Scientifically it's not *possible*."

"Everything you dream of is possible, Anouk. Sometimes you have simply dreamed too soon."

I watch him lift the nozzle and step toward me.

"What are the greatest mysteries, do you think?" he asks. "Life, of course. And death. We have solved them." He smiles, quick and pointed, his lips curling back from his teeth with a wet sound. "But for everything there is a price. You."

Palais du Papillon, Chambres du Morelle Noir— 112 feet below, 1790

The creature speaks, the cuts in his face flaring wide, glistening like the sliced bellies of eels.

"*Bonjour,*" he says, and his voice is thin, sharp, almost pitiful: a childish whimper that only adds to the wrongness of him. He makes me think of a bird spliced with a man, an insect dressed in a coat of human skin.

I look at Jacques pleadingly. He stands no more than four steps away, but in this dead, electric space it feels like an ocean. We cannot reach each other. *He is not on our side,* I want to scream. *You said so yourself; he is evil!*

"Who are you?" I say again, louder. "Answer me!"

"They call me their butterfly man," the creature says. He sounds shy, and as he speaks he lifts one of his small hands to his face, as if to hide it. His eyes glimmer from between his fingers, black pools without pupil and without iris. "They said if I helped them, they would make me whole. They would

love me, fix my ruined flesh. I could leave this place, be free."
His voice slips up, high and piercing. "They lied."

I begin edging over the floor toward the door to the hallway. Jacques shakes his head, his face crumpled in agony.

"Jacques," I whisper. "We cannot trust him. Bernadette,
take your sister. Run, *run, all of you, GET AWAY!*"

I clutch Delphine and dash toward the door.

Jacques is yelling. Charlotte screams. The butterfly man
hardly moves, only turns his hands, palms outward, and
there is a flash of blinding white light, unfurling toward
me. Something immensely hot strikes me, and I stumble,
Delphine slipping from my grasp. The air is forced from my
lungs.

"Aurélie," the butterfly man says. "Why do you run
from me?"

Jacques is bounding toward me, but he approaches so
slowly, as if through water or a dream. I am gasping in
pain, vivid clouds of colored ink blossoming across my
vision.

"Do you fear me?" the butterfly man says, and I see he is
smiling at me, a false, studied smile, as horrible to behold as
the splits in his skin. "The others fear me, too. Frédéric cannot bear the sight of me, though he is my father. Havriel is

disgusted by me. They want me only as a tool for their own wicked schemes. Even the servants, when I strap them to my table, shriek and cover their eyes."

"Please let us go," I whisper. "We want nothing from you. We—"

"But you do want something from me." The butterfly man is standing directly before me, the force of his presence like a horrid iron weight. One hand drifts toward me. When it touches my cheek, my skin aches as if I have been pricked. I bring my fingertips up. They come away bloody. "Jacques Renaud has made a bargain. His service in return for your freedom."

"You're lying," I say, but in the same sick moment, I realize he is not.

Jacques has reached me. He takes my arm, whispers in my ear: "I will find another way, Aurélie. Go to the inn, ask for Madame Desjardin, and tell her Margeaux's son sent you, tell her you are a friend—"

The butterfly man's dark glow intensifies. Pain opens like a white-hot rose inside my skull. "Do not speak," he says, his voice like a spike. "Listen to me. You will be my comrades." He smiles again, his expression unreadable. "All of you."

Jacques moves in front of me. "I will kill you if you lay a

finger on them. The deal was for me. I would serve you, and the Bessancourt sisters would go free; that was your promise!"

"Promises are like bones," the butterfly man says. "Easily broken."

Somewhere I hear Delphine crying, my sisters calling out. I feel the flutter of my heartbeat, wild through my bodice. And suddenly Jacques goes flying to the side, as if glancing off an invisible wall.

"No," says the butterfly man. "You will not."

I stumble backward, my hands finding Bernadette's, Charlotte's. I gather my sisters behind me, lifting weeping Delphine again to my hip. Jacques stands and pushes in front of us. But he has begun to bleed, tiny cuts forming on his head and neck.

"You must get away. I *will* find you— I'm sorry, Aurélie," he says through clenched teeth.

"*Jacques!*" I scream. I push Delphine into Bernadette's arms and lunge. The pain strikes me like a savage headwind, but I grit my teeth against it, pressing into this strange darkness, one foot, then another. My hand finds Jacques. "Leave him!" I beg the butterfly man. "Please, what are you doing? *Let him be!*"

But the butterfly man does not hear me, or else he does not care to listen. I pull at Jacques with all my strength. He will not move, and with a start, I see his feet no longer touch the floor. He is hanging in the air, the toes of his boots inches above the carpet. His muscles are straining, but he cannot move. Only his eyes stir. And his lips.

And even though he is bleeding, he smiles, and I see him sitting on a stool in a grimy cottage, his sisters and brothers hanging from his shoulders and bouncing on his knees. His mother sits by a little stove, her knitting needles going *clack-clack*, and sage and lavender are drying in the rafters, and a cat stretches in the sunlight from the window, and Jacques is smiling, just like that. But as I watch, his smile breaks. His skin drains of life and color, freezing gray and blue like a field in deepest winter.

I grasp his fingers, try to pull him down, crying and screaming.

"Aurélie," the butterfly man says, close to my ear. "You will be my ally in this long, slow game. And you." He nods toward Jacques. A deep, rumbling cloud seems to strike me, strike us all, and I am drifting backward, my hair floating around my face. I watch as the butterfly man folds Jacques into his horrible embrace and draws him away from me. "You are nameless. You are lost."

Vous êtes perdu.

51

"You were very difficult to track down, you know." Havriel is seated casually, his shoe buckles gleaming, artifacts from a different time. I hear the metallic glide of the nozzle's tube, dragging over the floor as he fiddles with the head, passing it from hand to hand. "Adopted."

I ignore the bait. I'm not discussing my parents with him. "You didn't have to do all this," I say quietly. "You didn't have to go through all this trouble if we're just bodies for you to harvest."

He looks up at the ceiling. "But you are not simply bodies. Haven't you realized that yet? There were no other candidates. No elimination rounds. We have been hunting you, and others like you, all these years. From France to Mumbai to Wellington to San Diego. All this time you have been asking: *Why me? Why me?* Because you are a Bessancourt, Anouk. You are a part of the family."

"I'm not related to you," I spit. "I'm not a friggin' Bessancourt—"

But I'm seeing it now: Tall kids. Blue eyes. *Maybe we have something else in common? Something we don't even know about* . . . I feel the pieces grinding together, meshing in place.

Havriel laughs. "You don't know *who* you are, so why be upset? Now you know exactly where you belong. You know exactly what your purpose is."

It feels like my entrails are sliding through me, pooling around my bare feet. "My purpose?" I say. "My purpose is to die miserably so you can keep existing forever?"

Havriel doesn't answer. It's like he blanked me out right there. I need to stall. Once he stops talking to me, he's going to kill me.

"Even if we are related," I say, my toes digging into the carpet. "You guys fly us here, let us eat at your table, send us entire folders full of lies. You could have just stolen us off the street. Stuffed us in a van, knocked us out with some chloroform. We never had to meet."

"But I wanted to meet you!" says Havriel. "As times become less desperate, there becomes space for formality; as in society, so also in families. And so for this harvest, we devised a little . . . a little party. You must understand that despite how you may view the situation, you are not simply victims. You are our offspring, our precious progeny. So we found a way to connect you to your rightful place in this world, letting you know a little, not too much and not nothing at all, letting you meet others of your kind within your ancestral home."

"So, basically, you murder us *after* dinner. And I thought *my* family was dysfunctional."

Havriel crosses his legs in a quick, sharp motion. He doesn't seem to appreciate his thinking being questioned.

"Anouk, we are entirely functional. We are like a great machine, our family. My brother and I are the engine. You are the fuel. We extended to you the honor due you as scions of a noble bloodline. We gave you every comfort. Brandy in the bathroom. Dinner. A private jet. We treated you with respect. We needed you as close to the Palais du Papillon as possible, as the harvesting of the genes is a complex process and must be handled quickly and delicately after death of the donors—"

I snort. "It's not a donation if you rob the freaking bank."

Havriel ignores me. "And Frédéric does not like to

leave the *palais*. He can no longer abide the surface with its many contagions. So what better way than to bring you here in style, give you a proper send-off, make you all feel special and important, as if you were picked for something great. Because you were. Don't you see? You are a very valuable person, Anouk."

The words ignite something in me, a pathetic, involuntary response. I look at him in surprise and stupid hope.

"Your death paves the way for our family's continued success and dominance. It is not in vain."

The hope vanishes. *What about my life? What about who* I *want to be?*

"And the Sapanis? They're just a front? An alias?"

"The Sapanis are what we called ourselves as we reemerged from the palace during the Reign of Terror. We could not gain a footing in France under the Bessancourt name. We did not wish to emigrate. And so before we went into hiding, we devised a plan. We signed the château and its grounds and all our monies over to the brothers Wilhelm and Ehrfurcht Sapani. Ourselves. Twenty years later, we started anew under Napoleon. We opened a gunsmithy, then an armament factory, and slowly, crawlingly, over the decades and centuries, we rebuilt our dynasty. And now here we are! The most powerful supplier of weapons and technology in the world. They say it's those with the money who make the rules, but really it's those who can steal the money from anyone, any country and government. It is those who are *feared* who make the rules. The truth is, there are no Sapanis. There is no Monsieur Gourbillon finding a crater in the wine cellar, no Project Papillon. My brother is a shy man. We prefer to run our business ventures in private. . . ."

He trails off. His eyes fix on mine, and my blood runs cold. "Now, Anouk. I think we've chatted long enough." He bows his head respectfully, and the silver spike rises, his fingers wrapped around the nozzle like it's the head of a snake. "I will ask you one more time: where are your friends?"

52

Sinking. That's how I feel. Sinking down-down-down, into an endless, crushing blackness. This is too big for me. Too big for all of us. Lilly, Jules, Will, Hayden, and I—we're just tiny, rusty wheels in their huge plan, squeaking desperately. There's no way on earth I'm getting out of here alive.

"I don't think you know where they are," Havriel says. "I think you're lying."

"I do. I know where they are."

"Ah! So tell me. I upheld my end of the bargain."

He gazes at me expectantly across the tip of the nozzle, his eyes glittering.

I hesitate. Just one second, one flicker of confusion while I sort through possible lies I can tell. Havriel sees it. He smiles.

"I'm afraid we'll have to find them on our own,

then. It was lovely speaking to you, my dear."

Behind him, the man in the red coat strikes something—a sharp, crystalline note against one of the figurines on the mantelpiece. My eyes flick toward the sound—

Havriel lunges. Grips my shoulder and tries to spin me, jamming the nozzle toward my spine. I wriggle out of his grasp, knee him in the stomach. Whirl, looking for somewhere to run. The two men are between me and the door. Havriel's moving, the nozzle raised. I dive through the bed curtains. Crawl over the sheets and slip out the other side.

You still think you can escape . . . live happily ever after. No. Not really. But being realistic doesn't get you anywhere. I guess that's just what humans do, keep holding out for something, even if it never comes, even when there's only the tiniest, tiniest hope.

I hear Havriel coming after me. I'm pleased to note he's breathless from my kick, a rasp at the back of his throat. He emerges around the bedpost. I try to dash across the bed again. He catches my ankle and yanks me toward him.

"Do not make this more difficult than it has to be,

Anouk," he spits, and I roll over and kick him in the face with my free foot, over and over again, pummeling his cheeks, his nose. He catches that foot, too. But he has to drop the nozzle to do it. I wrench myself upright, grab the nozzle, and stab the sharp silver tip straight at Havriel.

The spike embeds itself in his shoulder.

He lets go of me with a howl. I launch myself back out the other side of the bed, scramble to my feet, and run for the door.

The marquis is right in my path. I slam into him. I expect him to topple over. At least move backward a few inches. Nope. It's like hitting a sack of bricks. I reel back. He shoves me. I stumble into the center of the room.

Havriel is hulking toward me, one hand clutching the small red puncture in his velvet coat.

I try to stand tall, dig my fingers into my palms. The pain in my rib cage is excruciating. It makes me mad. It makes me proud. *The chandelier didn't kill me. The psycho butterfly thing didn't kill me. Hayden didn't kill me. You're going to kill me, but hey, I made it all the way to the end, boss. That's not too shabby.*

Havriel doesn't even blink. He lashes out with the

nozzle. I duck, drop to the floor, and scrabble away on hands and knees—

And now I hear something behind me, coming from the double doors. The *click-click* of a handle being tried, cautiously.

Havriel kicks me in the shoulder. The pain is unreal, more like a white shower of sparks, like my nerves can't even really deal with that much anymore. I'm reeling, dragging myself over the floor.

The doors are opening.

I look up.

It's Lilly.

No way.

But it is.

Lilly, standing in the doorway, her face filthy, her clothes torn and ragged, grimy with sweat and blood. She's not crying. She's holding an old-fashioned flintlock pistol. She pulls back the hammer and raises it at Havriel.

Seeing her makes me smile like nobody's business. "Shoot Havriel!" I shriek from the floor. "I mean Dorf, *shoot Dorf!*"

The marquis starts toward her from the left. She wheels around, pointing it at him.

I start to crawl for the door. Havriel lets out a low growl and comes after me, fast and liquid like a panther.

Lilly jerks the gun back and forth between them, confused. The marquis is digging something out of his pocket, another glinting bottle—

"Lilly!" I scream. *"SHOOT THEM!"*

The gun goes off. There's a bright flash, a dull cracking sound, and a puff of gray smoke.

Havriel freezes, inches away from me.

Who's been shot?

They're both still standing. I get myself upright. Hobble toward Lilly.

The bottle falls from the marquis's grasp. Bursts against the floor. He brings his hand down to his stomach.

"Aide-moi, mon frère . . . !" the marquis breathes. And he collapses, folding at the knees, the waist, neatly, like a length of fabric.

Lilly points the gun at Havriel. Aims at his leg and pulls the trigger. Nothing happens. She pulls again.

One shot, Lilly. Flintlocks have one shot.

She throws the gun full force at Havriel's head, grabs my arm, and we race out of the room.

I glance back. See Havriel kneeling next to the

marquis, pressing his hand to the wound. He'll be up in a second. Maybe the marquis will be, too. Can these people die from bullet wounds?

We're in a long hallway. It's blazingly bright, and it only seems to get brighter up ahead. Wild, crazy elation bubbles up inside me. I feel weightless. I'm gripping Lilly's hand, and she's got mine, and we're running so fast. We're flying.

"Where are we going?" I shout.

"The boys!" Lilly shouts back. "I found the boys!"

Palais du Papillon—Chambres du Morelle Noir— 112 feet below, 1790

I watch from the ceiling, my gown drifting about me like a pulsing black stain. A girl lies below me. Her body is fetal, her knees drawn up to her chin. A younger girl darts around her, trying desperately to drag the dead girl upright. I see the younger girl's tears, watch her mouth open in a wail, but I do not hear the sound she makes. Everything is silent. Calm and warm, like floating on a pond, in a boat, in summer.

A small, pale man drifts into the scene below, his crimson coattails like twin fangs, or a dark cloven hoof. He is circling the girl on the floor, drawing nearer, nearer.

Aurélie!

It is Delphine. I hear her now. She turns her tear-streaked face and looks up at me, hovering just under the ceiling.

Aurélie, wake up!

The butterfly man leans down over the girl on the floor. His satchel lies open against the wall. He is lifting something out of it, a glass bottle tipped with a long, silvered needle. The bottle's contents pool at its base, black and oozing.

Pain explodes in my arm. I am on the floor again, in the cage of my body, and something is buried in my wrist. White fingers are pressing, pressing a vile serum into my veins, and I see it wriggling below my skin like dark snakes, crawling into me.

A wretched burning sickness rises in my chest. Images flash before my eyes, nightmarish concoctions, empty faces and roiling skies, snippets of sound and color—

I return to consciousness with a gasp. I am lying on the floor of the boudoir, four empty glass bottles lined up beside me, and Bernadette, Charlotte, and Delphine huddled close by, their faces stricken, peering at me through their tears.

I see their arms. I see my own. We all bear the same marks: four red entrance wounds and something spreading away from them, stretching up through our veins like dark trees, branches and tendrils reaching toward our shoulders, our necks, our hearts.

"What has he done?" I whisper. I prop myself onto my elbows, fear rippling through me. "Where is Jacques? Where is he?"

"There are garments here for you to wear. Rise quickly, and change."

I gasp, turning in the direction of the voice. The butterfly man stands by the door to the hall, statue still, eyes fixed on me.

"They will help you go undiscovered."

He gestures, and I see a stack of striped cotton, aprons and bonnets, spotted with age, folded neatly against the skirting board. Servants' clothes, well worn.

"Bring him back!" I cry out, and my voice is a savage, broken wail. "Where is he? What have you done?"

"Do not think of Jacques. Listen to me: you will return to the surface. You will leave France behind you. My masters have been given what they most desire. They will live twenty years longer, perhaps thirty. Then they will die. My discoveries shall be safe from them."

I drag myself to my knees and raise my head. The pain in my arm is fading, but the veins are still darkened, purplish threads swollen grotesquely.

"What have you done to us?" I say to the creature. "What is this?"

Bernadette is beside me, crying and picking at her arm, as if she might somehow pull the veins from her flesh and fling them away.

"I have made you a vessel," the butterfly man says. "A carrier. Were my masters to possess the serum that I have created, they would wish to live a hundred years and a hundred more. I would be held captive to their foolishness, their greedy whims. They would live forever. They could never be sated."

I stand and stagger toward him.

"And so I have put it inside your veins. You and your sisters shall be my strongboxes. You will take it far from here. The wondrous potion shall be passed down through generations, locked away in safety—"

"No . . ." I want to scream the word, but my throat closes. "We do not want your vile discoveries. You cannot do this! Take them yourself and leave!"

"Aurélie," the butterfly man says softly, and his hands go to his face, to the cuts, his fingers moving quickly and nervously across the carved-open skin, as though he is trying to close them. "Were you not listening? I cannot escape. They build traps to keep me contained. They hang mirrors in every chamber to repel me, to remind me of my place in this world. I know what would become of me were I to walk among your kind: I would be detested. I would be hurt and imprisoned, some curious wretched specimen, wrapped in chains and bound to a flaming pyre, or sunk to the bottom of the sea. They would call me a demon. I would have nowhere to turn. Here, at least, I am safe. They protect me. . . ."

He trails off, his fingertips hovering over his throat, a sliver of white skin visible above his collar. He drops his hand abruptly, as if only now realizing what he is doing.

"Do you know, they made me hideous so that I would be meek? Knowledge and power and eternal life I could have, but they would not give me beauty. They would not give me love or kindness. For then I would have more than they have themselves. I would have everything. I desire *everything*. Such is the folly of man. And such is my folly, too."

"To be unhappy?" I ask. "To be cruel?"

The butterfly man does not move, and it is impossible to tell if he is pondering my words.

"Change out of your finery," he says at last, drifting out of the room. "Follow me. Your name shall be the strongest shield, your skin the hardest iron. To harvest the precious material inside your veins would require your death. I do not think they would kill their own children."

My head throbs. The door stands wide now. The lights in the hall are blazing.

Bernadette and Charlotte are crawling over the floor.

Delphine is clinging to my skirts. Jacques is gone. And suddenly I feel as though I am standing at a crossroads under a fierce blue sky, and on one hand there is a girl lying in the dirt, weeping and unable to move. It is her right to weep; she has been lied to and betrayed, locked away in solitude, and I see the darkness under her flesh; her own veins are treason against her. The other road is empty, stretching away, because that girl has already gone far down it, running fast and desperate.

"Aurélie," Charlotte says. "What will we do?"

I stare at the open door. "We will go, of course," I say. I dash to the heap of clothing. I help my sisters change. Now I dress myself, slipping the rough woolen skirt over my head. It smells of lye and dirt, the stench embedded so deep in the threads, it has become a part of them. I reach the doorframe and see the butterfly man far down the passage, his back turned, waiting for us.

"Follow me," he says over his shoulder, and I lift Delphine up and hurry the others in front of me. We follow him down the hallway, the chandeliers passing overhead like watchful, glittering spiders.

We come to the corner. The butterfly man is gone, but I still hear his voice, crawling through the arteries of the palace, flooding every passageway and chamber, flowing like putrid water up the walls.

"*Go now*," he whispers, and I leave the girl in the road, leave her to weep and mourn. "*Run far with your precious cargo and do not let them catch you.*"

53

I'm pretty sure Lilly's lost it. She's laughing hysterically, crying, swooping her free arm in circles like some kind of demented windmill.

"I found them! I found you! We're getting out, Anouk!" She screeches it at the walls and the chandeliers: *"We're getting out!"*

The screaming is not a good idea. Someone's going to hear. But I'm laughing, too, running as fast as I can in my Pilgrims-R-Us nightgown, and I feel like I could run forever. Everything's crazy. Everything's awful, but I'm alive and Lilly is, too, and Jules and Will are, too.

"Where are they?" I shout, and we skid around a corner, into a room that seems vaguely familiar—a spinet I recognize, a portrait of the woman in the red dress, only she's wearing summer silks here and smiling kindly, and her eyes are cornflower blue, and she looks a bit like me. It's somewhere we trekked through before. Maybe somewhere near the library.

"I'll show you. I think they're knocked out, but they're still alive. Hayden must have just hidden them and gone to look for us. I don't know what happened to him, but he is *not* on our side. Better hope he doesn't come back until we're gone."

We slam through a door, into the *salle d'opéra*. A vast theater. Red seats curve like rows of bloody gums. Gilt figures extend up every armrest and pillar, mermaids and cherubs and bundles of pikes wrapped in thorns. I glance up. The ceiling is one huge butterfly, translucent and ghostly, spreading its massive wings over a stormy sky.

"How long were you on your own?" I ask her.

"Ages. It was fine, though. The trick is to get off the main floor plan of the palace. There are servants' passages *everywhere* and spy holes—"

Lilly points to a pillar in the far wall, crusted with gilt leaves and a shield. "See that pillar over there? There's a door in it and a glass hallway like the one we ran down when we first got here. I think it's the emergency exit. Maybe the one Perdu meant. We're getting the boys and we're getting out of here."

I think of Lilly on her own, fighting her way through the palace while the rest of us were busy getting captured and falling out of chandeliers.

"Lilly?"

"Yeah?" She's not listening, just running, dragging me up some steps and along the rippling midnight-blue curtain.

"Thanks for coming back."

"Duh," she says, and we stop, right at the center of the stage. We turn and face the theater. At the back of the theater, the silhouette of a huge figure is growing against the frosted panes of the doors. A hand is placed flat to the glass. Behind it, I see more shapes, tall, dark shadows.

"Point your toes," Lilly says urgently. "Hold your breath and keep your arms in."

"What?"

"You know how to swim, right?"

"What?"

The doors at the end of the *salle d'opèra* burst open.

Lilly stamps a tiny wire prong sticking up through the boards. And the floor drops out from under us.

I scream so loud it's like my throat is ripping. We're

falling like bullets into the dark, wind whizzing in my ears—

"Point your toes!" Lilly shrieks, and a second later I'm burbling, plunging into black water. It's shockingly, painfully cold. I'm gulping it, sinking. But Lilly's got hold of my arm and she's kicking upward, pulling me with her. We break the surface.

I drag myself up onto a stone ledge, gasping.

"Are you insane?" I sputter. I'm shivering violently, wiping my face, trying to catch my breath. It's so dark I can't even see my hand in front of my eyes. "What was *that*? What—"

"Anouk," Lilly says softly, and I hear her digging around in her sopping wet clothes. "They're going to come after us. We have to hurry."

She's shaking something. By the metallic rattle coming from it, I'm assuming it's a flashlight. A broken one.

"Oops," Lilly says. Giggles nervously. "There's light farther down. Come on."

She charges off into the dark and I follow, stumbling blindly. My nightgown is soaked, sticking to my skin. My feet are bare. The ground is weirdly sharp, full of welts and holes, like volcanic rock. As my eyes adjust, I see the barest outline of where we are: a low stone tunnel, hacked into the bedrock.

The ground becomes metal grating. We're on a walkway now, suspended high up in the air. Dull-white lightbulbs inside cages blink on as we pass them. The walkway is sloping downward.

"How far did you go?" My teeth are chattering. I can barely talk. The grating of the floor is cutting into my skin.

"Far enough to find them." She glances at me, and she looks scared suddenly. Exhausted. "Far enough to find a lot of things."

We're at the end of the walkway, turning onto a circular stairway. We stagger down, farther and farther underground. The sound of our descent seems to echo forever. Beyond the lights all I can see is thick, uniform darkness. And now we're at the bottom, in a huge vaulted space. A clammy, stone-cold copy of the *salle d'opéra* high above. The floor is covered in shale and huge triangular shards of rock, like this place was blasted out and never properly cleared.

The light is surreal—a dark, chilly green. Fluorescent tubes are bolted at random intervals across the ceiling, like glowing staples closing up a wound.

Lilly leads me along the wall. We're trying to be quiet, but if someone's within a hundred feet of us they heard us clambering down those stairs. I look up at the wall. It's scrawled with dripping words. Names. Numbers. Some of them are huge. Others form tiny, shaky sentences.

L'enfer, I read under my breath as we hurry past the uneven letters. *I am Jacques Renaud.*

1775—1795—1885?—1912—2004—2016

Aurélie. Aurélie du Bessancourt.

Forgive me. I cannot find you.

I brush my hand along the wall as I run. Some of the words are gouged into the rock, deep.

How long is eternity?

She cannot return to me.

I am lost.

Mon nom est perdu.

The words terminate in an angry mass of blots and splatters.

We reach a pocket of light. A huge, shattered chandelier is lying between the rocks, cables snaking away into the dark. It's been laid at the feet of a crudely hacked sculpture. At first it looks barely human. On second glance, I think it's supposed to be a girl. Piles of trinkets and ancient paper are heaped around it and tangled through the prongs of the chandelier.

"It's like a shrine," I breathe. Lilly looks up at the disfigured stone face. "Come on," she says, and pulls me onward. "Come on."

We're coming up on something. At first it looks like Stonehenge, looming out of the dark, and now like a circle of ancient telephone booths, and now I see that it's a series of tanks, glass and heavy, bolted frames, standing end up in the center of this enormous space.

They aren't empty.

Lilly tries to pull me past them. I shrug her off.

"Wait." The water behind the thick glass is cloudy, yellow-blue. A figure is floating inside. My throat closes.

It's indistinct, drifting. Closer. Now farther. *A finger. A hand—*

A face slides forward through the murky fluid.

For a second I think it's Jules. It's got his black hair, the same narrow face and pointed chin. But it's not Jules. It's someone his age, a kid with a fuller mouth and muscled arms, and he's wearing a button-down shirt, wide '60s pants. He's suspended in the water, eyes closed. Definitely, inarguably dead.

"I don't know what those are," Lilly mumbles. She's watching me, not the tanks. She won't look at the tanks. "We need to go, Anouk."

I wrap my soaking arms around me. Start walking again, moving past the circle of tanks. I catch glimpses of a boy in knee breeches. A thin, dark-haired girl in a nineteenth-century gown. Her petticoats are floating around her. There's a black cavity in the back of her neck.

"It's everyone they've killed," I whisper. "All the people they got rid of to stay alive. It's their own grandchildren and great-grandchildren."

Lilly stares at me. One of the bodies floats against the glass with a *thunk*, wispy hair drifting around its head like spun gold. Eyes closed. Blue lips. It could be Lilly's twin.

These are our ancestors. Bessancourts. I wonder if they were dragged down like we were, if they ever got the chance to fight, how long they lasted. Or if they just never woke up.

Lilly grabs my arm. We stumble on.

"Look," Lilly says, and up ahead I see something. To the left, close to another bubble of light: two slumped shapes solidifying out of the dark.

It's them. Will and Jules. They're tied to chairs, backs toward us, heads to their chests.

And Hayden's with them. He's leaning over Jules, cupping something in his hands. A rococo table stands next to him, medical instruments laid out in two neat, glittering rows across the top.

Lilly doesn't hesitate. Neither do I. Lilly tosses me a jeweled dagger. Pulls a long, thin saber from her belt loop. We approach out of the darkness.

Hayden sees us. Grins.

"My friends have all returned to me," he growls, and it's not Hayden's voice. It's like a dozen voices at once, strand after strand of grating, whining sound. *"My lost brothers and sisters, fellow children of darkness."*

54

We're steps away when I notice the fourth figure. Standing behind Hayden, blending with the shadows. A small shape, like a little kid. He's wearing an old-fashioned frock coat with pronged tails, flickering like a dark red flame in the blackness.

I lunge forward and bury the dagger in Hayden's shoulder. There's almost nothing left of the guy in the private school blazer, swaggering up to us in JFK. His hair is falling out of his head in patches. His cheeks are shadowy hollows. His lips have started to draw inward, shriveling.

He doesn't even flinch as the blade goes through his shoulder. Doesn't move. He's looking past me, into space, his palms still outstretched like he's been frozen in place. The figure in the shadows remains motionless.

"Hayden?" I stare at him, horrified.

I jerk the dagger out. It releases with a metallic grating sound.

No blood. No reaction. Hayden's not breathing.

"Get them," Lilly says, in a tiny panicked whisper. "Hurry!"

I spin and start sawing frantically at Will's ropes. Lilly begins hacking at the binds tying Jules to his chair. One rope cut through. Two. I sling Will's arm over my shoulder and start dragging him away over the rocky floor.

He weighs a ton. I hear his breathing next to my ear, shallow and raspy.

"Lilly?" I whip around. She's following, Jules leaning into her, almost toppling her over. Hayden still hasn't moved.

But the small figure has.

His face is turned toward us. He's watching us drag the boys desperately away.

And suddenly Hayden starts after us.

"I can't let you do that!" he calls out, and he sounds like Hayden again, his East Coast accent, golden boy attitude, silver spoon confidence. But the voice came from the small figure in the shadows.

"Lilly, *RUN*!" I raise the dagger, hoping I can somehow

fend Hayden off. He's hulking toward us, head lowered, eyes flat and wet, reflecting the fluorescent lighting. His shirt's torn, and under it I glimpse metal, curling tubes, maybe glass, embedded in his chest. Deep, glimmering wounds. Too many wounds. You can't survive that many wounds.

I hear a new sound: the ring of dozens of feet clattering down the stairs.

Lilly reaches me. "Dorf," she whispers. "They're here."

I spin. The tanks stand silently, the bodies floating inside, calm and ghostly. The steps are still ringing with descending feet. And now I see figures emerging out of the dark, dozens of them, thrown into stark relief against the green glow: Havriel. Miss Sei. Row after row of trackers, red lights piercing the gloom.

"Found you!" Havriel yells, his voice booming up to the ceiling. I look over my shoulder. Hayden's approaching fast. We let Will and Jules down as gently as we can onto the ground.

Havriel breaks into a run. Miss Sei is gesturing sharply to the trackers. A black case is being passed forward through the ranks.

Havriel reaches us seconds before Hayden does. He

ducks under my dagger, whirling. Knocks me sideways. Pain lances through my shoulder. Lilly lets loose a banshee shriek and swings her sabre toward Havriel.

Now Hayden's smashing into me. It's like he doesn't even see me. My dagger catches on his arm. Hayden swings it toward me, dagger and all, and I drop, scrabbling over the stones. I'm surrounded by legs, screams. Lilly's swinging her sabre in desperate arcs, trying to keep Havriel at bay. The trackers are forming a ring, Miss Sei pressing to the front. I hear that buzz again, inching into my brain, and my chest is aching, my lungs pressing against my damaged ribs like they're trying to jump ship—

I stand just in time to see Hayden's head jerk and smash into Havriel's skull. Havriel retreats a step. But he's only caught off guard for a second.

"Have you become so pathetic and desperate"— Havriel wheezes, grinning—"that you must hide behind the corpses of your more comely family members? I was wondering where this one had gotten off to. Did you enjoy your little afterlife, Hayden?"

Havriel's eyes narrow. He steps forward again, and I see he's got a gun. He presses it to Hayden's stomach.

Shots fill my ears, ringing in the cavern, again and again, a deafening string of noise. Hayden lurches backward. Falls to the ground. Havriel keeps shooting, until the gun clicks. Smoke rises gently from Hayden's ruined chest.

Havriel tosses the gun aside and turns on us.

"Stay away," Lilly hisses. She places herself in front of Will and Jules. I stand next to her, dagger out. "Stay back!"

"Should I?" Havriel says, and he sounds jolly somehow, desperate and crazy and happy. "Do you know what you did? You, in your desperation to live out your tiny, meaningless lives, killed a great man. A man who had lived two hundred and seventy years, longer than any other. A man who influenced nations, built empires and watched them fall, constructed a creature impossible to this day. And he died like a dog at your hands. Do you think I appreciate that?"

Lilly's sabre whips out, slashing Havriel's palm. "Shouldn't have come after us, then."

His face turns hideous, a crinkled, vicious mask, teeth bared. He looks down at the cut in his palm, and for a second I think he's crying, his eyes squeezed shut. But it's a chuckle, a thin laugh, high in the back of his throat. He steps toward us, his bleeding palm raised. Lilly swings her sabre with all her strength. Havriel's eyes open wide. He catches the blade on his arm, loops it down. The tip hits the floor. Lilly loses her grip, and Havriel kicks the sabre away. It goes spinning and dancing across the stones, like a tiny wind spout.

"Oh, children," he says, and he's right there, right in front of us. His hand—bloody from his wounds, bloody from his brother's—clenches around my neck. "You should not have made me angry."

He lifts me up like I'm weightless. I claw at his fingers. He doesn't let go. Multicolored explosions bloom across my vision. The buzz is rising, painful, filling every crack and fissure in my head, and I don't know if it's just me dying, or if everyone hears it. I see the trackers pinning Lilly's arms while she screams and kicks. I see Miss Sei, pulling on a medical glove with a snap, kneeling next to Jules and Will—

Havriel's eyes flick away from my face. He's looking over my shoulder. I don't know what he sees, don't even care anymore, but his mouth goes slack. And something hits me, hits us all. A massive shock wave, soft and cold and crushing all at once. I'm flying, rolling across the floor. I see Havriel hurtling into the dark, picked up like a rag doll.

I lie for a second, gasping, choking. Push myself up onto hands and knees. "Lilly?" I cough. "Will?"

The trackers are on the floor, spread around me in a circle, like I'm the epicenter of a bomb. Miss Sei lies crumpled against a boulder about ten feet away, glassy-eyed. Not far away from her, Havriel is sitting up in the faint blue-yellow light of one of the tanks, brushing his hand delicately across a cut in his cheek. He looks almost disbelieving.

"That was unnecessary," he croaks into the darkness, and he must be talking to the pale thing, because it's walking slowly toward us, drifting over the rocks and the bodies. Its eyes are black, birdlike.

The butterfly man. It's got to be. It was controlling Hayden, but this is its true form.

"You brought us our runaways," Havriel says, pushing himself to his feet. His voice is becoming a strange mixture of contempt and groveling fear. "I am forever indebted, my dear boy."

Will and Jules are about six feet away from me, tangled

with the bodies of some trackers. Farther back, Lilly's trying to push herself out from under the mass of arms and legs. Her hair is sticking to her face in wet strands. I start crawling toward the boys.

The butterfly man passes me, black eyes pinned on Havriel. The whine rises the closer he comes, until it's all there is, the only sound I can hear. The butterfly man stops in front of Havriel. The buzzing cuts off abruptly.

"I have not brought you your runaways," he says. His voice is weirdly soft and uncertain. Almost sweet. Havriel is looking up at him, his expression horrified.

"I have returned them for myself," the butterfly man says. "I have been waiting for you to arrive, Havriel du Bessancourt. I was waiting for Father as well, but it seems he has been given his just rewards already. I cannot say I will mourn him. I wish to tell you that our long-standing alliance is terminated."

Lilly's up, stumbling over bodies to get to us. I try to stand, feel the black polymer suits against the soles of my feet, sticky and disgusting, the give of flesh-encased machines.

Out of the corner of my eye, I see Havriel moving, backing away from the butterfly man. "Alliance?" he says. "But we are not allies. We are brothers! Equals!"

"Equals?" The butterfly man lets out a high, chittering laugh. I notice a disturbance in the air around him, a dark, fuming mass, barely visible.

I've reached Will. I heave him upright.

"Equals," the butterfly man says again, softer, yearning. "You rule the world in secret. I wander a dungeon, alone. You keep me fettered in a gilded wasteland, at every turn a mirror to remind me of who I am and what you made me. No," the butterfly man says. "If we were equal, you would not fear me so."

The disturbance around him flares. Havriel goes slamming against one of the tanks. He slides down it, coughing.

"I have had enough of this arrangement," the butterfly man says, and the longing's gone from his voice. It's sharp now, malicious. "Enough of Father, and enough of you. There is only one cure for pining after something you cannot possess, and that is to destroy it entirely."

Will and I are moving now, squashing over limbs, tripping over helmets. Lilly reaches Jules. She's trying to shake him awake.

I feel something brush the back of my neck, an

awareness, like a million tiny needles prickling over my skin—

I freeze. The butterfly man: he's looking straight at me.

I stay perfectly still, trying not to breathe. Will's so heavy. My muscles are burning, aching.

"Bonjour," the butterfly man says, and I close my eyes, because I know he's stepping toward me. I can feel the air sharpening, becoming dense and charged. My back feels like it's being picked at, like my skin is releasing in particles and dissolving into the air.

Will stirs, his eyes flickering open. "Will," I whisper. "Will, wake up!"

I move, start dragging us away. I'm hunched double, and my entire chest cavity hurts, and my arm is digging into Will's shoulder blades painfully. I raise my head. The butterfly man is right in front of me, stock-still, obsidian eyes boring into mine.

"You are indeed Aurélie's descendant," he says. "Her own mother would not know the difference."

"We're not part of this," I whisper. "None of us are, just leave us alone—"

He's too close. The buzzing noise is back and it's

deafening, and that shudder in the air *hurts*. My lips are cracking. I can't hold Will up anymore. He slumps out of my grasp. I'm falling, too, dropping to the cavern floor.

"You *are* a part of this," the butterfly man says. "You are my long-lost comrades. Forsaken children of this wicked, greedy family. I have waited long for one of you to come so far. For you to slip their nets and fight with me."

I look up at him. He is standing over me, but all I can see now is a blurry oval, two black holes where his eyes should be.

"We have much to do," the butterfly man says. "We will return to the surface, you and Lilly and Jules and William. Together we shall end this once and for all."

What is he talking about? I push myself up onto my knees, gasping.

"End what?" I whisper. "What are you saying?"

"The cycle. The Bessancourts. This empire of suffering and pain. There is no end to it. There cannot be. When we are poor we wish to be rich, when we are rich we wish to be loved, when we are loved we wish for freedom from pain and endless life and unchanging happiness. It is a great, unstoppable conundrum. There is some sickness deep in our minds, a darkness that causes all ills. It cannot be helped. It can only be eradicated."

Eradicate. I remember Rabbit Gallery, the stolen artwork, the massive warheads, the weapons used in all the wars of the last two centuries.

"You did that?" I say. My voice takes forever to reach my ears. "You invented the weapons, and Havriel and the marquis got rich and took the credit, but you *wanted* it, you *wanted* them to kill people."

"You speak as though you do not approve," the butterfly man says. "But what reason have you to love the world when it has treated you so harshly? Do you not crave revenge? Do you not crave justice?"

Uh-oh.

The butterfly spreads his hands over my eyes. I feel the scream ripping out of me, but I can't hear it—

And everything's gone.

I see a billion people crowding a busy street, dirty faces, ragged clothing, an endless swarm under neon signs. I see troops trudging off to a war, mothers sending off their sons with flowers in their plumed helmets, boots shined, faces grim. I see smoke rising from roofs and spires. Streaks of flame raining down on low wooden houses and walled gardens, the sky between the power lines staining hot, ugly red. I see bombs tumbling like heavy birds onto a city, and I see the little mark on their rivets, a butterfly with human eyes in its wings. Péronne—the Bessancourts' own town—blown to smithereens, bodies lying along the roadside.

"This is what I have done," the butterfly man says. "I gave them the tools and they gladly used them. There is no hope for such a people."

The images keep rolling, wave after wave. My skull is being filled up, synapses crackling, nerves overheating. I see things from my life, from other people's lives: a beggar being beaten on a roadside by two men in elegant clothing. Mom smiling—bright lights—a neon frosted birthday cake—bodies leaping from the sides of a huge gray aircraft carrier as it burns. I see Mom turning slowly to face me in the kitchen, a horrible look of determination on her face.

The images speed up, burning snapshots, and I see Lilly, Will, Jules, and me on the floor in the library, laughing even though there was nothing to laugh about. Us helping each other after Jellyfish Hall, holding each other up. Lilly coming back for me, and running, running into the light—

"You are unable to understand," the butterfly man whispers. "We are all follies, hopeless and doomed to repeat our mistakes forever. Every organism will fight against its own demise. Even a virus. And in the end that is what mankind is: an endless, stubborn blight."

The pain is all there is now. It's enveloping me, flapping in my ears like feathery gray wings. "We're not all bad. We're not, we—"

It hurts to talk. To breathe.

"We've got something else, something you can't see, but . . . it's there, it's just . . ."

I can't do this. Can't talk anymore.

" . . . one little drop of . . ."

Of everything.

Starlight, darkness, divinity, love. And it makes all this worthwhile.

Somewhere far away, I hear Lilly crying. Maybe laughing.

"*They're awake!*" she wails. "*Jules is awake.*"

Something cracks.

I'm in the cavern again, hunched on the floor. The butterfly man is arching over me, his face so close I can see the muscles under his skin, layers of bone and sinew, exposed to the air. I wriggle onto my back. Lilly's sabre is embedded in the butterfly man's calf. Lilly is hunched at his feet. She looks at the sabre, looks up at the butterfly man. Whirls and runs full speed away.

"Anouk?" she shouts over her shoulder. "Get up!"

The butterfly man pivots. I watch the darkness gathering around him. Brace myself for the explosion, the shock wave that will knock me out for good. It never comes. Havriel is crawling toward us out of the shadows like a huge bleeding slug. The butterfly man is watching him.

"Stop this," Havriel rasps. "I will give you freedom if that is what you want. I will let you have the children, the palace, anything, but do not let me die. You must be reasonable!"

"I am nothing if not reasonable. That is how you made me."

"I did everything you asked!" Havriel shrieks. He's nearly reached us, and I can smell him, a vile, ancient stench, metal and death and rot. I see threads of black in the red dripping along his face, and they're slithering, squirming like they're alive. "What more do you wish for? I will give you a billion corpses!"

"You already have."

Havriel stares at the butterfly man, heaving. His face is a mask of fear and hate and pain. He gasps and spits between his teeth. One hand goes to his chest, fingers wriggling into his waistcoat. They emerge holding a black cylinder. A red light is sliding up its length, blinking frantically.

A detonator.

He raises his fist.

"You will not command me," he growls, and he smiles through the blood, the red teeth, the ashen lips. "There is no escaping the palace."

55

"Come ON!" Lilly screams. My skin feels cracked, scaly. I'm half blind. I push myself up anyway, start dragging myself across the cavern floor. Will is a few feet in front of me. He's standing unsteadily, cradling his bruised head in his hand. Farther back in the darkness, I see Lilly. She's got Jules by the shoulders. They're limping toward the metal stairs as fast as they can.

I haul myself upright. The sabre is still stuck in the butterfly man's leg, reflecting the darkness flowing off his body. He's starting to twitch. Will looks over at me, confused. I grab his good arm, and together we stagger after Lilly and Jules.

We reach the bottom of the stairs. Lilly and Jules have already started up them, and Lilly leans over the railing. "Hurry," she gasps. "You guys, run!"

And now we're clattering up the metal corkscrew, on

and on. All I can hear is our breathing, the ring of the grating under our feet. Maybe the butterfly man is still talking to Havriel, maybe they're arguing, but I can't hear them. We come to the tunnel. Hurry down the walkway, lights blinking on as we pass.

Just keep running, Ooky. Just keep running.

We're at the pool of black water. We start up a second staircase cut into the stone, the ones Havriel and his henchmen probably took, so that they wouldn't have to plunge forty feet into pitch-black water.

We burst out into the *salle d'opéra*, gasping.

Lilly and I skid to a halt. The boys stop behind us. The woman in the red dress is standing on the stage, right at the center. But she doesn't turn to us, doesn't even seem to hear us. She's facing the theater, her arms spread wide. Her face is tipped up toward the ceiling, like a singer basking in her applause.

Everything is so silent. Deathly still—

I feel the first detonation in my fingertips: somewhere faraway in the palace, a long, pulsating rumble. Dust sifts down from the ceiling high above.

"Who's that?" Jules mumbles, and we shush him, start running along the orchestra pit toward the pillar with its gold-encrusted shield.

Lilly drags open the panel. Behind it is the mirrored passageway. We start up it. I look back, see the woman on the stage, the curtains wrenching from their moorings and falling, swirling around her tiny form like swaths of deep blue clouds.

Another explosion nearly throws me off my feet. The walls of the passageway are shaking, the glass ringing. Up ahead is a circle of blue metal—a door like a bank vault. A ladder. We start up it. A third explosion, closer this time. Smoke billows up after us, enveloping us. The air is becoming hot. Too hot. The shaft shakes.

"We're going to make it!" Lilly's yelling. "We're going to make it!"

We climb faster. Jules, Will, me, Lilly. Below, the explosions keep coming, endless and teeth jarring. I imagine the ceilings cracking, the chandeliers tinkling and falling into Jellyfish Hall, Razor Hall, Rabbit Gallery. The earth burying everything, swallowing crystal and brocade, the blood and death and secrets.

We keep climbing, keep climbing, and listen to it all fall away.

Palais du Papillon—112 feet below,
ten seconds before the detonations

Jacques lies against the wall of the empty panic room. His blood is a red-black mirror beneath him, still as glass. The light buzzes. The distant sound of running feet reaches his ears, but it is echoing away, leaving him behind.

A shivering jolt reverberates in the walls of the capsule. He thinks of the girl with the black hair, a steel girl with a tiny wounded heart. He thought she was Aurélie at first. But what a foolish dream that was. *Aurélie is gone. Aurélie is free.*

The jolt comes again, closer. The entire capsule shakes. Jacques's thoughts turn to home. The dry clack of his mother's knitting needles. The smell of drying herbs and tallow candles and damp wood. It has been so many years. He hears the creak of a hinge and looks up. A face is peering in at him through the hatch. At first he does not recognize it. But now she smiles. . . .

"Jacques," Aurélie says, and hurries for him. She kneels

beside him. "Come, Jacques, we must go! Can you not hear them? They are waiting to see you!"

And suddenly the stuttering light, the cold metal and the blood, all of it twists away and fades. He can hear the waterwheel, Madame Desjardin's voice calling across the fields. Aurélie is pulling him to his feet, and he is in the woods outside Péronne. In the distance he can see his brothers and sisters just as they were when he last looked back at them in the road, not yet wizened and old, but young and ruddy faced, their hands raised to him, and he cannot say if they wave in welcome or farewell.

He feels Aurélie's fingers in his, and he feels the sunlight breaking and falling through a million leaves . . .

Palais du Papillon—96 feet below—1790

"Careful," I whisper, one hand on Charlotte's back as she grips the iron rungs and begins to climb. "Quick and careful."

Bernadette goes next, then Delphine; I make my way up the ladder last, now and then giving Delphine's heel an encouraging squeeze. Our feet tap up, up.

"There is a door here!" Charlotte calls down.

"Open it!" I shout. "Open it!"

The shaft has become wider, blooming into a small chamber, a tulip atop a long stem. We all reach up, hands grasping. We slide back the door, a square of iron into the stone.

And there is sunlight. Fields and wind and the smell of grass and the scratch of insects. And sunlight . . .

Delphine laughs and wriggles out into the brightness. Charlotte follows. Even Bernadette cannot help herself and laughs with the rest of them, her sour little face twisting, her hands shading her eyes against the sudden, painful light. I climb out last. The sun tickles my cheeks. I listen to my sisters' joyful shrieks, and I feel the darkness squirming beneath my skin, the sting of the deep red wound.

My fingers reach for the daisy in my apron pocket, and I twist it like a charm. "I will come back for you, Jacques," I whisper, and the breeze takes my words and folds them away. "I will find you."

It is a vain promise. Perhaps I will die tomorrow. Perhaps Father will send guards after us and drag us back into the depths, or we will be captured by *révolutionnaires*, and I will never see Jacques again. But in this moment, there are no truer words. I will find him. I will try.

We start off across the field. The wheat is a soft new green, waving in the breeze. The air is hazy with pollen. Trees border the field like a hunched gathering of giants. In the distance I see smoke rising from the chimneys of a farmhouse. I hear the splash and babble of water, the gentle *creak-creak* of a waterwheel, rolling tirelessly nowhere.

And I decide then that I dare not think of tomorrow. I dare not think of hours or days or years at all. I will think of Mama, smiling at me from under the apple tree. I will think of the wind and the wheat and the sound of the birds, and how, if I could, I would take my sisters by their hands and we would leap into the air like little starlings and let the breeze wheel us away. I will think of a tall boy and a tall girl, far underground.

I have this moment in the sun. I have had many before it. Come what may, they will be mine forever.

Epilogue—217 feet above sea level, Pitié-Salpêtrière Hospital, Paris

We crawled up somewhere near the outskirts of Péronne, in a freezing green field. We dragged ourselves about three hundred feet to a little farmhouse. Nearly gave the elderly couple living there a heart attack when we asked to use their phone. The police came, ambulances bleeding swirling lights onto the snow.

I'm lying in a hospital now. Lilly is one bed over. Across from me are Will and Jules. They kept us together, probably for security reasons. Four teenagers purported dead in a plane crash emerging alive from a series of unexplained subterranean explosions is a bit of a sensation, apparently. Journalists, the *gendarmerie*, folks from the U.S. embassy; they're all waiting to talk to us. Our room's been quarantined, a guard from the special police stationed right outside. We're being spared for now.

Bright winter sun streams through the blinds, and

I feel heavy and weightless, sad and happy. But more happy than sad. A lot more happy. Happier than I've ever felt in my life, which is ironic because there's a drip stuck into my arm, and Hayden's dead, and we're going to be explaining this for a long, long time.

I look across the room at Will. He's sleeping, his face bruised, one arm slung across his forehead. Jules is awake. He catches my eye and starts making winky faces at me until I grin.

"Anouk?" I glance over. Lilly's propped up on her side, peering across the gap between our beds. She looks hollowed out and tired. Her head is bandaged; both fists, too, like a boxer. But now she grins, and there she is again.

"Yeah?" I say.

"We made it."

"We did."

"Parts of us." Will's awake now, too. His hand has gotten a real bandage, and I think he looks great, all things considered. Who needs ten fingers anyway? We sit up in our beds in our white, sterile hospital room, and we stare at each other like *Well, that was crazy.* Down in the street journalists are screaming, cars are passing, pigeons are warbling, but in here it's just us. And I smile at the others. Really smile, a bright, warm smile that I feel in my chest.

"Thanks," I say.

I doubt they have any clue what I'm thanking them for. But I know, and they smile back, and that's all I wanted anyway. I think of flying back across the ocean, talking to my parents, hugging Penny. Technically this whole thing was a massive failure. But *I* don't feel like a failure. I feel like I've done something great. Something awesome. I see a black Mercedes, speeding toward a pale château and an underground palace full of monsters. A girl with her head against the cold glass, thinking, *There's this special talent humans have that they can be unhappy no matter where they are.* But humans have another special talent: We can be happy almost anywhere, too. We can be happy because we're not alone.